D1053419

RANDOM HOUSE TRADE PAPERBACKS
NEW YORK

AN ACCIDENTAL AMERICAN

...

A NOVEL

ALEX CARR

A Random House Trade Paperback Original

Copyright © 2007 by Jenny Siler
Dossier copyright © 2007 by Random House, Inc.
© 2007 Maps by David Lindroth

Published in the United States by Random House Trade Paperbacks, an imprint of The Random House Publishing Group, a division of Random House, Inc., New York.

RANDOM HOUSE TRADE PAPERBACKS, MORTALIS, and colophons are trademarks of Random House, Inc.

ISBN 978-0-8129-7708-0

LIBRARY OF CONGRESS CATALOGING-IN-PUBLICATION DATA

Carr, Alex.
  An accidental American: a novel / Alex Carr.
    p. cm.
  ISBN-13: 978-0-8129-7708-0 (trade pbk.)
  1. Forgers—Fiction. 2. Terrorists—Portugal—Lisbon—Fiction.
3. France—Fiction. 4. Beirut (Lebanon)—Fiction. 5. Intelligence
service—United States—Fiction. I. Title.

PS3569.I42125A63 2007
813'.6—dc22   2006045764

Printed in the United States of America

www.mortalis-books.com

9 8 7 6 5 4 3 2 1

Book design by Simon M. Sullivan

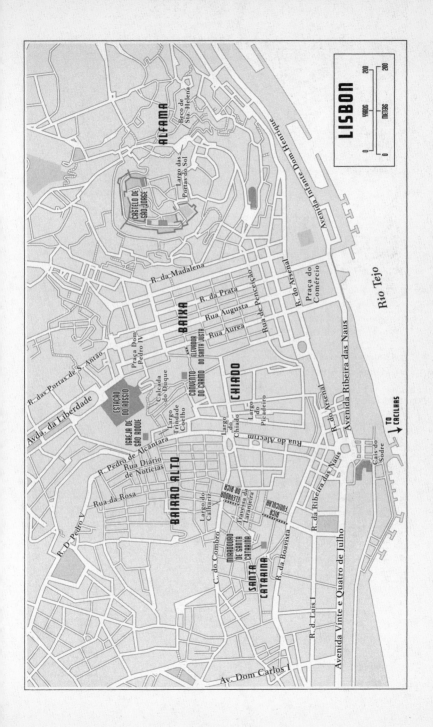

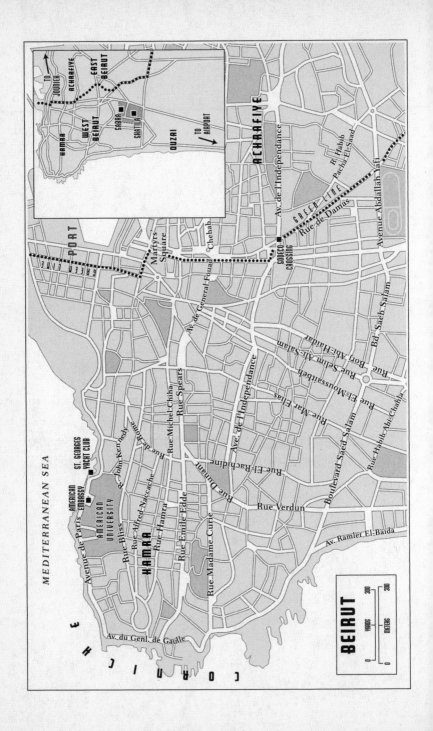

BEIRUT

AN ACCIDENTAL
AMERICAN

ONE

■ ■ ■

HOME, SABRI KANJ reminded himself as the jet touched down and the massive engines whined themselves to sleep. Home, he thought. Fairuz on the radio, his mother singing along in the kitchen. Lamb sausages on the grill. A memory to see you through, his friend Khalid had told him once, speaking from experience. Something they won't be able to take from you.

The plane paused, and Kanj could hear the two Pakistanis who'd accompanied him laughing in the front of the aircraft, then one of the men lumbered back and unshackled Kanj's feet from the metal bar beneath his seat. An oddly intimate act, Kanj thought, as the entire business had been, the man leaning against him as he had earlier, when they'd stripped and blindfolded and diapered him for the trip. All of it meant to humiliate him, to cow him for what lay ahead. Though Kanj knew all too well where they were taking him, understood as they could not that fear never promised salvation.

"Stand up," the man said. He was so close that Kanj could smell his most recent meal. Stale cooking grease and green meat. He put his hand on Kanj's shoulder to steady him, and Kanj winced. The Pakistanis had broken his collarbone in the raid, leaving it tender and raw. Kanj quickly checked himself and the pain, then shuffled into the aisle and started forward.

"Where are we, stewardess?" he asked with mock cheer, expecting no answer and getting none. Instead, the plane's front hatch popped open, and the stink of jet fuel filled the cabin. Somewhere not far in the distance, another plane was taking off, its engines laboring the giant craft skyward.

From out on the void of the tarmac, Kanj heard a snippet of Arabic, the accent clearly Jordanian. Not that it mattered. They could be in any of a handful of places: Syria, Egypt, Morocco. Black holes all, places where a man could get lost, where humanity held little sway against power.

Kanj squinted into the darkness of his blindfold, conjuring the house in Ouzai again, the sound of his mother's voice. Prettier than Fairuz's, he'd thought at the time, and she had been prettier as well. This, before the war had ravaged them all. In the living room his older sister was scratching out her math homework, her chin propped in her left hand, her dark eyes studying the page. The smart one of the family. A doctor or a scientist in some other world.

The man touched him on the shoulder, and Kanj felt his gut tighten for an instant. "Step down," the Pakistani commanded.

Some other world, Kanj reminded himself, putting his foot forward, feeling the edge of the stair, the drop down toward the tarmac. This memory and the secret he had hoarded along with it all these years. One or the other would save him in the end. A car door popped open, and the man forced Kanj's head and shoulders down, stuffed him into the seat. Then the door closed behind him and Kanj was alone, his skin prickling in the air-conditioned chill.

They drove for what Kanj guessed was an hour. No turns, just a straight line out into the desert, though in which direction Kanj couldn't be sure. South, most likely, or east, for they had not encountered the city. In Kanj's mind, the map of Jordan didn't stop at the great river but pushed like a fist into Israel's gut, with Syria edging in from above. And above Israel was Lebanon. Beirut and home again. The Corniche and the sea curving around Pigeon Rocks. The unrestrained bustle of Martyrs' Square. The cafés along the rue Bliss, girls from the American University sunning themselves at outdoor tables. The city as it had been, once, and was no more.

It was evening when the car finally stopped and Kanj was pulled from his seat. There was a smell to the air that told Kanj the sun had just set, the perfume of relief and release. The memory of another home. The dirt beneath Kanj's feet was fine as flour, packed hard by thousands of years of sun and wind, the rare wash of rain.

No one spoke here. There were only hands. Hands that led him down into the earth. Fingers that chained him to the floor. The sting of an open palm across his face. Then the blindfold was off, and Kanj was blinking up into the face of the man from whom he knew everything now would come. Pain and fear. Hope. Salvation, even.

His new god, Kanj thought, though the man didn't look the part. He was short and stocky, his underarms ringed with sweat, his bald head glistening in the light of the room's single bare bulb.

Kanj took a deep breath and raised his head, readying himself for what was to come. "I want to talk to the Americans," he said, the same words he'd repeated over and over in Pakistan. It was all they would get from him.

TWO

■ ■ ■

I KNEW THE FIRST TIME I saw John Valsamis what he was. It was a warm afternoon, one of those early-spring snaps that won't last. Barely March and shirtsleeves weather, the streams fat with runoff, the first green shoots of the crocuses struggling up toward the light. I had taken Lucifer out for his walk, and when we came home, Valsamis was parked on the road just outside my driveway, a small neat man in a white Twingo, a rental. Though I didn't know why, I knew as surely as if I had invited him that he had come for me.

He could have been any tourist, I suppose, a solitary American lost in this unimportant corner of the world. A wrong turn on the way to Tautavel or one of the Cathar fortresses, and this stop just to check his map and get his bearings. Could have been but wasn't. Even Lucifer could tell something was wrong. Impatient to get home, he'd taken off ahead of me, but when I rounded the last corner toward the house, he was stopped dead in the middle of the road.

An ex-con like me, the old shepherd-cross mutt knew the meaning of loyalty, the value of a good home. I'd rescued him from the shelter and the imminent jaws of death, and he repaid the favor each day with his own fierce brand of love. His ears flattened now and his tail lowered, curling between his powerful back legs. The dark fur along his neck grew stiff as a straw broom. He turned his head briefly in my direction, then let out a low growl. I had to walk on ahead of him, pretending everything was all right, and even then I was halfway down the drive before he gave up his post and followed behind.

Valsamis stayed in his car while the dog and I went inside. I could see him from the kitchen window while I got Lucifer his food, the car framed perfectly by the single pane of glass, as if he'd parked there deliberately, wanting to give me a view. His face was unmoving behind the windshield, half masked by the reflections of the bare trees overhead. I didn't recognize him, couldn't remember what might have brought him to find me. He didn't look like an old client, and he wasn't a cop, of that I was sure. If anything, he seemed more like a con.

I gave Lucifer his bowl, then went into the pantry, climbed up past the shelves of homemade apricot jam and pickled beans I'd put up the previous fall, and took down the battered old twelve-gauge I'd found in the attic when I first moved in. It wasn't much of a gun, but I felt better having it, and it was loud enough to convince the foxes that had ravaged my henhouse that there were better places in the valley for a free meal.

Hoping it would do the same for my visitor, I hefted it prominently in my left hand and headed out the kitchen door. I wanted to get a better look at the man, wanted to let him know for sure I knew he was there, but when I stepped outside, the Twingo was gone.

I stood on the gravel drive, wishing I hadn't quit smoking, wishing I had a cigarette to steady my hands. The wind kicked up just slightly, and the brittle branches of the trees in the garden lifted and resettled against one another, the rustling like gossip spreading through a crowd. Rubbing my bare arms, I smoothed away goose bumps and scanned the empty road, then turned back inside. Gone, I told myself, and maybe I'd been wrong. I'd let the old paranoia get me, the old prison fears. Not every parked car held some dark specter of the past. And yet I didn't believe my own story.

THREE

■ ■ ■

I SPENT THE REST of the afternoon putting the finishing touches on a copy of the new Angolan passport I'd been working on. The geeks at Solomon, the document security firm for which I freelanced, had come up with a new kind of multilayer infilling system that was a bitch to beat, but I'd cracked it in the end, and my final result was about as close to perfect as possible, a far better match than what would be needed to fool the immigration officers in Luanda. Bad news for my employers, but that's what I was paid to deliver. If I could beat their security, there were others out there who could get around it just as well.

It was close to five by the time the FedEx truck came to collect my package for Solomon.

"Running late," the driver, Isham, offered breathlessly as he fished in his pocket and pulled out a biscuit for Lucifer. "Sorry."

I smiled. "Did Madame Lelu need your services?"

Isham nodded. "The lightbulb in her bedroom was out again."

"Of course," I remarked. "And you're so tall."

My neighbor down the hill and her less-than-subtle attempts to lure the young man inside were a running joke between us.

Isham patted Lucifer on the head and grinned up at me. "You know how it is with these lonely older women," he countered playfully.

Isham was a nice kid, a first-generation Frenchman with a good Arab name and manners to match. He took my ribbing in good humor and gave as good as he got, but I could tell by the way his face colored that Madame Lelu's attentions made him slightly uncomfort-able.

"You'll take some eggs, won't you?" I asked, handing him my pack-age.

Isham nodded, too polite to refuse, though the courtesy would make him later still. Then his eyes shifted to the shotgun propped up against the front hall table, and he stepped back slightly.

"*Le renard,*" I explained, my eyes following Isham's.

"*Oui,* madame. Of course, the fox."

"I've lost two hens already this week. I just want to scare him a lit-tle. And you know how Lucifer is, a softie at heart." I smiled easily, nothing more to it than that, then turned for the kitchen.

"They've been laying like crazy all week," I called as I grabbed the basket of eggs I'd reserved for Isham off the counter, then padded back into the foyer. "It must be the warm weather."

"Yes," he agreed, one foot already out the door as he took the bas-ket. "Or it could be the fox. I've heard fear will make them do that.

"*Bonne nuit,*" he added. Then he jogged across the gravel drive and swung himself up into his truck.

■ ■ ■

I watched the FedEx truck pull out into the lane, then loaded Lucifer into the back of the Renault and headed to town for dinner provi-sions. There was no sign of my visitor on the darkening road, but I was thinking about him. His disappearing act had made me nervous, as I was sure it had been meant to do.

I made several stops, and it was late when I got back to the house, well past dark. The Twingo was there again, though this time Val-samis had pulled right into the driveway. When I swung in off the road, my lights flashed across his back window, and I could see his head inside, his shoulders low in the bucket seat.

I cut the engine and sat for a moment, trying to decide how to play things. I've seen people run when they didn't have to and get into a lot of trouble because of it. On the other hand, I've always thought it best never to volunteer anything.

In the end, Valsamis made the first move. The dome light snapped on as he climbed out, momentarily revealing his trim frame. He had the body of a featherweight, compact and muscular, but he was dressed more like a salesman or a lost member of some middle-agers tour group: loafers, pleated chinos, a blue button-down shirt. In his right hand, he held a brown leather briefcase.

I opened my car door, and Lucifer leaped across me, paws scrabbling on the drive's loose gravel as he darted toward the stranger, teeth bared in an unfriendly greeting.

The man didn't flinch. He snapped his fingers once, and the dog quieted.

"Luce!" I called, patting my leg. The dog gave Valsamis one last look, then stalked back toward me, his shoulders rippling beneath his black coat.

Valsamis closed his door and the light switched off, leaving him in darkness again. "Hello, Nicole," he said, coming toward me.

"Did Ed send you?" I asked, bringing my right hand to rest on Lucifer's broad head. If the man was another con, I figured he must be a friend of my father's, that Ed had run out of money and sent one of his rummy pals to track me down.

But Valsamis shook his head, all teeth and eyes swaying slowly from side to side. "Why don't we go inside?" he proposed.

■ ■ ■

"You've got a nice life here," Valsamis observed as I closed the door and switched on a light. Lucifer squeezed past us, giving me a protective glance before heading for the kitchen.

"I don't have any money," I told him, struggling momentarily to make the transition from French. Like everyone else in my business, I spoke English out of necessity. I'd spent several years in the States, but French was what I'd grown up with.

Valsamis didn't say anything. There's a certain lazy arrogance that comes with being a native English speaker, a self-assuredness born of the knowledge that yours will always be the common language and that you will have a distinct advantage because of it. I could sense this conceit in Valsamis. He stood with his arms stiff at his sides and glanced around the old farmhouse. It was by no means a mansion, but it was nicer than what a lot of people have, nicer than anything I'd ever had in the past. It was a place I took pride in, each inch of centuries-old stone and wood restored by my own hands.

I moved back toward the kitchen, letting Valsamis get a good look at the twelve-gauge. I'd already decided I wasn't playing the guessing game with him. I had a talent for waiting people out, and sooner or later, I figured, he'd have to tell me what he'd come for.

He lingered a moment, then trailed after me, leaning in the kitchen doorway while I set down my groceries on the counter. He looked even smaller inside than he had in the drive, dwarfed by the doorway that had been built to accommodate a much larger frame. In the harsh light of the kitchen, I could see the coarseness in him, the way a flaw in a gem might be revealed under a jeweler's loupe.

I guessed him to be around sixty, though it was impossible to tell for sure. His age could have swung ten years in either direction. An affectation born of the system, I thought, the way it hardened and softened you at the same time. There were women like this at the Maison des Baumettes, ageless lifers, bodies slackened by too much starch, minds wound by fear. And Valsamis? Not prison, surely, but a captive nonetheless.

"Yes," Valsamis remarked. "It certainly is nice. Though it must be lonely up here, and quiet. You don't miss the old days? Lisbon? Marseille? Dinner at midnight on La Rambla?"

"What do you want?" I asked.

Valsamis was silent, watching me. "It was a shame," he said, "that business in Marseille."

There was menace in his voice. He reminded me of the floor

guards at the prison, dough-faced bullies with sticks and keys. Pussy-whipped, my cell mate, Celine, used to say of the cruelest. Though with Valsamis, there was a sense that the power was real.

"They don't know you're here, do they?" he continued. "The French, I mean?"

I looked up at him, at his predator's face. "I'm not hurting anyone by being here," I said. "My paycheck comes from England, after all, from Solomon."

"No . . ." Valsamis said, the remark part question and part answer. "But I seem to recall that there were some conditions on your release. Something about leaving the country, wasn't it?"

I felt my face tighten, and my gut went with it.

Valsamis looked around the kitchen one last time and out the double doors toward the dark garden beyond. "It would be a shame to lose it."

"I already told you," I said. "I don't have any money."

Valsamis shook his head and opened his briefcase, then pulled out a folded piece of paper. "Go on," he urged, holding it toward me. The knuckles of his right hand were mottled with old scars.

I took the paper and unfolded it. It was a computer printout, a black-and-white image and text. At the top of the page, in bold block letters, were the words RED NOTICE. An Interpol term, I thought, words reserved for only a lucky few, a growing cadre of men and a scant handful of women deemed serious terrorist threats by the international police organization.

Below the words was a picture of a man's face, a head shot taken, it seemed, for some official purpose, driver's license or passport. The man was looking directly into the camera, his delicate features expressionless, his hair cropped close to his scalp. It was a face I knew well, even after so many years, and the sight of it in such a context made me flinch.

RAHIM ALI, large text above the picture read. Beneath it, under the heading ALIASES, were some half-dozen other names: Ahmed Ali, Nassar Ali, Hassan Abdallah, Nassar Abdallah, Harun al-Nassar. Beneath the names was a long list of biographical information. *Place of birth: Morocco. Dates of birth used: January 15, 1959; April 2, 1961; March 19, 1962. Height: 6′2″. Weight: 180. Hair: brown. Eyes: brown. Complexion: dark. Scars and marks: none. Languages: Arabic, French, English, Spanish, Portuguese. Citizenship: Moroccan.*

Whoever had compiled the information had done a sloppy job. The inventory of aliases was woefully incomplete, as was the list of languages. When I'd known Rahim, he'd spoken fairly good Dutch and German, as well as a smattering of some of the Slavic tongues. He had a gift for languages, and it seemed unlikely that he wouldn't have added a few more to his résumé since I'd known him.

There was one other glaring error in Rahim's profile, four words that kept catching my eye. It was a small thing, really, one I shouldn't have been surprised to have seen omitted, but for some reason it bothered me more than any of the other errors. *Scars and marks: none,* I read again, and I could almost feel the raised wound on Rahim's stomach, the long gash just below his ribs that I'd liked to run my fingers over while he slept. His body's only imperfection, I'd thought at the time, like the toothed smudge of a potter's mark on smooth clay.

"Bring back memories?" I heard Valsamis say.

"Is this a joke?" I asked.

Valsamis cocked his head to one side. "Now, why would you say that?"

"This. All of this," I said, motioning to the paper. "He's not a terrorist."

Valsamis took a business card from the briefcase and handed it to me. JOHN VALSAMIS, it said. In the center of the card was an embossed seal, an eagle grasping three crossed arrows, and around it the words DEPARTMENT OF DEFENSE, UNITED STATES OF AMERICA.

"We'd like you to look up your old friend for us," he said.

So this was what he'd come for. Not me but someone else. What I could give him.

"I don't do this," I told him. "Besides, I haven't seen Rahim in years. I can't help you."

"We think you can." Valsamis said this as if it were a fact that had been clearly established, as if I and my opinions had little bearing on the situation.

"Well, you're wrong." I glanced down at the picture of Rahim. It didn't do him justice, didn't capture even half of the breath-stopping quality of his face.

Valsamis opened his briefcase and took out a thin manila folder. "The American embassy in Nairobi," he said. He slid an eight-by-ten photograph from between the tan flaps and offered it to me.

The picture was familiar, a scene that had been played and re-played on the news and in the papers when it had happened over four years earlier. It showed the charred hulk of a car and a vast mountain of rubble behind it. Some two hundred people, I remembered, mostly Kenyans, had died in the bombing, and another five thousand had been injured.

"Your friend," Valsamis said, "and his friends in the IAR."

"You've got to be kidding." I shook my head. "Rahim's not a radical. He's one of the least political people I've ever known." And hadn't we all been? Not a crusader among us, unless you counted money as a cause, and even that had its limits. I couldn't imagine Rahim working for the Islamic Armed Revolution, no matter what they offered him.

"Times change," Valsamis said. He handed me a second photograph, one that I hadn't seen in the papers. It was of a young Kenyan woman and a child. The woman was dead, tossed to the ground, both legs blown clean off above the knees. The child, a little girl of two or three, was alive. She stood next to the body of what had once been her mother with a blank look and a blood-spattered face.

"There's more." Valsamis flipped through the remaining pictures, offering glimpses of eviscerated bodies, shoes, tattered pieces of clothing, everyday objects juxtaposed against the horrific. A woman's handbag lay in a pool of blood. A framed photograph of someone's wife and children poked out from a heap of smoldering bricks. "I've been there," Valsamis said. "It was right in the middle of the city. Most of the people killed didn't even work at the embassy."

"It's terrible," I agreed, and meant it, meant more than that. "But you're wrong about Rahim. I know him. This isn't something he would do." I turned the pictures facedown, set them down on the counter.

"Rahim was recruited by the IAR four years ago. He made all the documents they needed for their part in the bombing. Apparently his older brother has been with the organization for some time."

"Driss?"

Valsamis nodded. "I understand you knew him in Lisbon."

I shrugged. To say I'd known Driss was an overstatement. Rahim's brother had stayed with us for a month on his way to France, but he and I had barely spoken.

"He did a stint in one of Hassan II's prisons, as I understand it," Valsamis remarked, producing three more photographs from the folder. "Some hole in the desert for dissenters. Not a pleasant experience, I'm sure."

Valsamis handed the first of the pictures to me. It was a photograph of Rahim and Driss, the two brothers caught unaware, walking together down a city street. "This was taken just last month," Valsamis explained, "in Lisbon."

"So Rahim's brother visited him," I conceded. "But even if Driss is with the IAR, this doesn't make Rahim a terrorist."

Valsamis nodded patiently, then put the second photograph in my hand. Some dozen men were seated around a long table, each in full military dress, each sporting a dark mustache. And at the head of the table, like a patriarch at a family dinner, his face unmistakable, sat Saddam Hussein.

"Ibrahim al-Rashidi," Valsamis said, pointing to the man to the immediate right of Hussein. "Saddam's second in command in Iraqi intelligence."

I shrugged again. "I still don't see what this has to do with Rahim."

Valsamis added the third picture to the stack. "We took this last week," he said. "Lisbon again."

It was Lisbon, all right. The picture had been taken at the Café a Brasileira, just off the Largo do Chiado. The café's trademark yellow umbrellas were a dull shade of gray in the black-and-white photograph, but I recognized them nonetheless. In the center of the picture, at one of the outdoor tables, two men sat over coffees.

"Al-Rashidi," Valsamis said, pointing to the man on the right. He was in civilian dress now, a dark business suit and tie. "I don't have to tell you who his companion is."

I looked down at the face, the eyes and lips fading into the paper's dark ink. Twelve years and I would have known him anywhere.

"We have serious and credible intelligence that the IAR is planning something with the help of the Iraqis," Valsamis said, taking a careful step back. "Something bigger than Nairobi, and Rahim is part of it."

I shook my head, flipped back and forth between the pictures, between al-Rashidi's face and Rahim's, not wanting to believe what I saw. "You're going to have to do better than that."

"You know I can't," Valsamis answered, but he paused as if considering breaking the rules.

Nuclear, I thought, or biological, like the attacks on the Kurdish villages. Or the Trade Center all over again.

"We need your help, Nicole."

I leaned back against the counter, fingering that phantom cigarette. "Get out of my house," I told him.

Valsamis took a step as if to go, then hesitated and turned back to me. He reached out and flipped the stack of pictures on the counter back over so that the girl and her mother were on top, caught forever in that moment of loss. "A car bomb," he said, tapping the photograph with his index finger, nudging it slightly in my direction.

The statement hit me hard, and my eyes flew to Valsamis before I could catch myself. Not luck, I thought, searching his face, not mere coincidence, this choice of words. And yet Valsamis's face betrayed nothing. His head was bent just slightly, his own eyes focused on the girl and her mother. No, I thought, pushing away the dark reminder, he didn't know, could not have known.

"Sleep on it," Valsamis said confidently. "I'll be back in the morning." Then he turned and headed for the front door.

FOUR

■ ■ ■

AFTER VALSAMIS LEFT, I poured myself a glass of wine and went out and sat on the back patio with Lucifer. It was a cold night, with nothing of the day's warmth left. The moon was up, fat and full, a silver coin just cresting the opposite hillside. A thick fog had settled on the valley floor, dense and pillowy, and here and there in the distance, a few lights were visible, mountainside perches like mine, twinkling in the darkness. Below, the town was just a dim smear, only its hilltop church shining above the mist, ancient windows blazing with orange light, stone foundation skimming the clouds. In the distance, a rough doppelgänger, the Château d'Aguilar looked down from its own aerie island.

This was not a life I had ever expected, but it was one I'd come to cherish, the rhythm of each day like that of the one before. Out in my garden, in the cold beds tidied and blanketed for winter, I knew the shape of each flower to come. First the bulbs, crocuses and tulips, then the bright orange of poppies. Blue and white came next, the towering spikes of delphiniums. And in July, the garish yellows and reds of the daylilies, before the August flush of pink phlox.

On my first day at the Maison des Baumettes prison in Marseille, my cell mate, Celine, had pointed to one of the photographs above her bunk, a bright color glossy of a little girl balanced on a black rubber playground swing.

"Find something," Celine had said, motioning to the child, legs dangling in midair, feet in scuffed red sandals, toenails glittering hot pink. And next to the girl, another picture, a man leaning against the side of a car, ankles crossed, hands in pockets, shirt untucked. "If you want to make it out of here, find something."

That night, in the institutional half-darkness, I'd lain awake listening to the sounds of the cell block, the clatter of keys, the muffled patter of the night guards, the slow breathing of some hundred pairs of lungs. Find something, I'd heard Celine say, but for me there had been nothing. No Kodachrome sheen, no girl on a green scrap of lawn. I was alone by then, my grandparents dead several years earlier, and my aunt shortly after, from cancer.

It took me almost half a year to find the one bright snapshot that would see me through my sentence, and in the end it had been not a lover or a child but a place. Not even a place but the memory of it. A town I'd been to some dozen years earlier, seventeen years old and working the grape harvest. A little valley in the Pyrenees. A bright café with cracked green walls. Stone streets leading up to a hilltop church. This was what I'd promised myself, those six long years in the gray hive of the prison.

When the doors had swung open on me that last day, I'd headed straight to Gare St.-Charles. And from there to Geneva, to a bank on the rue du Rhône, a quiet room in the basement, and a metal drawer that held everything I'd left behind. The few things my aunt had given me, pictures of another time, the letters she and my mother had exchanged during their years apart. And cash, enough money for an old farmhouse with a graying stone wall and a chicken coop. A garden set amid the scrub and limestone hills. Eggs so fresh they steamed in the cold morning air. This place. And the long-held promise that I would never go back to prison again.

All that I had in the world. And what had Valsamis said? *It would be a shame to lose it.*

Lucifer sniffed the wind and whined, the wolf in him straining toward the night's riot of scent. Damp rosemary and juniper. The mice in the hedge, the skunk in the old pine.

"Viens." I patted my thigh, and the dog lumbered toward me, cir-

cling the ground at my side before sinking to his stomach. He sighed, then rested his snout on his crossed paws.

I took a sip of wine and closed my eyes, trying to forget Valsamis's pictures, Nairobi and that little girl. But the images clustered in the darkness before me, the hands and faces of the dead jostling against one another like the dry husks of my pole beans on their weathered trellis. On the legless woman's cheek, a stray lock of hair. The girl looking slightly away, as if to shield herself from the immodesty of death.

In another place, at another time, a phone rings and my grand-mother answers, pushing her own dark hair behind her ear. A word and then silence. She turns to me, and I know something terrible has happened. On the other end of the line, there is panic, a garbled voice. "No," I hear my grandmother say, and then "Mina."

Mina, my mother's name.

It's the thing we've been waiting for, the thing we've all expected yet been certain would never happen. My mother is dead, caught in a random act of violence in the city she loved more than all of us, her life extinguished by a car bomb intended for somebody else, for any-one but her.

And what *did* I think Rahim capable of? I wondered. *You're wrong about Rahim,* I'd told Valsamis. *I know him.* But even as I'd said it, I hadn't believed it. For in the end, hadn't that been our problem? Hadn't the truth been how little we really knew each other? The di-vide we had been unable to breach?

Lucifer lifted his head and rose to attention, his ears stiffening, his eyes scanning the darkness. On the farm below, a dog started barking and another joined in as something wild and menacing made its way along the hillside. A fox or a skunk, or maybe even a wolf. Whatever it was, the dogs could smell it coming.

Something bigger than Nairobi, I thought, and I was back in Lis-bon then, back in our apartment in Santa Catarina. I'd said some-thing smart about Driss, I remembered, his first night with us, something about false piety and wanting what you couldn't have. We were standing in the kitchen, Rahim coaxing an omelet from the pan, and I remember how he turned to me, his whole body suddenly bristling with fury. He clenched his fists, and I thought he might hit me.

Times change, I heard Valsamis say.

FIVE

■ ■ ■

THROUGH THE GRIMY PORTHOLE in the kitchen door, John Valsamis could see his waiter, the man's pocked face and Gaul cheekbones. The owner's nephew, he thought, or a cousin. Who else would want to work here, grease-stained as it was, the air tinged with the odor of turning meat? The man lit a cigarette and scratched at the back of his neck, his fingers raking the oily fringe of hair above his collar.

Valsamis dipped the corner of his napkin in his wine and wiped the tines of his fork, suddenly wishing he'd braved the fog to find the restaurant two towns over, the one Dick Morrow had recommended back in D.C. The best cassoulet in France, Dick had boasted. True or not, it would have been better than the watery pot-au-feu Valsamis no doubt faced now.

In any other car, he would have made the trip, but he hadn't trusted his tin-can rental on the slick mountain roads. Valsamis silently cursed the rental agent in Perpignan, the girl's surly smile as she handed him the keys. "It's all we have left, monsieur," she'd said, and he'd seen there was nothing to be done except smile back.

The local wine was drinkable, a bit rough but with a character that Valsamis could appreciate. Like the wine his father had made each fall in their cellar in Anaconda, the stench of the fermenting fruit wafting up through the floorboards. Though those had been California grapes, shipped into Montana on a railcar for the Italian mine workers.

Valsamis took a sip, then slid his cell phone from his pocket and punched in the Virginia area code and Dick Morrow's number.

As always, it was Morrow who answered, his voice tight, slightly irritated. Midafternoon on the East Coast, Valsamis thought.

"I've found her," Valsamis said.

"She's agreed?"

"More or less."

Morrow coughed. "Which is it?"

"She'll do it," Valsamis assured him, thinking of the look on Nicole's face when he'd left, how she'd watched him. Yes, he thought, he had gotten to her. She would agree in the end.

"You're sure she'll be able to find him?"

"Yes," Valsamis said, though in truth he wasn't so confident. Twelve years was a long time.

There was silence on the other end of the line, then finally Morrow spoke. "I want you in Lisbon."

Valsamis flinched. "I thought you had someone else to clean up the Portuguese end of things."

"Change of plans," Morrow said, trying to sound just a bit too cheerful about it, as if the whole thing were a picnic that had been rained out and now they'd be eating inside instead.

They'd had him in mind all along, Valsamis thought, but hadn't bothered to tell him.

"I thought you'd be pleased, actually," Morrow continued. "After all, it's been your project, and it was your idea to use the woman. This will give you a chance to finish what you started."

"Of course." Valsamis recovered himself. "Just surprised is all."

Morrow cleared his throat. "I don't have to remind you, John. We can't afford to have anything go wrong this time."

No, Valsamis thought, it was he who couldn't afford another mistake.

"No loose ends," Morrow cautioned. "Understood? You'll take care of them when this is finished. Ali and the woman both." Not a question, not even a request, but a command.

"Yes," Valsamis agreed. So this was why they wanted him in Lisbon. For the dirty work as well as the clean. "I understand."

"Good." Morrow went to hang up, but Valsamis stopped him.

"Any news from the Pakistanis?" he asked casually.

"Not yet," Morrow replied. "But you know how it is. We've got to oblige our hosts. Let them at least believe they've got a hand in things. I imagine we'll be sending someone over in a few days. That'll give Kanj time to soften up, anyway."

Time, Valsamis thought, but not much, not enough. He'd have to work quickly, but if things went smoothly in Lisbon, he'd have all the time he needed. There was a dull hum of empty air, and Morrow clicked off.

Valsamis put away his cell phone and lifted his glass again. Yes, there was definitely something to the wine. Lavender and wild thyme and rosemary, the taste of the Pyrenean scrub.

He closed his eyes and thought of the house in Anaconda, the high-altitude sheen of Indian summer. In the backyard, his father's old winepress, the wood stained with dark juice, and his father smiling up at him, the neck of his shirt ringed with sweat, his big hands on the iron crank.

The kitchen door swung open and the waiter appeared. He set Valsamis's food down in front of him, a hunk of grisly beef, a few pale vegetables floating in a greasy broth.

"*Merci*," Valsamis said, but the man was already gone, leaving him alone again, the sole diner in the oversize room. He took a bite of the meat and chewed, the food no better or worse than he had expected.

Yes, he told himself, there would be no loose ends. He would find Ali, and he would put it all to rest.

■ ■ ■

Lucifer woke me at seven the next morning, huge paws prodding me through my blankets, wide-eyed as a puppy and ready for the day ahead. Such boundless energy that I had to let him out the back door while I gulped my first cup of coffee and slipped into my boots and coat for our morning walk. It was a cold day and clear, the fog peeled back to reveal the valley, the hills dew-drenched and glistening in the bright morning sunshine. I let Lucifer run ahead on our daily circuit, nosing his way briefly along the road, then up the narrow path that led to the windy ridge above the house and back again.

The dog had put a fair bit of distance between us by the time I emerged onto the road, but when he reached the driveway, he stopped, as he had the day before, feet frozen in the gravel.

"Good dog," I called, patting my thigh, urging him back to me, but he held his ground, his steely eyes shifting from me to the house and back again.

I didn't see Valsamis when I first stepped into the driveway. The little white Twingo was there, Valsamis's briefcase and a white paper bag resting on the hood, but the car itself was empty. At first I thought he'd let himself inside, but then the door of the henhouse opened, and he stepped out and came toward me through the side garden. His hands were up in triumph, and in each palm were two eggs.

"Breakfast!" he called out as I started forward, catching Lucifer by the collar, hooking in his leash.

"I stopped at the bakery," he said, nodding to the hood of the car, slipping the eggs into his pockets.

I watched his hands disappear, his meaty fingers against the clean brown shells. Lucifer growled, tugging at his leash, and I pulled him back.

Valsamis picked up his briefcase and the paper bag. "I was thinking you could make some coffee."

■ ■ ■

"You know, you're a hard woman to find," Valsamis remarked, settling himself at my kitchen table.

I stripped off my coat and filled Lucifer's bowl. The dog eyed Valsamis one last time, then warily began to eat.

"Even your father doesn't know where you are." Valsamis slid the eggs from his pockets and set them in the center of the table. Not breakfast, I thought, but a reminder of what he could do to me and when. "What is it, fifty, sixty kilometers from here to Collioure? And you haven't once paid him a visit."

I scooped some beans into the coffee grinder and turned on the little machine, then packed the espresso maker and set it on the stove alongside a saucepan of milk. "You didn't come all this way to talk about my father," I told him.

"You're right," Valsamis agreed. "I assume you've given our conversation some thought."

"Why me?" I asked. "I mean, why do you need me to find Rahim? Isn't that what people like you do? You found me."

"He knows we're looking," Valsamis said. "We need someone he trusts, someone who can ask around."

"And how do you know he'll want to see me? It's been a long time."

Valsamis opened the paper bag and surveyed the contents, then pulled out a *pain au chocolat* and offered it to me.

I shook my head.

"You were quite the couple once, as I understand it. Love of his life and all that," Valsamis observed.

"Well, things change, don't they?" I turned off the heat under the milk and poured out two mugs, then topped them with espresso and handed one to Valsamis. "Okay," I agreed. "Let's say he would want to see me. What makes you so sure he's even in Lisbon?"

Valsamis sipped at his coffee, then tore off a piece of his croissant and smiled slightly, clearly pleased at my capitulation, at himself for having known I'd eventually agree. "We have reason to believe it's in his best interest."

"I'll bet you do."

Valsamis ignored the remark. He opened his briefcase and produced a thick stack of euros. "*Pour les frais,*" he said. For expenses. "You'll leave this morning."

"I'm to drive?" I asked, momentarily thrown off by the language leap before finding my footing in French.

Valsamis nodded.

"And once I get to Lisbon?"

"There's a room in your name at the Pensão Rosa. Do you know the place?"

I shook my head.

"It's in the Bairro Alto. On the rua da Rosa. You'll find it easily. Someone will contact you when you get there."

His accent was immaculate, his French flawless, unquestionably better than my English, and this was a statement, I thought, as the eggs had been. A way of making me acknowledge the inherent inequality in our relationship.

Valsamis shut his briefcase and stood up from the table, leaving his coffee and croissant nearly untouched.

"And when I find him?" I asked.

"We'll worry about that." He started to go, then turned back to me as if he'd forgotten some important piece of information. "Just think of it as giving back to your country, Nicole."

■ ■ ■

I once heard it said that there is no such thing as an accidental American. That we are, all of us, citizens by conscious choice. Of course, it was a Frenchman who posited this, some self-proclaimed modern philosopher on one of the political discussion shows on France 2, so I've always taken the theory with a grain of salt. After all, to be an American has never been my choice. I was raised in Lebanon and have lived most of the rest of my life in Europe. I've claimed France as my home and chosen the one profession in which these things can be changed. I'm my own universal consulate. I can whip out any decent passport in a matter of hours.

If anything, I am a mongrel, the daughter of a father who was, himself, a drifter and a con man. My mother was a half-breed with

French and Maronite parentage and an Arabic name. A woman whose own country had been stitched together by naive outsiders to form an optimistic whole.

"Just this one thing," she used to say, speaking of her last meeting with my father and what little she'd asked of him. She was proud of the fact, proud to have done for herself. Six months pregnant and on her own, her possessions only what she could carry in one small bag. Two loaves of bread and a spare change of clothes.

And the one thing? Certainly not money. No, what my mother had wanted was merely a signature, an acknowledgment of paternity. The only thing of value she thought my father could give me.

Not a name or even legitimacy but a life she imagined for her child, a certain freedom and power. The amphibious vehicles of the Sixth Fleet swarming in the Beirut harbor. An adolescent memory of the young marines with their GI haircuts and broad smiles. Rock and roll and Jackie Onassis. Places my mother and her sister had visited four years earlier on a trip to New York City. Greenwich Village jazz clubs. Hordes of overcoated diners at Schrafft's. The crush of rush hour on the subway. Women in stockings and high heels. Women who worked.

In the scrawled slope of my father's name, she'd seen all of this. America, Americans, and what it meant to be one. And five months later, in a maternity hospital in Paris, still groggy from the drugs, my mother had fought for this one thing on my birth certificate. *Father's nationality: American.*

Not a choice, then, but a legacy, a truth from which I cannot ever fully escape. My name, my own blue passport in a drawer, the real one, the cover indelibly stamped with the seal of the United States of America.

So when Valsamis turned back to me, I stared up at him, trying at first to get the joke, then realizing he was serious.

"Which country is that?" I asked.

■ ■ ■

I waited until I was sure Valsamis was gone, then walked a sulking Lucifer down the road to his temporary exile at the neighbors' house and headed back home to pack. I found a small shoulder bag in my closet and tossed a couple of changes of clothes inside, clean underwear and the essentials, toothbrush and soap. Traveling light, as I'd always liked it. Traveling optimistically as well. And why not? A week at most, I'd promised myself. A week at most, and I'd be back to Lucifer and the hens.

When I was done, I made my way to my office and sent a short e-mail to Solomon to let them know I'd be gone, then headed downstairs again. Valsamis's uneaten croissant and cold coffee were still on the kitchen table. I cleared his place, washed the dishes, and took the full garbage bag from below the sink.

The photographs of Rahim and the embassy were on the counter where Valsamis had set them the night before. I picked them up, meaning to throw them away, then hesitated and, unable to stop myself, thumbed through them one last time. It was a narrative of violence, a reminder of what terror can do. On one end, Rahim. On the other, the child, the little girl. And on both their faces, the same expression of hopelessness, the same inward turning of self and soul.

And in one of the other pictures, something I hadn't noticed before. At the outer edge of the rubble, half buried beneath the twisted frame of a bicycle, a dog, someone's pet. Not a dog but part of one. Paw and leg and shoulder and half a face, the rest of the creature cleaved clean away.

"*Les brutes*," I could hear my aunt Emilie saying after we'd buried my mother. Even then I'd thought, No, animals wouldn't have done this.

A week, I told myself again, dropping the photographs into the trash bag, then opening the back door and setting the garbage on the steps. I would find him and I would come home. I would be back before the crocuses flowered.

■ ■ ■

Valsamis skirted Perpignan and nudged the Twingo onto the race-track of the A9, forcing the gas pedal to the floor, trying for power that just wasn't there. In his rearview mirror, he could see headlights fast approaching, then a brief blinked warning before one car after another flew by him. Valsamis downshifted and tried the accelerator again, coaxing another ten miles an hour out of the engine. Better, he told himself, but still, it was going to be a slow trip south. He'd have to make good time if he wanted to get to Lisbon before Nicole.

It was a clear day, the sky bright and cloudless, Mont Canigou visible through the sooty scrim of diesel haze, the city thinning to farm-land and vineyards, the rocky fields still bare, scarred by the plow. Valsamis relaxed into his seat, slid from his pocket the disposable cell phone he'd bought at the airport, and checked for reception.

No such thing as a valueless contact, Valsamis heard Andy Sproul say. A dead man's counsel, the first thing Sproul had told him when he'd gotten to Beirut. Valsamis hated advice, should have hated Sproul for his presumption. Still green as the Iowa cornfields in which he'd been raised, and already Sproul had the world figured out. Yet Valsamis hadn't been able to hate him. It just wasn't possible.

And now, all these years later, it was Sproul's advice that came back to Valsamis. Sproul's ghost, smiling out from beneath his blond mop of hair, thumbing the deck of cards he always carried with him. Good for a game of 41 or Basra with the old men who inhabited the Hamra cafés, and Sproul holding his own like a native. He'd been right, of course: There was no such thing as a valueless contact. But then Valsamis had figured that out long before Beirut.

Valsamis pushed Sproul to the back of his mind and dialed the number in Peshawar, heard the phone ring on the other side of the world. Sproul's wasn't the only ghost that had come back to haunt him these last few days, though not all were as pleasant.

The line clicked open on the fifth ring, and Valsamis was relieved to hear Kamran Javed's voice in his ear.

"It's me again," Valsamis told his old friend. "Any news on Kanj?"

"He was moved yesterday," Javed said.

An Audi sped by on the Twingo's left, and Valsamis's grip on the steering wheel tightened suddenly. "Where to?"

"Officially, Amman. I told you before, it was only a matter of time. I kept him here for as long as I could."

Valsamis looked down at his hand. His knuckles were white, his arm shaking. "Yes," he told Javed. "I know." But he was thinking: Not long enough.

SIX

■ ■ ■

THIS BEAUTIFUL TIME, my mother used to say, speaking of her country in the years after the Americans left and before the Six-Day War, before the flood of Palestinians from the south. The time in which she became a woman. In Beirut and along the coast, there was French champagne and American music. "Moon River" and the twist. And in Jounieh, at the Casino du Liban, women in Dior dresses clustered at the roulette tables, their wrists glittering with diamonds, their bare shoulders tanned by the Mediterranean sun.

For a few earnest students, the shadow of 1958 remained. In the Hamra coffee shops, Joan Baez and Bob Dylan warbled over fuzzy speakers. But for most of the country, there was hope, a peace that people convinced themselves might hold. More important, there was money. Money to fuel one long last blind hurrah before the looming specter of civil war.

It is difficult for me to imagine Lebanon as it was then, knowing it as I do, through the filters of childhood and war. Hard for me to imagine the things my mother and her sister so often described, the Eden of the American University, seen through the eyes of the two young students these women once were. Even as a child, I understood the power of nostalgia, time's ripening of memory. Even then I had my suspicions.

"We were arm in arm," my aunt Emilie would say, recounting the parties and concerts, the professors they had tormented, the boys with whom they had flirted. Muslim and Christian and Druze all united under the banner of youth and prosperity. "Arm in arm," she would repeat, looking at my mother for confirmation in those rare times when I knew them to be together, and my mother would nod, though in a way that made me think she wasn't quite so sure.

Of course, by the time my mother met my father, Lebanon had already begun to change. For the young and wealthy, there were still yacht parties in Byblos and winter weekends on the slopes at Faraya-Mzaar. But along the border, and in the refugee camps south of Beirut, the humiliations of the Six-Day War had erupted into rage. And in the mountains around the Qadisha Valley, young Phalangists trained for battle.

My father must have been one of the last of his kind to arrive before the war, drifting south along the Mediterranean, following the scents of Chanel and good Cuban cigars, the fading reek of other people's money. Not a fighter but a two-bit hustler from Buffalo with an expensive tuxedo and a nice face. A man who hadn't been born to privilege but who had studied it and knew how to work a room. A gigolo, my aunt Emilie had once called him.

My aunt had been there the day my parents met in the ski lodge at Faraya-Mzaar, and she had disliked my father from the start. Too loud and too flashy, she'd thought, but my mother had seen something else in the tall American. When they ran into each other again at the St. Georges yacht club, my mother suspected fate.

Three weeks later, the day after the Israelis bombed the Beirut airport in retaliation for an attack on one of their planes in Athens, my mother found out that she was pregnant. But by then my father was long gone, heading north across the Mediterranean with the son of a Texas oil tycoon. Cruising toward the Aegean and on to the French Riviera, riding the next wave of free hospitality. Not long after, my mother was on her way north herself, packed off to a convent in the Dordogne, the only respectable solution for a girl in her straits.

■ ■ ■

There was no view from my window at the Pensão Rosa, nothing to see except the dark rooms that looked back at me from across the hotel's narrow air shaft, and the collection of items that had mysteri-ously found their way to its bottom. Among the thicket of weeds and garbage lay a stained T-shirt, a pair of red lace panties, an old pillow, and a single brown shoe. Overhead, there was just a cramped square of sky.

Watching, I told myself, scanning the blank windows. Here and there, where the curtains had been left open and a light was still on, I could see the dioramas inside, the furnishings identical in their shabbiness, yellow walls and sagging chairs, beds cupped by the cu-mulative weight of all the bodies they had borne. Valsamis would be out there somewhere, watching. And listening. This, the price of his hospitality, this room so conveniently waiting for me.

I hadn't planned to go to our old apartment on the Travessa da Laranjeira that first night back, but the long drive had left me road-weary and restless, so I left my bag in the room and headed down again in the Rosa's rickety elevator.

Just a short walk, I told myself as I left the hotel and started up the hill, to stretch my legs and clear my head. But I headed almost instinctively for the Largo do Calhariz, then plunged down into the warren of streets that lay to the west of the Bica funicular.

What I had come for, I wasn't sure exactly. Certainly not Rahim, since the chances of his being here were slim to none, less than none if he didn't want to be found. Still, I was relieved to discover our old building as it had been, the plaster facade the same sooty shade of pink, the gutters still shaggy with wild mint. At the end of the street, the flowering almond tree, bare now save for its spring stubble.

The old gas streetlamps were lit, and the firelight flickered off the shuttered windows and crumbling railings. Beyond them, I thought, a double bed with an iron frame, a single chair upholstered in faded green tapestry, and a dark mahogany dressing table. At least there had been.

The windows that faced the street were dark, but back in the interior of the apartment, where the kitchen was, a light burned. Someone moved across the doorway; a head was all I could see from where I stood. Then, as if on cue, the bedroom light snapped on.

I held my breath and waited, watching a woman's silhouette skate into view, and behind her, the blurred shape of a man. The couple kissed briefly, their shadows merging, then the man stepped forward and brushed aside the curtains.

I don't do this, I could hear myself say as I watched the man lean out to pull the window closed. It was what I'd told Valsamis that first night in Paziols. And yet here I was.

But then wasn't this what anyone would have done? One life for how many others?

Still, when the gaslight caught the man's face, and I could see finally that it wasn't Rahim, what I felt was only relief.

■ ■ ■

Another March, the spring of 1990. After two years in America, I'd come home to a Europe transformed. On Karl-Marx-Allee, in the shadow of the deserted guard towers, East Berliners were hawking broken pieces of the wall. In the flea markets of Prague and Moscow, tourists could buy a Red Army uniform for the price of a bottle of cheap vodka. Communism was on sale, and no one wanted to miss out on a slice of the profits.

"Money to be made," my friend Martine had told me on my first night back in Paris, and she hadn't been talking about souvenirs. By then the whole Soviet arsenal was up for grabs. But while everyone else was heading east, I went south, down to Marseille and the southwest coast of France. Trying to pick up the scent of my old life, I told myself, past clients and connections. Though I was really looking for my father, hoping and yet not hoping to find him.

I was still nursing my wounds from the end of the venomous relationship that had taken me to the States. Swearing off men, I'd told myself. Swearing, even as I watched Rahim cross the room toward me one night at a party at a friend's house in Marseille. Knowing that if he offered, I wouldn't be able to refuse. And he had.

What I wanted from him that first night was shamefully little. A place to spend the night. The sweet consolation of his body. The cool forgetfulness of sex, the simplicity of it. Nothing more than what I knew he would be willing to offer, though what I had to give was less.

Ours was the kind of company in which it wasn't polite to inquire about income or means, but I could tell by looking, by the Swiss watch on his wrist and the buffed moons of his manicured nails, that Rahim had done well for himself. So I was surprised, later, when the taxi he'd called drove us up into the poor, mostly North African Quartier Panier and dropped us in front of one of the no-name immigrant hotels off the Place des Moulins.

It was late, but a group of young men had congregated in one corner of the square to smoke and talk. Someone had brought out a boom box, and the powerful beat of Algerian rai music hammered out onto the flat facades of the surrounding buildings.

"*Les hittistes*," Rahim said, glancing at the men as we made our way up the hotel's front steps. Realizing that I hadn't understood the immigrant slang, he explained, "They have no jobs, so we say they are holding up the walls. *Tu vois?*"

I looked back at the group, at their cigarettes weaving and bobbing in the darkness. Several of the men were resting with their backs against the building behind them, earning the nickname.

Inside, the hotel's narrow stairwell smelled of cooked lamb and spices, of garam and garlic and coriander. For an instant I was back in Beirut, in the hivelike streets of the old city. From behind the closed doors came the muffled reverberations of Arabic. The language of my country, though not my language, for in our home, as in others of our social class, French had been spoken almost exclusively, and my Arabic was poor at best. But there was something infinitely comforting about it, the sounds simultaneously exotic and familiar.

We reached the third-floor landing, and the automatic light clicked off, plunging the stairwell into sudden darkness. Rahim opened the door to his room, and through the open window, we could hear the music again, a man's voice singing over the drums.

"What is he saying?" I asked.

"It's a protest anthem." Rahim translated the Arabic into French. "'Where has youth gone? Where are the brave ones? The rich gorge themselves to death, the Islamic characters show their true faces. . . . We should run, but to where?'"

We were both silent, listening. Then Rahim reached out and put his fingers on the back of my wrist, and I could taste my heart in my throat.

SEVEN

■ ■ ■

IT WAS A RAINY MORNING on the Largo Trindade Coelho. On the steps of the Igreja de São Roque, four brave tourists huddled beneath umbrellas before disappearing behind the church's somber facade. Beneath the dripping awning of the coffee kiosk, the air was rich with steam and sweat, the pungent reek of espresso. *Uma bica*, the Portuguese call it, thimbles of pure adrenaline. Out on the rain-drenched square, a flurry of pigeons touched down, gray birds on gray stone.

I finished my Portuguese breakfast of coffee and more coffee, then slipped a handful of coins next to my empty cup and made my way across the square and down the dizzying steps of the Calçada do Duque.

As a general rule, criminals and cons tend not to stay in one place for long. Before my time at the Maison des Baumettes, I'd drifted not with the tides but with work, which often meant weeks or days before it was time to move on. Most of the people I'd known in Lisbon had lived in much the same way, but there were a few exceptions, old-timers with businesses or families, people who managed to hold the veneer of respectability. It was a short list, but a list nonetheless, and on the drive down, two names in particular, those of Amadeo and Gaspar Fielding, had percolated to the top.

The unlikely offspring of an English father and a Portuguese mother, Amadeo and Gaspar ran Saudade, a tourist shop on the rua Augusta named for the particular form of longing that is Portuguese melancholy. The store housed a dubious collection of "native" wares, but the brothers' real bread and butter was in the more upscale merchandise at the back of the shop.

Dinosaurs of the Baixa, the Fielding brothers sold just about anything that could be faked. Louis Vuitton handbags, Dunhill cigarettes, Calvin Klein perfume, whatever their Calcutta supplier had in stock. They'd had the store for years when I'd known them, and I figured if anyone was still in business, it would be Gaspar and Amadeo.

It was midmorning by the time I found my way to the orderly streets of the Baixa. The rua Augusta was bustling with pedestrians, sophisticated Lisbonites and tennis-shoe-wearing tourists braving the soggy weather. The windows of Saudade were brightly lit, showcasing the same dusty merchandise I remembered from over a decade earlier. Gaudy pottery and Nazaré fishermen's sweaters, linens from Madeira. Closing my umbrella, I ducked out of the rain and into the store's warm interior.

A young man peered out at me from behind the counter. Gaspar's taste, I thought. Dark eyes and dark hair, lush curls falling around his face, with an adolescent slimness, the hips of a young girl. Amadeo, I remembered, appreciated a rougher, more muscular look.

"How can I help you, senhora?" The clerk smiled, immediately sizing me up, taking me for the foreigner I was. His English was perfectly flawed, airy and seductive.

"I'm looking for the brothers," I told him. "Are they here?"

"They are expecting you?"

I shook my head. "Old friend."

"Your name, senhora?"

"Nicole," I told him. "Nicole Blake."

He nodded, eyeing me skeptically as he picked up the phone, punched a second line, and relayed my request in rapid Portuguese.

There was a moment's hesitation, then the clerk set down the phone and blinked up at me from beneath his full lashes. "Gaspar will see you," he said condescendingly, then motioned toward the rear of the store.

I wasn't expecting a hero's welcome, from the Fieldings or from anyone else in Lisbon. I'd done my time in Marseille, done it fair and square, but I knew from experience that I was irrevocably tainted by my brush with the justice system. Prison is a desperate place, and any number of things can happen on the inside; any number of deals can be made, even by the best of us. But I knew Amadeo and Gaspar as well as I knew anyone, and I was hoping their good manners wouldn't let them forsake me completely.

Gaspar was waiting for me outside the office door. He had changed little since I'd seen him last. He was older, of course, but well preserved, still in his standard uniform of a blue blazer and a neat bow tie.

"Nicole Blake," he said. "Christ, it's been a long time." His accent was perfect British uppercrust, an unnecessary affectation, for it was common knowledge that his origins were less than pure. He planted a hasty kiss on both my cheeks, but I could sense a wariness beneath his warm facade.

"You look fabulous, as always," I told him.

He dismissed me with a wave of his hand, then opened the office door. "Amadeo!" he called out as he ushered me inside. "Look who's come to pay us a visit!"

The office was small and cramped, the single desk piled with unruly mounds of papers and disheveled files. In the center of the space was a massive armchair, its velvet upholstery mottled with stains. In the chair, like a dowager at a garden party, sat the older of the two Fielding brothers.

"It's Nicole," Gaspar said, raising his voice. "Nicole Blake."

Amadeo leaned forward, squinting to see me better. He was wrapped in a thick afghan, his feet encased in wool slippers, his papery cheeks rouged with neat red circles. On his lap was the day's *Diário de Notícias,* the paper spread out across his blankets.

It took an instant for him to place me, but when he did, his eyes flared in recognition. "Yes." He beamed. "Yes, of course. Nicki." He clapped his hands. "I'd say a celebratory drink is in order," he directed Gaspar in the same theatrical English his brother used. He turned to me. "It's been the ruin of me, you know. Too much of a good thing."

"I doubt Nicole has come to celebrate," Gaspar said, focusing his gaze on me. "Now, have you, dear?"

I shook my head, but Amadeo wasn't going to be denied.

"Don't be such a pill," he told his brother. "Besides," he offered, motioning to the newspaper in his lap. "There are the Turks to toast as well. They've told the Americans to go screw themselves, you know?"

I nodded, though I hadn't known, hadn't given any of it much thought. I glanced down at the paper. TURKISH PARLIAMENT VOTES AGAINST U.S. TROOPS, one of the headlines read. "I don't think there's much anyone can do to stop the Americans now," I remarked. "They'll be in Baghdad in a matter of weeks."

Amadeo shook his head vigorously.

"My brother, the eternal optimist," Gaspar said, his voice touched with just a hint of paternalism.

"Not at all," Amadeo protested. "But I do believe it's up to the mongrels among us to care. After all, we're the only ones who can really see, aren't we?"

"I'm afraid Amadeo believes rather irrationally in the triumph of goodness. I, on the other hand, see this for the pissing contest it is. It makes me wonder if your president isn't compensating for something." Gaspar winked at me. "Not at all like the last fellow."

Amadeo nodded appreciatively. "Clearly size wasn't an issue for him."

"Clearly!" Gaspar agreed. He cleared a stack of books from a chair and motioned for me to sit, then settled himself behind the desk, having either forgotten or chosen to ignore his brother's earlier request for a drink.

"In France now, aren't you?" Amadeo asked me. "I seem to remember hearing that."

Gaspar cleared his throat and shot his brother a look of warning.

"Oh, yes!" Amadeo said, disregarding the reproach. "Marseille, wasn't it? Maison des Baumettes. It's nothing to be ashamed of, my dear. Just a little vacation is all. Time to catch up on one's reading, make some new friends. How long have you been out?"

"Three years," I told him.

"And you're still in the business?"

"In a way. I took a job with Solomon," I answered. "Can't begrudge a girl trying to make a living."

There was no use in lying. As quickly and as far as rumor traveled in these circles, it was a good bet the brothers already knew about Solomon. If they didn't, they could easily find out.

"Of course not," Amadeo said kindly, but Gaspar seemed less forgiving.

"And this visit?" the younger brother said, smiling coolly. "As pleasant a surprise as it is, I can't believe you've come all this way just to see two old men."

"I had some business in Seville," I lied, poorly. "And a few days to spare."

"Nostalgia, then," Amadeo observed.

I nodded, biding my time. How to sound eagerly disinterested? "Not many of us left from the old days, are there? Though I hear Rahim's still in town."

"That's right," Amadeo said. "I'd forgotten you were a couple once." He turned to his brother. "We saw him just the other day."

Gaspar shook his head. "You're mistaken," he said flatly.

"But yes," Amadeo persisted. "It was at Eduardo's, remember? He was leaving just as we were coming in."

"Eduardo Morais?" I asked, remembering the old watchmaker from twelve years earlier.

Gaspar cleared his throat, then smiled apologetically. "You'll have to forgive my brother," he said, ignoring my question, bringing his gaze to rest on Amadeo. "He has an old man's memory, I'm afraid.

The truth is that we haven't seen Rahim for some time. I wouldn't be able to tell you if he was still in Lisbon or not." He opened one of the drawers of his desk and drew out a bottle of port and three glasses. "How about that drink, then?" he proposed.

"Yes," Amadeo stammered. "Yes, of course." He looked greedily at the wine, then turned to me. "An old man's memory," he said, tapping the side of his head. "Sorry, my dear. I can't imagine what I was thinking."

I lowered my eyes, a girl looking for an old love, a man she'd once lost herself with. "It's been a long time," I conceded.

Gaspar poured out the three glasses and passed one to each of us. "To old friends!" he said, hoisting his glass.

I raised my glass in return, touched it to the brothers', and took a sip of the port.

Amadeo downed his wine, then winked at me. "To love," he said, raising his glass, then emptying it once more.

■ ■ ■

Not love, exactly, but something close to it. The idea of love, maybe. A symmetry of desire. Two in the morning, and out the window the coast rushes by, scant, scattered lights of tiny port towns, terrestrial constellations vanishing into the void of the sea. In the compartment next door, a party is brewing, three American boys and three dark-haired Italian girls we saw smoking between cars earlier. The melancholic sounds of Brazilian jazz serenade us through the wall, the faint odor of hashish.

Not that we mind being kept up. It's been three days since we've slept, since that night on the Place des Moulins. Three days, at the end of which Rahim has surprised me by asking me to come with him to Lisbon. And I have surprised us both by saying yes.

Rahim gets up and opens the window, and night air floods the compartment, the deafening clatter of the rails. Against the glass, his body is perfect, naked as the dark earth beyond. He bends down slightly to light a cigarette, holding his hand to protect the flame, and his palm and face flicker and glow. Three nights, and I have yet to tire of looking at him, nor does it seem possible that I will.

He hands me the cigarette and I take a drag, but it is not really what I want.

"Come here," I say, taking his fingers, pulling myself up to meet him. It is not in my nature to succumb so completely to pleasure, and yet I am learning. I slide up just slightly so that our bodies come together perfectly. Face and hips and feet like two seamless halves of a single creature, two wings folding forward to touch. And in that moment it seems impossible that we should ever not be.

Rahim is hard again, his lips soft and warm on mine. I can taste the tobacco in his mouth, the cheap red wine we drank earlier out of paper cups. But even in getting what I want, there is little satisfaction, just my need for more, the sense that such wanting could kill me.

I put my legs around his waist and lift myself toward him, trusting him to hold me. From next door, laughter, and then quiet, sudden and still. And out the window, the ceaseless motion of the wheels, sheer force and power carrying us into the night. The train lunges slightly, shimmying on the rails, and Rahim puts his hands under my naked hips, steadying me against him.

EIGHT

■ ■ ■

NOT SHOPPING, VALSAMIS THOUGHT as he sat in the rain-spattered window of the café across from Saudade and nursed his syrupy coffee. It had been a good half hour since Nicole had disappeared into the horrible souvenir store, and Valsamis was beginning to think she'd slipped out the back on him.

Out on the rua Augusta, a river of black umbrellas swirled and eddied, sweeping past the bright storefronts. Inside, two old men played dominoes, a group of students smoked cigarettes and laughed while they talked, and three workers in blue coveralls with nothing better to do lingered at the stand-up bar.

The communal life of a European city, Valsamis thought wistfully. The smells of tobacco and fresh bread rolls and hot cod fritters. A pair of elderly women stepped inside, shaking the rain from their umbrellas. Each was immaculately turned out in stockings and a neat wool suit, sensible pumps and dark gloves, and a matching hat.

Yes, Valsamis thought, this was where he wanted things to end. If not Lisbon, a place like it, somewhere civilized, an apartment in Hania, perhaps. Three rooms overlooking the Sea of Crete. This was where he would grow old, walking along the waterfront each morning and into some little café. Drinking thick Greek coffee, rotting his teeth on ouzo.

This home, not the place he'd left, fast food and cheap clothes, windowless buildings full of shoddy abundance. The students stood to go, and Valsamis glanced up from his coffee, catching the eye of one of the boys, a slim young man in a black sweater and blue jeans.

Valsamis smiled and the boy smiled back, shrugging into his coat and book bag. A slightly dreamy smile, as if he were looking past Valsamis.

Yes, Valsamis agreed as the young man smiled again, this is where I belong. Suddenly he was weary of it all. Weary of what he had done and what he would have to do, the presumption in Morrow's voice. *You'll take care of them when this is finished. Ali and the woman both.*

The students pushed out the door, and Valsamis's gaze slid to the street, to a girl outside, waving and smiling, waiting to greet the boy as he emerged. For a brief instant Valsamis saw himself for what he was, a strange man at the edge of the boy's line of vision, an awkward tourist drinking coffee in the window of a café on the rua Augusta. A fool.

Across the street, beyond Saudade's dusty display windows, a figure moved. The door swung open and Nicole stepped out onto the street. She headed south, down to the tram stop on the rua da Conceição, and that was where Valsamis lost her. Somewhere in the bustle of coats and umbrellas, in the push to board the tram, she saw him and stepped back out of the fray. It was too late by the time Valsamis noticed, the doors already closed, the tram clanging toward the Alfama and her face slipping away behind him, her shoulders framed by the dark canopy of her umbrella.

■ ■ ■

Laundry as bright as confetti. The yellow flutter of a caged canary. An old woman grilling sardines beneath the window of our apartment in the Bairro Alto. This was our Lisbon. A summer reduced to a tourist's snapshots, to one warm night at a café on the Miradouro de Santa Catarina, the sound of a *fadista* in the distance.

In the morning we would lie late in bed, listening to the neighborhood through our open window, the tsk-tsk of the woman next door sweeping her steps, a bundle of old men gossiping their way down the street. In the evening Rahim would make large, elaborate dinners for the ragtag community of drifters and students who found their way to our apartment each night.

These were Rahim's multitudes, the same *hittistes* we'd seen that first night on the Place des Moulins. Young men who'd come north to escape the repression and hopelessness of their homes, who'd found a different kind of hopelessness waiting for them. Immigrant poverty. The scorn of European women. Rahim fed them all, though not out of charity, for they were his bread and butter.

At the time he did identity papers, mostly. French work permits for the steady stream of Moroccans and Algerians heading north, and the occasional passport or student visa. Rahim was a stickler for secrecy, for keeping his work and personal lives separate; he'd rented a space out on the northwestern fringe of the city, a shabby little studio tacked on the back of a widow's house, in the shadow of the old aqueduct. He told his landlady he was an artist.

When he had work, he would go there in the afternoons. Sometimes I would go with him. On a few occasions I even helped. But mainly, during the hours when he was gone, I just waited. I hadn't really worked in months, hadn't needed to.

Often I would walk around the city, up across the hills and through the ancient alleyways of the Alfama, or down the wide Avenida da Liberdade to the sprawling Parque Eduardo VII and the glittering glass dome of the Estufa Fria. Or I would take the train out to Belém and sit in the tower park and watch the mammoth container ships heading out to sea. Even this was part of the waiting, and the waiting itself was something I had become. Not myself but a perversion of myself, surrendered to the fetish of longing.

■ ■ ■

I saw John Valsamis as soon as I stepped out of Saudade, his silhouette like a clenched fist in the window of the café across the street. It was hardly a surprise, part of the game I'd known to expect. All the same, I hated the thought of being shadowed. I let him follow me down to the tram stop on the rua da Conceição, then slipped back out of the crowd just before the number 28's doors banged shut.

A lie, I thought as I watched the tram start the long climb up the hill, and caught a passing taxi instead. I didn't believe for a minute that Amadeo had been mistaken about having seen Rahim. And who was Gaspar protecting? Rahim? Himself? Or was it just instinct? I was an outsider now. Or was it Eduardo Morais whom Gaspar was trying to shield? Though neither of the brothers had confirmed my guess, it made sense that Amadeo would have been referring to the watchmaker.

Rahim and I had visited Morais many times, summoned for dinner or an afternoon of port and cards on his little back patio. Never business—Morais was a man who worked alone, an artist of the old school, meticulous in his skill—but as much as Morais preferred to work in solitude, he loathed the thought of drinking alone.

Morais lived not far from the Igreja de São Miguel, on a tiny alley in a honeycomb neighborhood at the bottom of the Beco de Santa Helena. It was a warren of streets far too narrow for a car, so I had the taxi driver let me off at the Largo das Portas do Sol. It was still drizzling when I stepped out of the cab, and beyond the rain-lacquered railings and dripping foliage of the old square, the Tagus was shrouded in mist.

Twelve years had all but erased the exact location of Morais's house from my mind, and it took me a good hour of wrong turns and backtracking through the impossibly narrow lanes to find Morais's distinct green door and the elaborate azulejo that topped it, a tile-work portrait of Saint Vincent.

The house lay at the very back of a dead-end street, squeezed in against its neighbors and a slender flight of stone stairs that connected to the alley above. It was an unassuming structure, two stories of badly flaking plaster, windows underscored by once-elegant wrought iron. A narrow loggia ran the length of the second floor, the sagging balcony crammed with potted palms and unruly tomato plants.

I knocked once on the peeling door, and the sound echoed in the quiet street. In the doorway of the house opposite, an old woman huddled against the day's chill, grilling sardines on a makeshift brazier, impassively taking me in.

I knocked again, louder, and heard someone move inside. After a few seconds, the green door swung open and a young woman looked out at me.

"*Bom dia,*" I said in my best guidebook Portuguese. "*Queria ver Senhor Morais.*"

"My grandfather is working," the woman answered, her hand on the door, her black eyes hard on my face.

I smiled reassuringly. "It's important," I told her. "Please."

She hesitated, lingering on the stone threshold. She was thin and elegant, her long hair swept up and back, dark and shiny as polished ebony. "He knows you?"

"Yes." And I know you, I thought. A barefoot girl on Morais's back patio, gangly limbs tanned the color of caramel, lips stained with pomegranate juice. "My name's Nicole," I told her. "Nicole Blake."

She opened the door a few inches wider and reluctantly motioned for me to step inside. "Wait here," she said, leaving me in the dark hallway.

I heard her move through the back of the house, doors opening and closing as she went. She returned a few moments later. "Grandfather will see you," she said grudgingly. Then she led me through the same series of doors.

The low room that held Eduardo Morais's workshop had changed little since I'd been there last. Half a century of clutter lined the walls, disemboweled timepieces and boxes of scavenged watch works, tiny gears and pins. On a workbench near the one small window, a tall cabinet clock lay like a patient on a stretcher, its face dismantled down to the clockwork bones.

There was an unusual smell to the room, oil and metal, and something entirely unrelated to watchmaking. A printer's smell, achingly familiar. Ink and acetone and unblemished paper. The tools of a forger.

A watchmaker by trade, Eduardo Morais was a man with an eye for minutiae and the patience for painstaking detail, two qualities that had also made him one of the best counterfeiters in Europe. He'd learned his craft long before the era of the computer knockoff, before Xerox and Hewlett-Packard had helped make forgeries a home business, and when I knew him, he still worked by hand. It was slow going, but Morais turned out quality instead of quantity, single documents that more than paid for his time. If you wanted quickie car papers or a residence card, Eduardo was the wrong man to ask. But if you were looking for a clean U.S. passport and you were willing to pay, Morais could do the job better than anyone.

Morais was hunched over a drafting desk when I entered, his shoulders silhouetted by the bright lamp that illuminated his work. He made a slight movement of acknowledgment, hand flicking over his shoulder, then secreted whatever task was at hand into a large leather folder before pivoting his chair to face me.

He had not aged over the years so much as he had shrunk, his body caving in on itself, bones and skin sagging under the pressure of time. Another year or two, I thought, and he would disappear entirely among the clocks and tools.

"What a pleasant surprise," he said in easy French. He motioned to a fraying chair just an arm's length from his own. "Will you sit?"

"I don't mean to stay long," I told him, grateful for a common language other than Portuguese. "You're busy."

He shook his head. "Nonsense. *Pas du tout.* I've asked Graça to bring us some tea. Now, please, sit."

"Thank you." I stepped forward, following his gesture to the dusty armchair. His fingers were smeared with ink, his cardigan mottled with black stains. "I'm afraid not everyone has been so gracious in their welcome."

Morais nodded sympathetically. "I'm too old for petty suspicions," he said. "Working for Vanguard, aren't you? I seem to remember having heard that."

"Solomon, actually," I corrected him. "And some freelancing here and there. There wasn't much else for me. Once I got out."

"Yes," Morais agreed. "Better not to waste your talents. Though with you there, I'll have to be on my toes."

"Hardly." I doubted there was much I could throw at Morais that he wouldn't be able to get around.

"The straight and narrow must agree with you," Morais commented. "You look good."

I smiled. "So do you."

"Old, you mean."

"Not at all."

"Don't lie," Morais scolded. "Now, tell me, my dear, what can I do for you? I'm right to assume this visit isn't purely for old times' sake?"

I shook my head. "I hear Rahim is still in Lisbon."

Morais smiled knowingly. "Of course," he teased. "I should have guessed."

There was a soft knock from the hallway, then the door opened and Morais's granddaughter appeared with a tray.

"You've met Graça?" Eduardo nodded at the young woman.

"Yes," I replied.

"Graça thinks I'm old," Morais remarked. "And foolish. Don't you, my dear?"

The girl scowled. "Of course not, Papi." She set the tray on a low table between us, then leaned down and kissed Morais on the cheek.

"Senhorita Blake is an old friend of Rahim Ali's," Morais said, addressing his granddaughter in Portuguese. "Perhaps you can tell her where to find him?"

The briefest shadow of panic darkened Graça's features. Then she shrugged petulantly.

"*Nao?*" Morais prodded. "I felt sure you would know."

"*Nao,*" Graça replied coolly. She poured out two cups of tea, then turned and made her way out of the workshop, closing the door behind her.

After watching her go, Morais reached under his desktop and produced a ring of keys. "I'm at her mercy," he complained, bending down to unlock the lower drawer of his desk, producing a pack of cigarettes. "Otherwise there would be port instead of tea. Everyone thinks they can live forever these days. I'm afraid I don't see the point." He tapped a cigarette from the pack and offered me one, but I shook my head.

"You are staying in the city?" he asked.

"In the Bairro Alto, at the Pensão Rosa."

Morais lit the cigarette, closed his eyes, and leaned back to inhale. "I can't be sure," he said, his words obviously chosen with care, "but I've heard he has a workshop in Cacilhas. In an old dairy, not far from the ferry dock."

Three old men, I told myself, thinking of the Fieldings. Three old minds, memories slipping like worn gears. It was hard to know whom to believe, impossible to separate lie from mere confusion—though I was more certain than before that Amadeo had been right, that he had seen Rahim here. Yet if Morais was willing to tell me where Rahim's studio was, then why would he lie about this?

I reached for my cup and took a sip of the tea. Not panic but fear, I thought, remembering the look on Graça's face when Morais mentioned Rahim. It had been an odd exchange, and though Morais had chosen to speak to the girl in Portuguese, I couldn't help but feel that it had been for my benefit.

NINE

■ ■ ■

THOSE FIRST YEARS MY MOTHER AND I spent in Paris are hardly a memory to me now, just a few hazy scenes conjured up from the dim vault of childhood: a particular pair of brown leather pumps, the chipped rim of our old bathtub, the sounds of one of my mother's students playing the Kreutzer études in our living room, or the same scale over and over, the same missed note each time.

It was my aunt Emilie who sketched in the details of that time, what took my mother from Beirut in the first place, and what led her back. My mother and her sister had not lived in the same city since my mother first left for France. By the time we returned to Beirut, my aunt had already married and moved to Bordeaux. But the sisters had kept a faithful correspondence, and it was through my aunt's secondhand retelling that I learned about the convent in Dordogne. How, faced with the only respectable choice—that of giving me up—my mother had chosen a different path entirely. How she had cobbled together a life for us in Paris, at first sleeping on the floor of a friend's studio near the Sorbonne and, later, in our drafty apartment on Montmartre.

A few months before Emilie died, she gave me the entire record of her correspondence with my mother, an old Dior shoe box crammed with yellowed paper. It was a gesture of reconciliation on my aunt's part, I know that. But to this day, I have not been able to bring myself to read the letters.

We all carry the dead within us, as we wish them to be. To my aunt, my mother was never anything other than the one who'd stood up to their father and won. To her father, my mother remained a slightly serious girl on the stage of the recital hall at the American University, her hair bound in a tight bun, her chin and shoulder curled around her violin, her whole body swaying with the effort of a Dvorak concerto.

And to me? The person I've carried for so many years is yet another incarnation of the woman we all knew. My mother was a breathtaking skier, as fearless as her compatriots but with a certain grace that transcended the characteristic Lebanese recklessness. It is this version of my mother I try to hold on to now: her black hair flying loose behind her, her skis carving effortlessly through the snow at Faraya-Mzaar, her body not wrecked as it was at the end, but whole, powering its way down the mountain. The only reconciliation I need.

■ ■ ■

"A milkmaid," the old man said, his false teeth sliding in and out of place as he contemplated my question. Then he put his finger to the side of his head. "Yes! Yes! The old dairy." He smiled and turned, gesturing out the café's front window toward the bus station across the street and a narrow lane that disappeared behind it. "Down there and take your first right."

"Thank you." I slid a ten-euro note onto the counter and waved the barman over, adding another of the pensioner's *medronhos* to my bill before gathering my things to go.

It was a wretched afternoon in Cacilhas, sodden and gray, the air above the waterfront thick with yellow smoke from the factories below. Beneath the beneficent arms of the Cristo Rei, tugboats shuffled back and forth across the harbor, their red and white hulls bright as songbirds against the dark river.

At night, well-heeled Lisbonites crossed the Tagus to visit the seafood restaurants clustered along the riverfront, but during the day, unless you lived or worked in Cacilhas, there wasn't much reason to make the trip. It was a hardscrabble little town, made more so by the rain and chill, the dull patina of wet mud and soot that glazed the streets and sidewalks.

To my surprise, the man's directions proved to be accurate, and I found the old dairy easily, about halfway down a dead-end alley. The azulejo that had served as the dairy's billboard had seen better days. Some of the tiles were cracked or missing, and those that were left were scarred and stained, but the milkmaid, sketched in delicate blue, was as lovely as ever, her ample bosom and coquettish smile perfectly intact.

Other than a black-and-white cat curled in the shelter of a nearby doorway, the alley showed no signs of life. The ramshackle buildings were closed up tight, windows shuttered and locked. The dairy itself had obviously been vacant for some time.

I started into the overgrown passage on the building's left side, and the cat climbed out of her doorway and bounded ahead of me, meowing loudly as she scaled the rust-pocked iron stairway that led to a small landing and windowless door on the dairy's second floor.

Searching the ground for something to get me past the padlock that I could see hanging just above the door's knob, I picked up a broken piece of iron railing and started upward.

The cat mewled again and scratched impatiently at the door. Waiting for something, food, water, affection, or all three, something she'd gotten here in the past. She looked well fed, but in a strange way, all belly. Pregnant, I thought.

Nudging her gently aside, I wedged the tip of the broken rail beneath the hasp and pulled, praying the corroded iron would hold. The screws groaned and snapped, threads tearing through the jamb's ancient wood. I pulled again, mustering all my strength, throwing my weight behind the bar, and the screws popped free.

With the hasp gone, the door opened easily. The cat rushed past me as I tightened my fist around the iron rail and made my way forward, taking in the makeshift apartment and its spartan furnishings.

Along the far wall was a narrow cot, the mattress dressed in mussed sheets and a blanket. Next to the cot, a doorway opened onto a rudimentary bathroom. Closer to the front door was the kitchen, with a refrigerator, a grimy sink and hot plate, and two rows of open cabinets that held a coffee canister and an assortment of chipped dishes.

In the middle of the room was a crude desk, a long, thick piece of plywood propped on four hefty crates with a powerful swing-arm lamp attached to either end. Clues to the apartment's real purpose, I thought. Bulbs bright enough to see the tiniest mistake by. And on the floor to the right of the desk, a combination digital printer, copier, and scanner.

In my day we'd had the one-hour rule, the time it took to clear a space of anything incriminating. And by now? I wondered. Twenty minutes? Ten? The way things worked today, a laptop was enough computer for almost any job, and in the end you could just fold it up and walk away. No doubt that's exactly what Rahim had done, for there was no computer to be seen, and nothing else of any interest, either.

Making my way to the copier, I lifted the lid and looked inside. It was an unlikely hunch, but I figured it was at least worth the effort, the last thing copied or scanned easily overlooked. But the glass plate was empty.

The cat snapped at me from the kitchen, a sharp meow this time, her hunger desperate.

"Don't get your hopes up," I warned her, crossing to the refrigerator, kneeling to open the door. But she was right. On the wire rack was a half-full bottle of milk, and beside it, an opened tin of sardines. The milk had turned, but the fish was still good. I put the tin on the floor, and the cat set greedily at it.

"Good girl," I told her, reaching down to run my fingers along her back as she ate. She licked the tin clean, then stopped suddenly and lifted her head, her whole body tensing, her eyes on the open door.

Outside, something snapped in the passageway, feet rustling the weeds, the stride quick and purposeful. I crossed to the front window and peered out through the grime-streaked pane. A figure moved in the shadows below. Not Rahim. A woman.

Gripping the bar, I ducked into the bathroom and flattened myself against the wall. The woman started up the stairs, her shoes reverberating on the iron treads. Then she stopped on the landing, and I could hear her lingering in the doorway.

"Rahim?" she called. And then, in Portuguese, "Are you there?"

The cat answered with a plaintive meow, and the woman tried again, her voice quieter, more tentative. "Rahim?"

She waited for a moment, as if debating whether or not to come in. Then I heard her footsteps on the stairs, going down this time.

I waited for her to finish her descent, then stepped out of the bathroom and made my way back to the window. A woman, I thought, watching her go. If she had known to come here, there must have been something beyond the casual between her and Rahim.

She turned out of the side passage and started down the street toward the bus station and the docks. Even from a distance, I could tell that she was not unattractive. She was tall, dressed in a long wool coat and boots, her black hair cascading over her shoulders and down her back. She walked to the end of the street, then turned to look back before disappearing around the corner, and I caught sight of her face for the first time.

Graça Morais.

TEN

■ ■ ■

TAZMAMART. WHAT WAS IT VALSAMIS had called it? *Some hole in the desert for dissenters.* The worst thing a man can do to another man, Rahim had said. Ten years we can't even begin to imagine. Forsaken completely, crouched in a tomb in the sand, living off roaches and fetid rainwater, a single vent and a thin slice of sky. Ten years during which Rahim had prayed each day that his brother was dead.

Driss had been a student when they arrested him, a reckless young man preaching democracy on the streets of Rabat. But Tazmamart had changed all that. The Driss I'd known in Lisbon was sober and stooped, with the air of an ascetic. And though he stayed with us through most of August, he and I barely exchanged a dozen words.

He didn't like me, treated me with the same scorn so many of Rahim's Moroccan friends so obviously felt toward me. It was a stigma I'd grown used to, the woman they all wanted to fuck yet hated for making them want her. Driss's scorn had extended to Rahim as well, I'd thought, to his Swiss watch and German stereo. I was merely another possession.

Driss had brought a shortwave radio with him, and after dinner he would sit in a corner of the kitchen listening to the BBC or Radio France. The Iraqis had invaded Kuwait by then, but the faraway skirmish was not something to which any of us gave much thought.

But Driss was listening, and slowly, the others were, too. I could hear them after I went to bed, voices in the darkness, the Arabic harsh and guttural. Moroccan Arabic was an even greater mystery to me than its Lebanese counterpart, and aside from the odd word or two, I could understand very little. But their anger and outrage were clear.

At first it was mainly Driss who spoke, then slowly the others joined in, faces I recognized from Rahim's dinners, desperate men who came to the apartment for a week or two and were suddenly gone.

And then, finally, I could hear Rahim's voice as well.

■ ■ ■

John Valsamis crossed to the window and peered out across the air shaft at Nicole's half-closed drapes, the swath of dark room visible in the space between the two long panels. Up before dawn and gone. And now, coming into evening, there was still no sign of her. Valsamis could hardly blame her for her disappearances—no one wants to be followed—but still, he didn't like it that she'd been gone all day, plus the day before.

Valsamis's cell phone rang, and he hit the mute button on his TV remote. CNN dropped into silence. On the screen, a handful of white SUVs, each marked with the plain black letters UN, pulled into a fenced factory compound, their wheels kicking up clouds of fine desert dust. FALLUJAH, IRAQ, the banner across the bottom of the screen read.

"Yes?" Valsamis said into the phone.

"Any word on our Moroccan friend?" Morrow's voice, and the cough again.

They were getting old, Valsamis thought, all of them. "Not yet."

"And the girl?"

Valsamis hesitated just a moment too long.

"You said she would get this done," Morrow snapped.

"She will."

A woman's voice sounded in the background on the other end of the line. "Cocktail," Valsamis caught, "darling." And then Morrow: "Tell everyone I'll be right there, dear."

That life, Valsamis thought, and that house. Rain falling quietly on the towpath, on the cobbled Georgetown streets. And inside, only what he imagined, waxed wood and tastefully worn rugs, dinner dishes shining in the firelight, a woman in a plain cashmere sweater and a simple silver necklace. Furniture isn't something you buy, it's something you have, he thought, trying to remember who it was who'd told him that. Someone in the Agency, back when he was first starting out. Valsamis had been careful never to bring anyone to any of his apartments after that.

"Remember," Morrow said. "No loose ends." Then the line clicked dead.

■ ■ ■

November 29, 1990. The end of a rainy fall in Lisbon. On our kitchen table, a bowl of tangerines, an empty bottle of vinho verde, and half a loaf of bread. Dinner dishes in the sink, and on the floor a plate of fish bones for the silky black cat who has adopted us. Leila, Rahim calls her, the Arabic word for "night." Out the open window, rain drums on the rooftops of the Bairro Alto, on the foot-worn cobbles and glistening streets tumbling down toward the black Tagus.

Driss has been gone for three months now, but in the living room, the radio he left hums low, the almost inaudible drone of a woman's voice, a proper British accent punctuated by the hush of static. The BBC. It's late and the others have gone, but Rahim is still listening. In the news today, an ultimatum, a UN resolution for force. The beginning of something we have been expecting and other things we can't yet imagine.

In the dark bedroom, on the old green chair, a chocolate-brown sweater and black jeans, underwear trimmed in lace. To be in love, I think, to want nothing more than this. The radio clicks off, and I hear Rahim moving down the hallway. He climbs into bed, and I put my mouth on the crest of his shoulder. He is as comfortable in his own skin as a wild animal.

Nothing more, I tell myself again. And yet when Rahim turns toward me and slips his hand across my stomach, I can feel a knot there, like a secret waiting to happen. The thing that will divide us, though I don't yet want to know it. At the moment there is only a feeling of apprehension, a vertiginous sense of choice. And in the darkness, the rain's thrum, the sound of Leila in the kitchen, the clink of the bones against the porcelain bowl.

■ ■ ■

It was well past dark when I finally made my way back to the Pensão Rosa. There was a light rain falling, a fine Atlantic drizzle gently settling on the city's red roofs and stained cobbles. In the Bairro Alto, the old gas lanterns were lit, their sooty flames shadow-dancing off the cracked plaster facades of the old town houses. Along the rua da Rosa, the first stirrings of nightlife could be heard. The click of glassware and billiard balls, a snippet of fado.

> *Quanto sou desgraçada*
> *Quanto finjo alegria*
> *Quanto choro a cantar . . .*

Up the hill, the Rosa's front door opened and a couple stepped out into the street, walking arm in arm. Out of the corner of my eye, I saw a figure move in the doorway opposite, shoulders and head ducking out and back again, eyes and teeth winking in the darkness. A man, his movements familiar, I thought, even in the guttering flame of the old lanterns.

I stopped, then stepped toward the dark doorway. "Rahim?" I called quietly.

Something rustled in response. Fabric moving against fabric, what could have been shoes on wet stone. Then, except for the nighttime respiration of the Bairro Alto and the chatter of rain, all was quiet.

"Rahim?" I called again. But there was no one in the doorway's dark rectangle, just a narrow passageway burrowing backward. At the end of the passage was a dimly lit courtyard and a bare and crooked olive tree.

ELEVEN

■ ■ ■

THIRTY-FIVE NOW, THIRTY-SIX, RAHIM THOUGHT, ducking farther into the shadows. He did a quick backward calculation in his mind, remembering just how young Nicole had been before, how young they'd both been.

Her hair was still the same dark brown, though shorter than he remembered, cut back to show the slope of her powerful shoulders. Her face was just a shade narrower, a trick of memory or age or both, and her dark eyes were set back into the pale oval. But there was something about the way she carried herself that was fundamentally changed.

What prison will do to a person, he heard his brother say. Six years in the Maison des Baumettes. Six years that had hardened her, and that was saying a lot. She'd always been tough as nails, with the guarded independence of a stray cat, even in bed. It was a kind of aloofness that offended him in other women, this eternal holding back. But there was a depth to Nicole's reserve that had made him want her more.

She'd always been good at her craft, and Rahim had been surprised when he'd first heard about the mess in Marseille, surprised to find that Nicole had thrown herself back in with Ed in the first place. Even among people who lied for a living, Ed Blake had a bad reputation. He was the kind of hustler who would have cheated his own mother. Or, in this case, his own daughter.

Rahim didn't know the details, only what he'd heard through the grapevine. Something about a car scam, reselling rentals with phony pedigrees. It was just the sort of thing Ed would have cooked up, crude and old-fashioned. Somehow he'd talked Nicole into doing all the paperwork, the *cartes grises* and the credit cards and licenses they'd used to lease the cars in the first place.

The way Rahim had heard it, Ed had cut and run at the first sign of trouble, leaving Nicole to pick up the pieces. And when the French police, alerted by a string of bad credit cards, finally caught up with him in Val d'Isère, he'd offered Nicole up, talking his way into a nice neat six-month sentence.

But Nicole had done her time, every last day of it, as Rahim would have expected her to. Not someone who would sell others out to save herself, Rahim thought. And the last Rahim had heard, she'd taken a consulting job with some document security firm. Out of the life, and who could blame her?

Out of the life, and yet she'd come back after all these years. Come back and was asking about him. Rahim couldn't help but wonder why.

■ ■ ■

At first it's just a feeling, nothing more, the internal knowledge that something has changed. Two weeks later, I know for sure. Rahim has gone out, and I'm standing in our chilly bathroom, bare feet on the cold tiles. In the silvered mirror above the sink, my own face stares back at me. On the rim of the sink, balanced carefully on the curve of white porcelain, is a slender finger of plastic.

Outside, on the rua da Moeda, the Bica funicular groans up the hill. Ninety-nine, ninety-eight . . . I start a long count backward from one hundred, listening to the car fade slowly into the distance, teeth grinding at the worn rails.

Eighteen, I count, seventeen . . . On the sink, in the tiny window, a thin blue bar has appeared. No question, no doubt, except for the choice that is now waiting to be made.

The front door opens, much earlier than I had expected it would, and I hear two voices in the living room, the guttural reverberations of Arabic. Rahim and one of his Moroccan friends. I take a deep breath and gather myself. Out in the living room, the radio comes on, Europe 1, from France. I will have to tell him, I think. If he hasn't guessed already, he will.

I tuck the plastic stick in my pocket, open the door, and start down the hall. Rahim is in the kitchen making tea. He nods silently at me, spooning dried mint into the ornate pot Driss brought with him as a gift from Morocco. Rahim's friend Mustapha shouts something from the living room, and Rahim answers back, his tone angry.

This is their nightly ritual now. Mint tea and the news and, later in the evening, a bottle of cheap port. The long slow countdown to January 15, the deadline given to the Iraqis by the Americans for withdrawal from Kuwait. The long final breath before war. By now we all know Saddam Hussein will never back down.

In the other room, Mustapha lights a cigarette, one of his shaggy roll-your-owns, and the smell of the tobacco makes me gag.

Yes, I think, I will have to tell him, but not now. Not like this.

"*Je sort,*" I say. I'm going out.

■ ■ ■

Even with the hindsight of history, it's difficult to pinpoint the exact date on which the Lebanese civil war began. Aftershocks from the 1967 Arab-Israeli war, in the form of a massive influx of Palestinian refugees, had shaken the foundations of Lebanon's delicate political balance for some time. In the ensuing struggle for power, violent confrontation became more and more common, as the Lebanese army and the Christian Phalange Party, led by the Gemayel family, pitted themselves against the Palestinians and the militias of Kamal Jumblatt's left-wing Lebanese National Movement.

The gradual buildup of hostilities continued until the spring of 1975, when three of Pierre Gemayel's bodyguards were shot in Ain al-Rummaneh and the Phalangist militia ambushed a bus of Palestinians in retaliation. The incident sparked a wave of revenge killings and anarchy, and within a month Lebanon had descended into the bloody war from which it would not fully emerge for almost twenty years.

Two decades, an entire generation of violence, and yet there were periods of calm, beats like the stalled pulses of a failing heart during which people could begin to imagine that the worst might be over. Days or even months, and sometimes just long enough for a quiet meal. A hundred and fifty short-lived cease-fires in the first eight years of the war alone.

It was during one of the first and longest of these lulls, the summer of 1977, that my mother took a job teaching violin at the American University of Beirut, and we moved back to my grandparents' house in Achrafiye. My mother had heard enough of the war and had decided it would be better to witness the reality than to imagine the worst from afar. The Syrians had come by then, and after the crushing horrors of the previous two years, most people were convinced that the peace would last. In August, the St. Georges yacht club hosted international waterskiing and water-polo competitions. Julio Iglesias even stopped in Beirut on his world tour.

I was seven when we returned to Lebanon, too young to understand the war or what my mother's choice meant, how hard it must have been for her to watch from a distance while the city she loved destroyed itself. But I remember my first glimpses of Beirut from the deck of the cargo ship on which my grandfather had arranged our passage, and the short drive from the port, the faceless houses along the rue Georges Haddad, their interiors exposed like those of a doll's house, rooms half intact, beds and sofas listing toward collapse.

When we finally pulled up in front of my grandparents' house, my mother climbed out of the car and went to her father. "No one can stay angry forever," she said.

She was a woman who was right about many things. Even as a child, I understood this. But standing there outside the apartment in Achrafiye, with war's carnage fresh in my mind, even I had to wonder whether she would be wrong this time.

■ ■ ■

TWELVE

I WOKE THAT NIGHT IN MY ROOM at the Rosa, my sleep interrupted by desperate howls. The alarm clock by the bed read 2:09. Down in the air shaft, two cats were mating, their cries like those of an abandoned child. Rolling out of bed, I made my way across the dark room, pulled the curtains back, and slid the window open. From the floor below me came a string of curses in an unfamiliar language. Swedish, maybe. And then, in the darkness, a third window shushed open and a voice yelled in Portuguese. Something was thrown and landed with a rustling thump. The cats let out their last yowl, then ran off together through the weeds, offended, licking one another's wounds.

I closed my window, then climbed back in bed and shut my eyes, imagining the growing pile of discarded missiles at the bottom of the air shaft. Spare sandals and half-smoked packs of cigarettes, coat hangers and ashtrays. Whatever was handy in the wee hours of the morning.

Out in the corridor, someone moved. A latecomer from the bars, feet stopping just outside my room. My neighbor across the hall, I thought, a pale, middle-aged English woman with a dog-eared *Lonely Planet*; I'd encountered her when I first arrived, though I hardly would have pegged her as a night owl. The door was so thin that I could hear her coat rustle.

I rolled over and waited for the sound of her key in the lock, but it never came. There was something else, something closer. More rustling, paper on the floor. In my room now, I was sure of it. I threw the covers back and stood. In the thin bar of light that crept in beneath the doorjamb, I could see a white square, an envelope. There was a knock and then the footsteps receded, louder and faster than they had come.

The corridor was empty by the time I got to the door. I picked up the envelope and put my hand on the light switch, then stopped myself. Through the open curtains, I could see one or two lit rooms on the opposite side of the air shaft, and the dark windows around them. Valsamis was somewhere behind one of the blank panes. And if I was awake, I thought, it was a good bet he was, too.

His prerogative, I reminded myself, as I had that morning. And why wouldn't he be watching? But still.

Skirting the bed, I made my way to the bathroom and closed the door, then turned on the lights over the sink, greedily tore open the envelope, and pulled out the single piece of paper.

It was a brief message, the words handwritten in dark ink, but I knew exactly what it meant. *Adamastor,* it said. *6:00.*

I put my free hand to my face and could feel the flush in my skin, the heat of my whole body drawn upward. There was only one person who would have left such a note, who would have wanted to meet at the statue of the old sea monster on the Miradouro de Santa Catarina.

Rahim.

■   ■   ■

It's late when I get back to the apartment, moving toward the early hours of the morning, but more of Rahim's friends have come since I was gone, and they are clustered in the dark living room. The television is on, and on the screen an otherworldly ballet is unfolding. Dark sky, luminous pearls of anti-aircraft fire, the Baghdad skyline washed with the aqueous green of night vision.

It's happened, I think, the Americans have finally gone in. Knowing better than to intrude, I stand in the doorway for some time, listening to the broadcast, the contained panic of the American reporters and their cameraman as the bombs begin to fall.

For the first time that I can remember, everyone is silent. No one, not even Rahim, acknowledges my presence, and at first I think he hasn't seen me. But when I turn to start down the hall to our bedroom, he looks up at me, angry, accusatory, and in that moment, I think, I am every failing that has ever divided him from himself, every weakness that has kept him from his god. I am one of *them* now, and nothing will ever be the same between us.

■ ■ ■

Something bigger than Nairobi, I thought, Valsamis's words ricocheting in my head. Turning off the bathroom lights, I made my way back out into the dark bedroom and fumbled in my coat pocket for the pack of Portugués Suaves I'd bought on my way up from the docks. Not for smoking, I'd told myself then and reminded myself now. Just an old habit for my hands.

I closed my eyes and could see the pictures again. Not the ones of the Nairobi bombing but the others, the images we all see in our dreams and wish we didn't. The blurred body of a plane hurtling forward. The giant tongues of fire. Smoke like some mad dark river churning into the blue sky. And in one of the towers' windows, a man, a tiny figure desperately waving a makeshift white flag.

What would it take to change a person, I wondered, to bring him to this place? Anger distilled to its purest form.

During my six years at the Maison des Baumettes, I lived among women who had done the unthinkable, who had murdered their husbands or drowned their children. Monsters and yet not. In truth, there was very little that separated these women from the rest of us, from the forgers and junkies and thieves, even from those on the outside. We are all, in some way, overtaken by our lives, shaped and molded by the glacial forces of time and family until the person we are and the self we recognize no longer agree.

And my own life? And Rahim's? There was Driss, of course. And there was the war.

"If you were to leave," Rahim had told me once, before such things seemed possible, "if you were to leave, I would go home to the mountains, to the old Berber sheepherders. There will be nothing left for me here." I'd laughed then, laughed at the impossibility of it. But I had left.

And in the end he had not gone to the Berbers. He had not chosen the rocky wilderness of the High Atlas, as he'd promised, but some other, fiercer wasteland.

I tapped the unopened pack of Suaves against my palm and felt the cigarettes shift. There was a certain satisfaction in the gesture, in the promise, however false, of pleasure.

Six o'clock at the statue of Adamastor. Not a betrayal, I told myself, putting down the cigarettes, making my way toward the door. Not a betrayal but simply what had to be done. And yet somehow I had imagined more time, days in which to get used to the idea, in which to convince myself I was doing the right thing.

I punched the wall switch and the overhead light glared on, illuminating the room in all its shabbiness, all the ominous and unidentifiable stains that accompany the human condition. In the window I could see my own blurred reflection, pale arms and legs framed in the room's entryway. And my hand, raised now, the note clutched in my fingers.

At the time it seemed like I stood there forever, but looking back, I can see how quickly it all happened. How little time it took for the phone to ring and for me to answer.

■ ■ ■

"We just need to talk to him," Valsamis told Nicole. "Find out what he knows."

Nicole didn't say anything. From his window, Valsamis watched her sit down on the edge of the bed and put her free hand, the one that wasn't holding the phone, over her face. A gesture of despair.

Valsamis turned and glanced at the Ruger on his bedside table. Four more hours to keep her on track, he thought. Or he could do it now, quick and quiet. Though if anything went wrong in the morning, if Rahim got spooked or didn't show, he'd have nothing to fall back on.

"Nicole?" he said again, and this time her voice came back to him. "Yes?"

"You've done the right thing, Nicole."

THIRTEEN

■ ■ ■

IN THE EARLY-MORNING DARKNESS, Santa Catarina rose like some madwoman's wedding cake, each dark tier sugared and frilled with the city's wild sprawl, palm fronds and rooflines and intricate Manueline facades, stone twisted and curled like icing from a piping bag. And on the hill's southern flank, the long narrow gorge of the funicular tracks, like a greedy finger dipped in and drawn upward.

On the Largo do Calhariz, at the top of the Bica funicular, the windows of a coffee kiosk blazed out onto the silent square, onto the handful of tables and upturned chairs, the umbrellas folded in on themselves like the wings of sleeping bats. Inside, a barista and two customers, three curls of smoke wreathing up toward the fluorescent lights.

Down on the Tagus, the Ponte 25 de Abril shimmered like a bracelet on the river's black wrist. And on the far bank, the great Cristo Rei statue, lit as if from within, arms outstretched toward the city.

I paused in the kiosk's glare, facing into the darkness, and slid the Suaves from my pocket. *We just need to talk to him,* I could hear Valsamis say, his assurance when I'd called to tell him about Rahim's message.

Though of course this was a lie. I knew what the Americans did to people like Rahim. We all knew.

Greedily ripping the cellophane wrapper, I shook a cigarette from the pack and lit it, then cupped my shaking hand around the match's delicate flame, succumbing to the warm rush of smoke, the taste of tobacco.

■ ■ ■

Twelve years between them, Rahim thought, stepping back into the doorway as he watched Nicole turn onto the rua Santa Catarina and make her way toward him. Twelve years, and why she had come back to Lisbon, Rahim couldn't say. Whatever the reason, it wasn't safe for her to be asking about him, wasn't safe for either of them. Even now he was aware of the danger, aware that someone could be watching. This was why he'd chosen to wait here instead of on the belvedere.

A gust of wind whistled up from the river, and Nicole pulled the collar of her coat tight, hunching her shoulders against the cold. She was close now, just a couple of meters away, passing into the bright arc of the nearest streetlamp. Her hands were bare, the knuckles red and chapped, and as she drew closer, Rahim could see the smeared salt stain on her cheek from where the wind had made her eyes tear. Not beautiful, he thought, for no one could have argued that Nicole was beautiful. But there was a primitiveness to her, her whole body as raw as those pale hands. And for all that had passed between them, he wanted her still.

■ ■ ■

Such a fitting meeting place, Valsamis observed, sliding his Ruger from his coat, checking the nightscope. Adamastor, this god turned by lover's rage to wind and stone, an embodiment of the dark and vengeful soul of the southward passage and the great African continent, what it had meant to those early sailors. Sea and storms determined to swallow them whole.

It wasn't quite dawn and the sky was coldly luminous, brittle and bare as ice on water. Out on the *miradouro,* the statue towered like an angry fist, body clenched in eternal wrath. Down on the Tagus, the first ferry to Cacilhas drifted out onto the river's empty oblivion, a night watchman's lamp slowly trolling from shore to shore.

Just get him to the belvedere. Valsamis repeated his instructions as he watched Nicole start up the rua Santa Catarina, her face a ghostly green in the scope's eye. That was all she had to do; he would take care of the rest. Nothing to go wrong, and yet so much. Nicole took a long drag on her cigarette, and her face caught for an instant in the ember's glare, her skin a light source in itself, like a figure in a Dutch painting.

Wet work, Valsamis thought. This, what separated him from Morrow and the others. What they would not have been willing to do. But, then, it was better to take care of these things yourself. Better to know there would be no mistakes.

Valsamis crouched down, as he had learned to do as a child in Montana. His father beside him in the darkness, beneath the snow-sodden boughs of the old ponderosas. His big burly arm around Valsamis's shoulder, steadying the Remington, the rifle still too big for the boy's hands.

"You've got to be quick about it," his father had told him in the truck driving up into the Pintlers, his only advice, and this from a man of great deliberation. Valsamis hadn't understood it at the time, and when the first elk dipped into the draw and moved down toward them through the waist-high drifts, Valsamis hadn't moved fast enough. He'd let himself be dazzled by the creature. And when he finally recovered, he'd missed his shot.

All these years later, he could still remember the exact feeling of defeat, the elk lumbering away into the underbrush, spooked by some force both unseen and unheard, the scent of Valsamis and his father drifting toward him across the snow, eggs and bacon fat, whiskey and Lucky Strikes, the stink of humanity.

It was the last time Valsamis had hesitated in the face of death.

■ ■ ■

I inhaled deeply, pulling the smoke into my lungs, and scanned the dark *miradouro* ahead, the stand of palms, elegant as a *fadista*'s fin-

gers on the neck of her guitar, and in front of them the massive silhouette of the sea god. Watching, I thought. Valsamis and others,
perhaps. And then, in the doorway beside me, something moved.

I stopped walking and dropped my cigarette to the ground, my
eyes straining against the darkness, my heart pounding. "Rahim?" I
called quietly.

All was silent. Mistaken, I told myself. Another ghost like the one
outside the Rosa. Then a face appeared in the doorway, features
slowly revealing themselves.

Twelve years, and yet Rahim's body was as familiar to me as my
own, his hair that smelled of saffron and black pepper. As if the rich-
ness of Africa had been born into him. And for an instant I understood what had brought us both to that place, the wound we'd each
carried all those years. Not a betrayal, I reminded myself, but still, in
that moment, I wanted nothing more than to run.

Rahim stepped toward me and opened his mouth as if to speak,
but he never got the chance. There was a whisper in the air, like
schoolgirl gossip.

Neither of us moved, then Rahim's left hand flew to his neck and
I could see the splash of blood beneath his fingers where the bullet
had hit.

"*Attention!*" he hissed, grasping my wrist and yanking me past him
and into the shelter of the doorway.

My back slammed against the wall and my breath was knocked
from my chest. When it came back to me, I could smell blood in the
air.

"*Tu es blessé?*" I gasped, turning to Rahim.

He shook his head, pressing his hand to his neck. But I could see
that he was wounded. His shirt was sticky with blood. His eyes were
panicked, his breath shallow.

I sloughed my jacket and helped him to the ground. "*Tiens!*" I
said, kneeling beside him, pressing the canvas jacket against his

neck. Hold this. I could smell the fear on him, the sourness of his sweat and breath. In a matter of seconds the jacket was soaked through with his blood.

"It's okay," I told him, wanting to believe myself, but even as I said the words, I knew they were a lie. "You're going to be okay."

I rose and started toward the doorway, but Rahim put his free hand on my arm and held me back. His grip was uncomfortably strong, his fingernails sharp against my skin. He reached into his pocket and took out a pistol, shoved it into my hand.

I looked down at the gun, then moved toward the doorway again, stepped out, and waved in the direction of the belvedere.

"He's hurt!" I called into the darkness, my voice echoing up the empty street, my own fear coming back to me.

Down on the river, a ship's horn sounded as if in reply, but from the belvedere, there was just silence. The wind picked up slightly and the palms shivered.

"We need help!" I called again, desperate now, trying to keep my voice under control.

This time the answer came almost immediately. A second shot hissed out of the darkness, clipping the stone doorway just above my shoulder. This bullet intended not for Rahim but for me.

Ducking back into the doorway, I lifted the pistol and ran my thumb across its body, feeling for the safety.

Rahim reached for my arm again, and I crouched down next to him. He was shivering, his skin cold and damp, his teeth chattering. He would die here. He would die here and there was nothing I could do about it.

"The invoice," he whispered, taking a slow breath, gathering himself for the effort of speaking.

"Ssshhhh." I put my hand on his forehead, then leaned toward the doorway and peered out into the dark street. Not blind, I thought. No, Valsamis could see us perfectly, must have been shooting through a scope.

"The invoice," Rahim repeated, louder this time, struggling to be heard. "At the dairy."

"I'm going to get us out of here," I told him.

"No," he rasped, pushing my hand away. "Go, Nic."

I shook my head, but he didn't see. His eyes were focused on the doorway, on something in the distance beyond my shoulder.

"The car," he said. "The lights."

I didn't understand at first, thought he was imagining something. And then from the hillside below came the groan of a car engine toiling upward.

"The lights," he repeated.

I nodded, suddenly understanding. If Valsamis was shooting through a nightscope, the car would be my only chance, the headlights the cover I needed.

I peered out again into the gloom and watched the two lights heading up the hill toward us. Yes, I thought, if I went behind them, I might just make it.

I looked back at Rahim one last time, and he nodded at me, as if giving me permission to go.

"Thank you," I told him, still not quite sure what had happened. Then I took a deep breath and rose up on the balls of my feet, legs tensed.

This way, I whispered, willing the car toward me. The lights washed forward, blazing a perfect path up the street, toward the belvedere and across Adamastor's flanks. The car passed the doorway and I leaped out behind it, rising toward the brilliance. In an instant I was safely through, back into the darkness again, my legs propelling me down into the wild maze of Santa Catarina.

FOURTEEN

■ · ■ · ■

THEY WILL MAKE YOU FORGET the taste of your mother's milk. What Khalid had said all those years earlier, the two of them huddled around a fire in one of the wrecked buildings on the green line they'd claimed as their temporary home. Burning books that night to keep warm. The previous inhabitant's collection of French mysteries, Simenon and Lenotre.

It was Kanj who'd discovered the apartment. A mortar had smashed into the roof above the living room, leaving a gaping, rain-logged hole around which a few sun-starved weeds had grown, but the rest of the space was miraculously intact. China in the dining room cabinets and expensive linens on the beds. And in the kitchen sink, unwashed breakfast dishes, a crust of toast, a brown smear of egg yolk, testament to the speed with which the war had overtaken the city.

Normally, Khalid didn't talk about his time in prison, but that night something had set him off. Kanj hadn't admitted it then, not even to himself, but he'd been afraid, terrified not so much by the pain of torture but by his own weakness, what he might say or do. Khalid must have sensed it, for after a good hour of talk, he'd grown quiet.

"It will surprise you," he'd said, stirring the ashes, "just how much the body can take."

This had not comforted Kanj at the time; he had not been able to understand what Khalid meant. But now he had come to see that his friend was right, that the fear of pain was worse than the pain itself, that once you surrendered to it, there wasn't much you couldn't bear.

Shift change, Kanj thought, listening to the sound of footsteps outside his cell, the scrape of a key in the lock. He took a deep breath and let his body relax completely, let the physical go. Then the door opened and he could see the man again, the familiar bald head and blunt hands. My best friend, Kanj thought, and my worst enemy. Soon, Kanj told himself, soon they would bring the Americans to him.

■ ■ ■

Taken, I told myself, shivering as I made my way down toward the river. My fingers were numb, my hands covered in Rahim's blood. I'd been taken, and good. I could hear my father laughing as he walked away from a shortchange he'd pulled at a bar in Nice, counting his money as he went, handing me a crumpled fifty-franc note. People see what they want to see, he'd said, his cardinal rule of the con.

I was sixteen at the time, a runaway from my aunt's house in Bordeaux, falling hard for the same man who'd seduced my mother all those years earlier.

"You don't know him," Emilie had said when I'd finally called to tell her I was staying. "He's just using you."

She'd been right, but at the time I'd wanted more than anything to believe she was wrong.

It was light when I emerged onto the waterfront, the morning dour and unwelcoming, clouds like bruised chilblains on the ashen sky. With nowhere else to go and Rahim's words still fresh in my mind, I'd decided to head back to the dairy. Invoice or no, I could lie low there for a while, at least until I figured out my next move. The Cacilhas ferry had just left the dock and was churning its way out onto the river. Its twin had cast off from the opposite shore, but it was still a good twenty minutes away, limping through the chop.

It was too cold to be without a jacket, the clouds halfheartedly spitting a few raindrops, and I needed to clean myself up, so I made my way into one of the dockside cafés and headed for the restrooms.

I washed my hands and face as best I could, then slid Rahim's pistol from my hip pocket.

It was a small gun, a Hungarian FEG SMC-918. Soviet firepower in a bantam package, its clip lined with six neat Makarov rounds. I put my hand on the grip, let my palm become familiar with the weight and shape. I hadn't had a lot of use for guns in my profession, but back before I'd gone to prison, I'd carried an old Luger, a Czech knockoff that my father had given me once in a rare gesture of paternal concern.

I'd used it only a few times, mostly on deadbeat clients who thought they could skip out without paying, and then just as a way to impress. But on a few occasions the gun had actually saved my life, and I wasn't unhappy to see the little FEG now. I checked the safety, slid the pistol back into my pocket, and headed out into the café.

The morning was in full swing and the establishment was buzzing, the windows white with steam, with the heat of so many bodies and the humid respirations of the espresso machines. Hands and toes tingling, I made my way through the crowd, squeezed in at the stand-up bar, and ordered a coffee and a bread roll.

I wasn't hungry, but I forced myself to eat anyway. Out in the cold, there hadn't been much room for thought, but as my mind began to thaw, I stumbled back over the morning's events, each time vainly hoping for a different outcome. But in the end there was no denying my complicity. Rahim was dead and I was alive, only because he had saved me.

I shook a cigarette from my pack, thought back to my first glimpse of Valsamis, his face through the window of the white Twingo. A con, I'd told myself then, and I hadn't been wrong. The only question now was how much I'd been played. There was a part of me that still wanted to believe Valsamis had been right about Rahim, that what had happened on Santa Catarina was merely a broken promise, that getting rid of me was just a way of eliminating any complications.

There was a sort of sweet absolution in believing this. Foolishness instead of guilt. My own skin all that mattered in the equation. But the better part of me knew the answer wasn't nearly so simple.

I lit my cigarette with my shaking hands and glanced out the café's front windows at the ferry, still a fair distance from the dock. There was a trio of old men at the bar beside me, part of the ubiquitous flock of gray-hairs and newspapers that populates every café from Athens to Lisbon, their blood thick with coffee and anisette.

"I'm telling you!" the pensioner closest to me insisted. "There is nothing to find." He unrolled his paper and set it on the bar in front of him, tapping the headline with a gnarled index finger.

His friends nodded in agreement, then the conversation moved on to football, a far more contentious topic.

I downed the last of my coffee and scanned the headline, slowly deciphering the Portuguese. UN INSPECTORS FIND NOTHING BUT SAND, DIRT. Beneath was a picture of an empty warehouse.

Here we all are again, I thought, twelve years on and back to the same argument. For a fleeting moment I was in our apartment on the Travessa da Laranjeira, back in the little front room listening to the throaty hum of the radio. Waiting, still waiting, for Rahim to come to bed.

I closed my eyes and fought back the memory.

■ ■ ■

The young desk clerk flicked his eyes upward and watched Valsamis enter the lobby. He'd been reading a paperback western, the frayed cover showing a virile man on a muscular horse and a bronze-skinned woman in tight buckskin cowering seductively beneath him.

The romance of the American Indian, Valsamis thought, remembering the Blackfeet and Salish of his childhood, dirty kids in ancient cars, a boy his age he'd seen outside a bar on the way to Great Falls one winter. Twenty below and a good foot of new snow on the ground and the boy had been waiting outside without shoes or a coat, his bare feet red and raw, his matchstick arms mottled and bruised.

Too lazy and too stupid to take care of their own, Valsamis's father had said. But when they got in the car to leave, Valsamis's mother had reached back and untied Valsamis's scuffed brown boots, taken them and his coat, and trudged back to where the boy was waiting.

Nine years old, maybe ten, and even then Valsamis had understood the significance of his mother's action, the boots and coat, he'd been reminded over and over, not merely clothes but some defined portion of his father's life. A certain number of hours inside the smelter. A sacrifice made for them. And yet when they'd pulled onto the two-lane highway and Valsamis had started to complain, his father, without looking, had reached back and slapped him, hard.

Valsamis watched the desk clerk turn back to his book, then started across the lobby and up the stairs to his room. He'd had her, he thought, angry at himself for having bungled things, angry at Morrow for having sent him to Lisbon in the first place, when what he wanted was back in France, back in Paziols, when he should have been clear of it all by now.

Just a temporary setback, he reminded himself as he unlocked the door and let himself into the room. But there was no time to spare now. The drapes were open and he could see Nicole's room across the air shaft, her window dark as well. She wouldn't be coming back here, but that didn't mean he couldn't find her.

■ ■ ■

It was a short walk from the Cacilhas dock to the old dairy. Ten minutes and I found myself at the pale feet of the milkmaid. Remembering the cat, I'd stopped and bought a dozen grilled sardines from the old man who kept a cart near the pier. I was glad I had, for she was there to meet me, pacing back and forth on the landing like an impatient lover.

I climbed the stairs and let myself inside, fumbling in the darkness for the light chain I remembered from my earlier visit while the purring cat twined herself around my ankles. The room was ugly in the unshaded glare of the bare bulb. Narrow cot and empty shelves, everything dirty and worn. Not much, I thought, but it would do for tonight.

I set the fish on the tiny kitchen table and unwrapped the paper. The sardines were still hot, their skins crisp and charred, the fish nestled tail to tail like a bouquet of silver flowers, heads and gills blossoming upward. The cat jumped up beside me and snatched a sardine for herself, then tore greedily into the flesh, resting her belly on the table while she ate.

Due any day now, I thought, watching her chew through the soft bones. Her stomach was tight, her nipples swollen and pink, her body no longer her own. She adjusted herself slightly and one of the kittens rippled beneath her mottled fur, nose or paw rolling upward, looking for a way out.

I ran my palm across her back and she stopped eating to glare defiantly up at me, as if daring me to go on. Taking the hint, I left her to her meal and made a slow circuit of the apartment, carefully checking the old cabinets, running my hand between the toilet and the wall, under the cot, anywhere I thought Rahim might have stashed an invoice. But the search seemed senseless, the possible hiding places almost infinite. And that was if the invoice existed at all.

The mind's tricks, I told myself, remembering the last frantic moments with Rahim, his desperation to tell me. From two breathless words it was impossible to know what he'd really meant, or even if he had understood. Though he'd been right about the car lights, right about Valsamis's nightscope, and I had doubted him there as well.

The cat jumped down, landing with a heavy thump on the old floorboards, and sauntered across the room, drunk off the fish. She stopped next to the printer/copier and ran her whiskers across the corner of the machine.

As stripped down as the apartment was, there was something wholly incongruous about the printer. It was a quality piece of equipment, a step up even from the digital multitasker I had at home, and certainly more sophisticated than anything I'd known Rahim to use in the past. Though I wasn't really surprised, for the sophistication of documents had changed markedly over the last twelve years, and Rahim would have been keeping up.

No, it wasn't so much the printer as the fact that Rahim had left it, especially since he'd so obviously cleaned the apartment of everything else. If it had been me, I thought, and I'd been running, I might not have taken it with me, but I wouldn't have left it behind, either.

Crossing the room, I lifted the lid and checked the scanner plate again, then pulled out the tray and leafed through the blank sheets of paper. Nothing. I put the tray back and pressed the power button, watched the little green light blink on.

The machine was silent at first, but as I moved to stand, some internal mechanism clicked inside. There was a hum and then the sound of paper sliding from the tray. Whatever Rahim's last command to the machine had been, he'd turned off the power prematurely. Now, back online, the printer spit out its long-hoarded task.

Taking the document from the tray, I switched on one of the swing-arm lamps and set the paper on the makeshift desk. It was a shipping bill of some sort. An invoice, though for what I couldn't be sure. The bulk of the document was printed in Russian, but the letterhead stood out in English. BSW AIR CARGO INTERNATIONAL, it read. And the address: a post office box in Sharjah, United Arab Emirates. The date at the top of the page read April 11, 2001.

Language is an integral part of forgery—I've worked in dozens of languages in my time—but fluency is never a requirement. Where opera singers learn their parts phonetically, I've often learned mine by shape, perfecting whole documents without ever deciphering their meaning.

Russian had been a minor exception; I'd attained what I called bar fluency, enough knowledge to order a drink. And, from my few forays into Soviet commerce, the basics of official language. But all that had been a long time ago. I didn't work in Cyrillic at Solomon; there were specialists for that.

I read over the body of the document, stumbling through the text, trying to conjure up the ghost of my lousy Russian. Most of the copy was gibberish to me, but a few words stood out, confirming my first impressions. In the space that called for a *description of goods,* my Russian failed me completely, but I managed to decipher the next few lines. *Country of origin,* I translated, and, in the space provided, *Trans-Dniester.* And below, *Port of origin, Odessa.*

The next few lines were shipping technicalities, weights and measurements, but there was one other piece of information that caught my eye, a single line close to the bottom of the page. *Port of entry,* it read, *Basra, Iraq.*

■ ■ ■

Valsamis rolled onto his side and put the pillow over his ear. On the chair by the window, his coat pocket was ringing, and not for the first time that morning. It would be Morrow, Valsamis thought, counting out the four long rings, waiting for his voice mail to kick in. Valsamis had forgotten to turn off the ringer earlier, and now the idea of getting out of bed and walking across the room seemed like too much effort.

He was hoping that if he ignored the phone, Morrow would give up. But the ringing started again almost as quickly as it had stopped, just enough time in between for Morrow to hang up and redial.

Valsamis pushed aside the covers, swung his legs off the bed, and padded across the room. Fishing in his coat pocket for the little phone, he flipped open the receiver. "Yes?"

"Well?" Morrow's tone seemed presumptive, accusatory, even. Too confident, Valsamis thought, that something was wrong.

"There won't be any more problems with Ali."

"And Nicole Blake?"

"I told you, I'll take care of her." Valsamis winced, wishing he had lied.

"There are people in Lisbon I can call if things get out of hand." Morrow's words were more warning than assurance.

"They won't," Valsamis told him.

Morrow hesitated. "One more thing, John."

Valsamis felt suddenly sick. He leaned toward the window and pushed it open, hoping to temper the lingering odor of stale cigarette smoke, but it was no use, the room was saturated.

"We should take care of the Morais girl as well." Morrow's voice was dispassionate, contained. "And the old man, too. Loose ends, you know?"

FIFTEEN

■ ■ ■

FOR SEVERAL MONTHS AFTER our return to Lebanon, it looked as if my mother might actually be right. There was a fragile concord that fall and winter. Not so much a peace as a common acknowledgment of the lunacy of war. For the truth of the early conflict was that the rifts it had revealed ran far too deep to ever be forgotten again. And yet, in our eagerness, we all believed.

In Beirut there was an almost hysterical scramble for normalcy, as if people knew the worst was yet to come. There were concerts and dinner parties, even the return of ordinary crime, of holdups and burglaries and murders of passion. In January, Fairuz sang the Rahbani brothers' *Petra* at the Piccadilly Theatre, and my grandfather took us all to the opening night.

I was eight at the time, too young for the theater, far too young to understand what the performance meant to a city struggling to forget civil war, but I still remember the spectacle of that evening, the competing smells of expensive perfumes, the textures of the women's gowns as I moved among them in the foyer. The crush of silk and sequins and fur.

Onstage, her robes catching the lights like the feathers of some exotic bird, what we had all come for, the poor printer's daughter from the Zuqaq al-blat who had conquered the world, the woman whose voice was our own. Goddess, I'd thought when the curtain first parted to reveal Fairuz standing there, and the entire audience had caught its breath with me.

At intermission someone gave me my first glass of champagne and

I wandered, light-headed, through the dark sea of tuxedos, hot and itching in my stockings and tight shoes. When the houselights blinked to signal the end of the intermission, I looked up to see my grandmother pushing her way through the crowd.

She was a beautiful woman, even at her age, slim as a girl from her regular tennis matches at the Summerland Hotel, her hair dark and glossy. She'd worn a red dress that night, an elegant sheath that clung to her waist and thighs, and as she came toward me, I could see the powerful muscles in her arms and legs.

"Where's your mother?" she asked, bending toward me.

I shook my head. "She said she was going to the bathroom."

She took my hand and started back into the crowd. The lights blinked a second time, and people began to file slowly back into the theater, reluctant, it seemed, to get back to the story. Even I knew it would end badly. My mother had told me everything in the car on the way there, how Petra refuses to betray her country and how her daughter is killed because of it.

We neared the ladies' lounge and my grandmother stopped abruptly. "Go back to the theater," she said, letting go of my hand.

I moved slightly, trying to look past her, but she positioned her body as if to shield me from something.

"Go to your seat," she hissed. This time there was an edge of threat to her voice, as when I crossed her at home.

I turned to leave, craning my neck as I went, peering past her. I could see my mother in the far corner of the lobby, talking animatedly to a man in an elegant tuxedo who seemed to be listening intently. The man looked to be about my mother's age, tall, with a neat dark beard and dark eyes.

My mother was leaning with one shoulder against the wall and her back to us, sweeping her hair over one ear as she spoke, a gesture I recognized as one of nervousness. She was wearing a dress not unlike my grandmother's, only black, and from the back the two women looked so much alike that it would have been difficult to tell one from the other had I not already known who was who.

"Go!" my grandmother repeated sharply.

My mother and grandmother were late getting back to their seats. By the time they joined us, they had missed an entire scene. After she sat down, my mother turned to me and smiled. Her face was open, her expression meant as a gift of reassurance for me, but even in the darkness, I could tell she had been crying. My grandmother sat rigid beside her, looking straight ahead toward the stage.

■ ■ ■

It was late morning when I left the dairy and headed back to the docks, the dim day dimming even further, the sky sliding from pearl to dove gray. The wind had picked up, cold and gusty, straight off the Atlantic, and there was a steady rain falling, with no break in sight. I'd found a worn peacoat, presumably Rahim's, back at the apartment, and I was grateful to have it as I stood on the waterfront watching the ferry come in.

I rode back across the river, then headed up into the Chiado, to a cybercafé on the Largo do Picadeiro that I'd noticed the day before. I needed help with the invoice. Normally I would have taken the document to Eduardo Morais, but with Graça and possibly Morais himself involved, I wasn't sure how much I could trust him or anyone else in Lisbon.

With my local contacts out of the question, my best bet for help was my friend and colleague at Solomon, Sergei Velnychenko. A crackerjack forger, Sergei was a man who knew firsthand the ugliness of the Russian prison system. Legend had it that Sergei had made a good name for himself in the Russian mob, managing to keep his free-agent status and operate within both the Odessa and the Moscow mobs at the same time. Things would have stayed rosy if he hadn't made the mistake of screwing one of the big Muscovite's wives and getting caught at it. The man had seen to it that Sergei spent the next five years in a prison in Siberia.

Like most of the scattered workers at Solomon, Sergei and I had never actually met. With all the bad blood dogging him in Russia, and few employment opportunities waiting for him upon his release, he'd taken Solomon's offer straight out of prison and moved his paycheck and his computer to a new home in the British Virgin Islands. But sometimes you don't have to meet people to know them. I'd spent enough time online with Sergei to know that if there was one person I could trust to keep a secret for me, it was him.

Checking my watch, I found a free computer at the café and logged in to the Hotmail account I kept for personal use. Still early on Tortola, I thought, though Sergei wasn't much for sleep. *Need your expertise on a document,* I typed, hoping to catch the Russian at his computer fulfilling some early-morning fantasy, figuring he would know from the Hotmail address that my request wasn't work-related. Ten minutes, I told myself, hitting send, watching the message evaporate. If there was no reply by then, I'd check back later.

I sat back in my chair and glanced around the café at the midmorning clientele, a hodgepodge of students and artists and pensioners, each intimately connected to something or someone on his or her screen. They'd be looking for me eventually, probably already were. Valsamis and whomever he was working for.

On the far side of the café, a girl rushed to greet her friends clustered at the coffee bar, and for half an instant, seeing her dark hair and long coat, I mistook her for Graça Morais. It wasn't much of a surprise, I thought, that Rahim had chosen her. She was so much of what he'd always liked, young and pretty with a hard edge. But I was taken aback by his choice nonetheless, almost insulted, though I couldn't quite say why.

I checked my watch, and my empty in-box stared back at me. Then a message popped onto the screen, another Hotmail address, Fernando76. Sergei Velnychenko was an ABBA fan.

Sergei's answer was as short as my request had been: *Send it my way and I'll see what I can do,* he replied in his impeccable English.

Waiting for your answer, I wrote back. Then I hastily slipped the invoice from my pocket, ran the document through the café's communal scanner, and e-mailed the image to Sergei.

I didn't have to wait long. Not even five minutes later, Fernando76 had a new message for me. *Standard shipping invoice,* Sergei wrote, confirming what I already knew. *Five crates of steel cables from Trans-Dniester to Basra via Odessa. Nothing unusual.*

And BSW Air Cargo? I e-mailed back.

Owned by Bruns Werner, old friends say main cargo gladiolas. As for Werner, armor-plated. Meaning somebody was looking out for this Werner. Someone with a lot of pull. As for the gladiolas, it was a word Sergei had used before, and not in reference to flowers. Gladiolas had been the cover Sergei's bosses in Odessa had used when helping to clean out the Ukrainian supply of Soviet-era weaponry. In other words, Bruns Werner was an arms dealer.

Another e-mail followed. *Dimensions fishy,* Sergei had written. *Do you mind if I ask around?*

I hesitated, my hands hovering over the keyboard while I thought about Sergei's offer. Nothing unusual, he'd said, but that in itself was strange. You don't forge a copy of a shipping invoice unless there's something unusual about it, and I was fairly certain the invoice was a fake—not just because I'd found it in Rahim's printer. There was a slightly flawed quality to the white spaces where the shipping information had been penned by hand. It was a shadow of a shadow, nothing I could put my finger on, nothing someone who didn't know exactly what he was looking for would find, but it was there nonetheless.

Of course, with the sanctions, almost anything going into Basra would have been contraband. But then why put Iraq as the destination? Especially with a home base like Sharjah, a well-known convenience port, a shell game for ships and cargo flights heading to the

Mid-East and Africa. A commercial no-man's-land where, for the right price, almost anything, including a plane's official destination, was negotiable.

And then there was the question of Trans-Dniester, a strange little country carved from the remnants of the Soviet Union. Famous more because of its unaccounted-for supply of Soviet weapons than its steel cables. The breakaway republic had won its hard-fought independence from Moldova in the early 1990s, right before I'd gone to prison, and I remembered the frenzy then, every arms dealer and hack smuggler looking for a piece of the cash pie. No, something didn't make sense.

Be discreet, I typed.

The answer from half a world away: a pixilated face, a yellow moon winking at me. *As discreet as a hundred-dollar whore,* Sergei had written. *Check back* P.M.

■ ■ ■

Rush hour, John Valsamis thought, checking his watch, doing a quick backward calculation. He punched a number into the disposable cell phone he'd bought on the rua Augusta and imagined his call rocketing straight toward the pandemonium of the Beltway, the phone on the other end chirping its insistent message. A favor called in, but then he was owed, had more favors coming his way than he could ever use. A Cold War's worth.

From somewhere in the Maryland countryside, the voice of Hank Kostecky snapped onto the line. "Hank here!" In the background was a woman's voice, a single word carefully repeated. Kostecky's Arabic lesson, Valsamis thought. Berlitz for the spy. Fifty-odd years of Russian, and now there wasn't an intelligence man out there who could so much as order a glass of tea in Baghdad.

"Johnny the Greek!" Kostecky quipped at the sound of Valsamis's voice.

Valsamis blanched. The big Polack was the only man who could get away with calling him that, but Valsamis didn't have to like it.

A Westerner by habit and a Greek by blood, Valsamis hadn't known quite what to make of the Agency's social code. Part Southern and part military, Langley's mores had both confounded and irritated the working-class kid from Montana who'd grown up in the rough-and-tumble melting pot of a copper boomtown.

He and Kostecky had met in Peshawar, back in the early eighties. Kostecky was just starting out then, and Valsamis had recognized himself immediately in the son of an immigrant steelworker from Pennsylvania.

"I need a favor," Valsamis told Kostecky now.

"I'm listening."

Valsamis could hear the woman's voice in the background. *"Fein yimkin ana akra beshkleeta?"* she asked patiently. And then, in flaw-less English, "Where can I rent a bicycle?"

"I need your ears for a few days," Valsamis said.

"Anyone special?" Kostecky asked.

"Her name's Nicole Blake. American citizen living in France. A lit-tle town in the Pyrenees called Paziols. She's a freelancer for Solomon, the British document security firm."

"What are we talking about here? Phone calls, e-mail?"

"Whatever you can get that will help me find her. I lost track of her a couple of days ago in Lisbon."

"I'm on it," Kostecky told him. "How do you want me to reach you?"

Valsamis rattled off his number. "You know the drill," he reminded the other man. "This is strictly between us."

"I know the drill," Kostecky replied, then paused. "I guess you've heard about Kanj."

"I heard the Pakistanis finally caught up with him," Valsamis said. "Everyone must be chomping at the bit to get a piece of the action."

"Word is Near East is prepping for him in Amman. But officially he's still a ghost. No Red Cross visits for that boy." Kostecky laughed crudely, then muttered something to himself.

Valsamis could hear the woman again. "*Ey kar yamshee ila al-qasr?* Which bus goes to the palace?"

"You ever get the hang of this piece-of-shit language?" Kostecky asked.

Valsamis smiled to himself. "I get by."

■ ■ ■

I was soaked through and shivering when I finally turned off the Beco de Santa Helena and onto Eduardo Morais's narrow street. I stepped into the shelter of the loggia and knocked once on the old green door, turning my face up to Saint Vincent.

It was Graça who answered. Graça, in designer jeans and a black turtleneck, her hair falling across her shoulders.

"My grandfather is asleep," she announced, staring out at me defiantly. Her feet were bare on the tile floor of the foyer, her nails lacquered a dark plummy red.

"I haven't come to see Eduardo," I told her.

"No?"

A piece of work, I thought, everything about her meant to unnerve. Though there was something about my having known her before, something about my memory of her as a child, that made the act less intimidating than I knew she wanted it to be.

"Rahim's dead," I said, my rickety Portuguese allowing no room for subtlety.

Graça shifted slightly in the doorway, her hand moving to the door frame, her face collapsing in on itself. All that hardness momentarily unmasked, and in its place a flickering of unsteadiness and grief.

"I saw you at the dairy," I told her. "Yesterday afternoon. That was me inside."

"What do you want?" she asked, rallying the old hostility.

I nodded to the dark hallway beyond her. "I want to come in," I said. "I need to know what Rahim has been working on."

Graça took a step forward, steady and sure, bristling once again, her body filling the doorway. "I don't know what you're talking about."

Twenty, I thought, counting back the years, twenty-one at most. She couldn't have been more than ten the last time I'd seen her.

"Rahim's dead," I repeated, in English this time, too tired to battle on, taking a gamble that her English was better than my Portuguese. "Someone shot him this morning on the Miradouro de Santa Catarina, and they would have killed me, too. It's only a matter of time before they figure out you two were together. Do you understand?"

Graça nodded. Scared, I thought, as she should have been, for her grandfather's name would not protect her from Valsamis or those who had sent him.

"These people don't mess around," I told her.

She took a step back, and I thought she might let me in, but she shook her head instead.

"I can't help you," she said, then swung the door closed.

SIXTEEN

■ ■ ■

IN HIS WHOLE LIFE, JOHN VALSAMIS had known his father to cry only two times. The first was on November 22, 1963, when John F. Kennedy was shot in Dallas. Valsamis was in school when it happened, and he'd come home to find the same man who once beat him for wasting food sobbing before the black-and-white footage of Jackie climbing down from the ambulance in her bloody dress.

The second time was almost ten years later, when Harry Truman died. No tragedy this time, just an old man gone at last, but still, Valsamis's father had cried like a baby.

Valsamis had been home from Vietnam at the time, discharged from the marines and staring down the rest of his life, the old brick smelter that had swallowed so many of his family's days and nights. Four brothers and a father working overtime. Three sisters married to the same kind of man.

On the plane from Honolulu, in the first-class seat they'd bumped Valsamis into, a different offer, a man in a dark blue suit who'd talked about Castro and Allende, who'd given Valsamis his business card before disappearing down the crowded concourse of the Los Angeles airport.

Valsamis's father was a devout anti-Communist, a former member of the National Republican Greek League, and a survivor of the ferocious civil unrest that had convulsed Greece after World War II. He'd been in the mountains along the Albanian frontier in the summer of 1949, and he hadn't forgotten what the Americans had done for them, the sound of Truman's air force humming in the west.

Valsamis and his father sat up late the night of Truman's death, toasting the former president, his father recounting battle stories over his homemade retsina, the tales legend now, each one told and retold, forged into myth. His life before eight kids and twenty-five years smelting copper, his body compressed by the weight of it all.

After his father staggered off to bed, Valsamis went to his room, fished the business card from the bottom of his old military duffel, and laid it carefully on his mother's yellowed quilt. CENTRAL INTELLI-GENCE AGENCY, it said. Beneath the letters, the official seal, and beneath the seal, a name.

Richard Morrow, Valsamis read, remembering the man from the airplane. Clean hands on the sweating tumbler that held his gin and tonic. Teeth and shirt so white Valsamis almost couldn't bear to look. And then, as the plane banked toward smoggy Los Angeles, his finger on the day's paper, the headline screaming failure in Vietnam, what Morrow had said. *Someone's got to make sure this doesn't happen again.* And suddenly Valsamis had gotten the feeling the good luck that had nudged him up from coach hadn't been luck at all.

Valsamis tucked the card carefully away, turned the light out, and climbed into his bed. Outside in the darkness, the wind was blowing hard, scouring the mile-high Anaconda plain, lashing at the house, the old windows and wooden clapboards creaking and moaning like a ship in a gale.

■ ■ ■

Nostalgia, John Valsamis thought, irritated by his own memories. Thirty-plus years on, his father dead for nearly a decade now, and it was this night that came back to him as he sat at the bar in the Café Nicola and watched two old men playing chess.

Even the Communists were gone, a failed experiment left to molder on some back shelf. In Beijing there was a brand-new television in every apartment and an Avon store on every corner.

The menace now is something none of us could have imagined,

Valsamis thought, something we will never understand. A rage born of being always left behind, an anger that worships everything American and hates its own idolatry. Worse, this enemy is a beast of our own making, stitched together from money and guns and oil, a fury that served us once and well, and that now threatens to destroy us.

Yes, Valsamis thought, ordering a second coffee, slapping a handful of coins onto the counter, someone has to make sure it doesn't happen again.

Valsamis's cell phone rang. "Yes?" he answered.

"We've got her," the caller said neutrally. The voice was bland, midwestern. A man.

"Where?" Valsamis asked.

"Lisbon. She accessed an e-mail account from a public server at 10 Largo do Picadeiro. Looks like an Internet café."

"She checked her e-mail?" Valsamis had used Kostecky's NSA connections a few times before, but he was still amazed at what they could do.

"Yes, sir. Just spam, from the looks of it. But she sent several e-mails to a private account."

"Were you able to get a name?"

"Yes, sir. The account's registered to a Sergei Velnychenko. The e-mails were received at a private address on Tortola, British Virgin Islands."

The man hesitated as if he had more to say but was waiting for further instructions. "Sir?" he asked finally. "I can read the transcripts if you'd like, sir."

■ ■ ■

Vanity, I thought, making my way back toward the Largo do Picadeiro, my own pride that had sent me here. All those years ago, a part of me had wanted Rahim wrecked by my leaving, gone, as he'd promised. Yet here he'd been, his life and his appetites still perfectly intact.

You're wrong about Rahim, I heard myself say that night in my kitchen in Paziols. *I know him. This isn't something he would do.* And yet hadn't part of me wanted Valsamis to be right? Hadn't my vanity wanted this weakness in Rahim, his rage at my leaving, some flaw greater than my own? Didn't a part of me still want this? That was the insult of Graça Morais.

I skirted the National Theater and headed across the square and in through the door of the cybercafé. The crowd had thinned since my earlier visit, and the establishment was nearly empty. Two bored employees lingered behind the coffee bar, a thin pale girl in a leather jacket and a nervous young man with spiky black hair. The only other client was a middle-aged woman in cheap office clothes. Miss Lone-lyheart, I thought, watching her face in the light of the monitor, her shoulders hunched over the keyboard.

I ordered a coffee, then took a computer at the back of the café and logged in to my Hotmail account. There was an e-mail from Sergei waiting for me, the message short and even more obtuse than his earlier one. There were no cute smiley faces this time, no fooling around.

Cargo likely labeled incorrect, he had written. *Search Alazan.*

I typed the word into the search frame and waited for a response. Several dozen listings flooded the screen, three pages of possible websites and articles. I skimmed through the descriptions, my eyes lighting on the same phrases over and over. *Alazan rocket. Weather control. Trans-Dniester.*

I clicked on the first listing, an article from a scientific journal. It was technical jargon, mostly, written with professionals in mind, but I managed to glean from it that the Alazans had originally been part of a Soviet weather-control experiment in which the rockets were launched into storm clouds as a way of preventing hail from damaging crops.

The second article on the search list, titled "Cloak and Dagger," was from a British paper, a description of two journalists' descent into the post-Soviet black market in arms. There was a long intro that narrated a shady meeting with a Ukrainian gangster named Dimitri in Trans-Dniester's frontier capital city of Tiraspol.

A typical exposé, I thought, the journalists more concerned with their own skin and careers than anything else. No doubt a con job on the Ukrainian's part, for I'd known enough Dimitris in my time to know they didn't do anything for free. And then, several paragraphs into the article, I felt my heart catch.

The Alazan rocket, the text explained, *initially part of a failed Soviet experiment in weather control, was later fitted with warheads containing radioactive waste. Now part of a huge stockpile of aging, unwanted weapons in Trans-Dniester, a 129-mile-long sliver of land on Moldova's border with Ukraine, the Alazan is considered to be an ideal weapon for terrorists.*

Dirty bombs, I told myself, glancing around the café, my eyes lingering on the single woman and the two kids behind the counter. My old prison paranoia at work again. I shuddered slightly as I remembered what Valsamis had said that first night. Something bigger than Nairobi. No, this was something much bigger. Somewhere just upriver from the Baltic Sea, radioactive missiles were up for grabs. And if Sergei was right, the invoice was a shipping bill for five of them.

SEVENTEEN

■ ■ ■

UP TO SOMETHING, EDUARDO MORAIS THOUGHT, rolling over in his bed, listening to the front door open and close, the latch falling softly into place. Through the slats of his bedroom shutters, Morais saw his grand-daughter emerge onto the lane below. She stopped in the gaslight and adjusted her coat against the night's chill, then started off again, the hard soles of her boots tapping on the alley's stone cobbles.

She was up to something. Morais was certain of it. Too young to know better and too old for him to stop her. But still, he didn't have to like it. He'd seen her with Ali, had heard the two of them in the house together when they must have thought he was asleep. A man twice her age, and an Arab.

Morais had been relieved to see Nicole Blake back in Lisbon, more than happy to help her find Rahim. The two of them had been in love once, and Morais was hoping Nicole's presence might distract Rahim from Graça.

Morais closed his eyes and tried to regain the gift of sleep, but it was no use. His bladder was calling, and in the end he would have to relent.

Sliding his feet into his slippers, Morais eased himself from the bed and padded down the hallway to the bathroom to face the first of the night's battles. This was the worst of the degradations of age, his old body failing so badly that every piss was work, every successful elimination a minor miracle. Flipping on the bathroom light, Morais flattened his left hand against the wall, took aim at the toilet bowl, and half missed, his sloppiness part accident and part spite.

He'd been so pleased when Graça had first come to him. Curious, as her mother never had been, and wanting to learn; Morais had been more than happy to oblige her. He'd taught her everything he knew, each careful skill, but in the end Morais had been unable to convince her of the merits of perfection. Like everyone these days, his granddaughter didn't have the patience for the old kind of quality. She'd preferred to do things her way, preferred the speed of the computer to the beauty of the human hand.

Downstairs in the kitchen, something moved. The cat door, Morais told himself, listening to the rasping of hinges, the quiet groan of the floorboards. His old tabby, Saramago, letting himself in from an evening of hunting. Squeezing the last few drops from his bladder, Morais shook himself off, tucked his flaccid penis inside his pajamas, and headed back out into the dark hallway. He would die soon, he thought, and everything he knew with him, the realization coming to him for no reason, as it did so often these days.

Morais stopped at the top of the stairs, contemplating the dark hallway below, the possibility of a nightcap. He fumbled for the light switch, his hand brushing the wall. Fifty years he'd lived in this house, fifty years of late nights and early mornings, of coming and going in the dark. Then last week he'd stumbled on the way to the kitchen and lain for two hours like a beetle on its back. Later, Graça had stood with him on the stairs and made him practice turning the light on and off, made him promise he would do the same when she wasn't there.

His hand touched the switch, but he hesitated, listening to the sounds of the house. A new sound now, in the front hall this time. Not Saramago. Something bigger.

"Graça?" he called.

But the only answer was the ticking of the house's old clocks.

"Saramago?" Morais tried. "Saramago!" he called again, his pupils wide, his eyes intent on the dim landing.

And then, finally, an irritated yowl, the cat's hungry voice.

"Yes, Senhor," Morais called down to the creature, "I'm coming."

Out of the darkness, two bright eyes appeared. And behind them, the body of a man.

Morais's hand hit the switch, and the stairwell was flooded with light. He saw the intruder below.

"Can I help you?" Morais blurted, for the man looked more like a lost tourist than a menace. An American, definitely an American, the kind you saw playing Pessoa at Café Nicola, or wandering with his *Fodor's* through the Alfama. Only there was something off about this one. Lonely, Morais thought. A stranger, always a stranger.

The man looked up. His face was blank, his eyes flat. He raised his right hand up the staircase, showing Morais the silenced pistol in his fist.

Briefly there was a disconnect between what Morais saw and what he understood. Between this strange man at the bottom of the stairs and the gun in his hand. The intruder looked past Morais, as if searching for something or someone, then his eyes narrowed and he focused in on the old man.

Morais put his hand up, the gesture part self-defense and part welcome. His last thought was of his workshop, of all that would be left unfinished, and his tools as he'd left them, each in its place.

■ ■ ■

Graça Morais tucked the cigarettes in her pocket and started back up the hill, leaving behind the little kiosk, the ancient owner's wizened face framed by the day's headlines. On the front covers of *Diário de Notícias* and *Público,* the scowling face of the American president. And in *Jornal de Notícias,* a beleaguered United Nations weapons inspector and the simple headline WHERE?

It wasn't so much the cigarettes Graça had wanted as an excuse to walk, to get out and get some fresh air and sort things through. Whatever she believed, something had happened at the Miradouro de Santa Catarina the day before. After the Blake woman's visit,

Graça had walked up into the Bairro Alto and stood behind the police barricades with the other gawkers, listening to the neighborhood gossips.

"Murdered," the old woman beside Graça had said to her friend, pointing her gnarled finger at her head, indicating a gun. The friend had looked back at her, her shock one step removed. And then, whispered: "They say it was an Arab."

Graça turned down the narrow lane toward home and picked up her pace, her boots pounding out a rapid staccato. She should have known, she thought, pulling her coat tight to stifle a shiver. She should have guessed there was something wrong with the job for al-Rashidi. Even Rahim had said it: It was too much money for what the man wanted. A handful of phony papers that any hack could have turned out on a PC. But Graça had wanted the job, and in the end Rahim had not been able to say no to her.

Up ahead, a cat darted from the shadows and into the gaslights, her grandfather's big tabby, Saramago, swaggering toward her. King of their street, as always. Graça bent down and put out her hand, and the cat nudged her palm, running the length of his back beneath her fingers, spine arching in pleasure. She brushed his tail and her hand came away wet. Not water but something sticky, the smear dark in the lamplight.

Graça raised her hand to her face and sniffed, pulling back in disgust, the smell of blood unmistakable. Not Saramago's, for the cat seemed fine. He darted ahead and stopped on their front doorstep, looking back at Graça, impatient as always, waiting for his servant to let him in, though he knew perfectly well how to use the cat door off the back patio.

Graça wiped her hand on her jeans and started forward, fishing her keys from her pocket. But as she neared the front door, she could see that she wouldn't need the keys. The door was open just slightly. A centimeter, maybe less, where the wood met the jamb.

Not her work, for she could clearly remember turning the lock behind her when she left. Clearly. It seemed odd that her grandfather would have come this way so late, unless the cat had been scratching to come in. But even then, left to his own devices, Saramago almost always went around to the back.

Graça put her hand on the knob and pushed. The door swung inward, revealing a slice of the front hall, the floor and wall lit by the light from the stairwell.

"Papi?" she whispered.

Saramago rushed past her, down the hallway and toward the kitchen. Something was wrong, Graça thought, the sound of the cat's paws like the slap of feet on a wet bathroom floor.

"Papi?" She took a tentative step, peering down the hallway as her hand pushed the door wide.

At the foot of the stairs, a large dark stain spread across the floor. Toward the kitchen, a neat set of prints, Saramago's staggered tracks fading like a printer's stamp run out of ink. And just to the left of where the cat had passed, a wide smear, the stain muddled where something large and heavy had been dragged across it.

Graça looked down at her own hand, at the faint patina of blood on her palm. "Jesus." She retched, doubling over, hand catching the door frame as she steadied herself. There was so much of it, she thought, too much.

Above her, in the back corner of the house, where her bedroom was, something stuttered across the old floorboards, a human foot and the weight it carried. Someone quietly searching.

Graça took a step back. Too much blood for anyone to have survived, she told herself, closing the door behind her. "Bless me, Father," she whispered, and the start of the Hail Mary, the words coming haltingly back to her. And then she was running, down into the darkness, down through the hive of houses and lanes.

■ ■ ■

I slept hard on the narrow cot at the dairy, swallowed whole by the great beast of exhaustion, gone, finally, to some other place. Years earlier, the train trip south with Rahim, and "The Girl from Ipanema" coming softly through the wall. In my mouth, as I woke, wine and cigarettes, the sour taste of shame.

It was early still and dark, the windows staring blindly back at me. The sky tinged a deep black ocher by the phosphorous lights of the port. The cat was asleep at my feet, curled up and snoring, eyes closed tight, whiskers twitching in her own fantasy. Thin again, and lithe, catching rats in the deserted dairy below.

I rolled over and tried to blink away the dream that had woken me, but Rahim refused to leave. I could see him still, slumped in the doorway, his head marked by Valsamis's bullet, by the dark wound of my betrayal.

Down in the side passageway, something moved through the weeds, bigger than a cat but almost as quiet. Snapping awake, I swung my feet to the floor and crossed to the window. At the bottom of the stairs, a figure moved, a black cap of hair and two thin shoulders. Graça Morais. She hesitated, looking up at the cracked windows and closed door. Then she put her foot on the first step and started upward.

■   ■   ■

"There was nowhere else to go," Graça said. She was shaking slightly, perched on the edge of a battered folding chair, her coat tight around her. On her jeans was a smear of blood, a long fading smudge where she'd wiped her hand. And on her skin the rusty tinge of it, darker where her fingers creased at the knuckles.

I took the stovetop coffeemaker from the hot plate, poured out two cups, and passed one to Graça.

"I used to give Rahim a hard time about this place," she said, cradling the chipped porcelain, glancing around the spartan space. We'd settled comfortably on English as a common language. Hers was better than mine, honed, like the English most of her peers spoke, on pop music and American television.

"All his secrets," she remarked. "How did you know?"

"Your grandfather told me."

She contemplated my reply. "Do you think it's safe here?"

I shrugged. "I hope so."

"Whoever it was was still in the house," she said, looking down at her cup.

"They saw you?" I asked.

"No. I could hear them in my bedroom upstairs."

Valsamis, I thought. He did not strike me as someone who would leave this kind of work to others.

"I found a copy of a shipping invoice when I was here the other day," I said. "For a cargo of cables from Trans-Dniester to Basra, Iraq."

Graça's head jerked upward, betraying what she knew. In over her head, I thought, watching the cool girl I'd met earlier evaporate.

"You knew about the invoice, didn't you?" I prompted.

She took a sip of coffee and squeezed her eyes shut.

"We can find a way out of this," I told her, not believing a word myself. "But I need you to tell me what you know."

She opened her eyes and stared back at me, hard now, who she was coming slowly back to her. "I remember you," she said. "From when I was a child."

For an instant I was back on Eduardo Morais's patio, under the shadow of his arbor, the broad leaves of the grapevines whispering against one another. On the table, the patter of gin rummy, the drowsy slap of the stiff cards against the old wood table. In the chair beside me, his face naively triumphant as it always was when he was about to win, Rahim. "Yes," I agreed.

Graça nodded, gathering herself. "What are you doing here?"

I let the words sink in, the question I also wanted an answer to. "I don't know," I told her. It was the best I could manage.

Graça got up, walked to the dirty front window, and stared silently out at the dark street. The cat followed behind, weaving back and forth between Graça's legs, brushing her calves.

"This job, the invoice," I said, not sure where to begin or how much to give away. "I was told Rahim has been working for the Islamic Armed Revolution."

Graça spun back to face me. "You're kidding, right?"

I shook my head, but Graça balked at what I was suggesting.

"Rahim hated those people. Cowards, he called them. I was with him last fall when the towers came down. He was disgusted by it, like we all were." She slid a pack of cigarettes from her pocket and fished one out. "Besides," she said, putting the filter to her lips, striking a match, "the Trans-Dniester invoice was my job."

"Your job?" I tried to hide my surprise.

Graça nodded. "Yes," she said proudly. "Al-Rashidi came to me."

"How long have you been doing this?" I asked.

"I've done a few jobs."

"And your grandfather knew?"

"He knew." Graça flicked the ash from her cigarette.

Knew, but not really, I thought. "How did al-Rashidi find you?"

"I did a job a couple of months ago for a guy named Vitor Gomes. Immigration papers. Al-Rashidi got my name from Vitor."

"And Gomes? How did you come by his patronage?"

"He came to my grandfather, but Papi wouldn't take the job."

"So you offered your services instead?"

"Yes."

"And did your grandfather say why he wouldn't work for Gomes?"

"You know him, yes?"

I nodded.

"Then you know how he can be. I thought maybe the job was too simple for him. No teeth, as he likes to say."

"And al-Rashidi's job, did it have teeth?"

Graça shrugged. "Enough." She turned her face down and away, but I could see the flush in her cheeks. She was a good liar but not good enough.

"You couldn't do it by yourself, could you?"

"I know what I'm doing," she protested.

"But you couldn't finish the invoice on your own."

"No." She took a long drag off her cigarette and wrapped her free arm tight around her chest. She was making an effort not to cry and just barely succeeding.

"What did Rahim say when you asked for his help?"

"He thought it was too much money for too small a job."

"And was it?"

"Ten thousand euros," Graça said quietly.

"On a fake shipping invoice?" It was a huge sum for what might have amounted to two days' work, a price that would have seemed too good to be true to any real professional.

Graça nodded. She'd made a mistake and she knew it, knew exactly what her miscalculation had cost her.

"But Rahim agreed to help you anyway?"

"Yes."

Yes, I thought, of course he'd agreed. And looking at Graça, I knew why.

"And did al-Rashidi pay?"

"The agreement was half up front and half on delivery," Graça explained. "I gave the invoice to him two weeks ago and got the last five thousand then."

"You delivered the invoice?" I asked.

"Yes. We met at Casa Suíça."

"Rahim was with you?"

"No."

"But the two of them must have met," I insisted, thinking of Valsamis's photographs, Rahim and al-Rashidi on the patio of Brasileira. "To discuss details of the job, at least."

Graça shook her head. "I was the only one who dealt with al-Rashidi."

"But you told him you were working with someone else."

"No." She finished her cigarette, walked to the sink, and carefully doused the coal.

Whatever adrenaline had carried her across the river was gone; she was tired and deflated, sagging against the old countertop. "I'm sorry," she said, in Portuguese now, speaking to no one in particular.

I opened my mouth to offer some form of absolution, then stopped myself. "That was the only time you met, then? To deliver the invoice?"

"We met once before," Graça answered. "At the beginning, to talk about the job."

I took a sip of my coffee, then fiddled with the cup's chipped rim, pondering what Graça had just told me, hoping and failing to find an answer in the momentary distraction.

"And Gomes?" I asked. "What do you know about him?"

"Nothing, really. Like I said, he came to my grandfather. He runs girls. Junkies, mostly. Africans."

"You know where to find him?"

Graça shook her head.

"Nice of you to help him out," I said.

Graça didn't flinch. She stared back at me, her eyes saying she knew I'd done worse.

I tossed my coffee into the sink. The grounds had been old and stale, and it was too bitter to drink. There was one more thing I needed to ask Graça. "Rahim's brother," I said. "Driss. Did you know he was here?"

Graça nodded. "He comes to visit every few months. He's got a mosque up in Toulouse."

"A mosque?"

"He's some kind of cleric," Graça explained. "Imam, or whatever they call it. I've never met him. I don't think he cares much for Rahim's lifestyle."

No, I thought. Some things didn't change. I set down the empty cup and motioned toward the back of the apartment. "You need to get some sleep," I told her. "Take the cot."

■   ■   ■

John Valsamis turned off the taps and stepped out of the shower. Two bars of cheap hotel soap whittled down to their flowery essence, and he could smell it still. The stink tenacious as the odor of a field-dressed elk on a cold morning. Not his clothes, for these Valsamis had wrapped tightly in three plastic bags, everything he'd had on, right down to his underwear, a neat package to be disposed of later. No, this stink was in him, the old man's blood in his nostrils and in the back of his throat.

It had been so long since he'd killed a man close-up that Valsamis had forgotten how much blood there could be. With Morais, so much had spilled out that it had seemed almost as if he'd been in a hurry to die, each ounce of his being rushing out onto the tile floor.

Valsamis had seen this kind of haste only once before. Years earlier, in a little village in the Annam highlands, just east of the Laotian border. He'd bungled that job, too. Green and scared, on one of his first trips out, and he'd stumbled across a young girl in the darkness, younger than he was, even. Pretty as a deer and quiet as one, she'd stepped out of the bushes in front of him. At the moment there hadn't been time for reason, just Valsamis's fear hammering him to action.

He'd shot her a good dozen times in the chest, and she'd been dead before she hit the ground. Vanished, Valsamis had thought at the time, her soul bled out onto the little footpath. As if she couldn't get away quickly enough, away from him and that place.

We should take care of the Morais girl as well, Valsamis heard Morrow say, the "we" echoing in his head. This from a man who'd spent Valsamis's war drinking cocktails at the embassy club.

Valsamis rubbed himself dry and padded out of the bathroom, securing the towel around his waist before reaching for the disposable cell phone on the bedside table. Things were getting ugly. Nicole Blake was gone, and now the Morais girl, and Kanj would find someone to listen to him soon, if he hadn't already.

Valsamis pressed the talk button, punched in Kostecky's number, and waited. Nicole would use her Hotmail account again. And when she did, Valsamis wanted to be the first to know.

EIGHTEEN

■ ■ ■

MY GRANDMOTHER WAS A METICULOUS WOMAN, raised under colonial rule, keenly aware of her place in Lebanese society, and of what that meant. Like other Christians of her age and class, my grandmother prided herself on her French, so it was French that was the language of our household. But that night, after we'd come home from the theater, it was Arabic I heard through my bedroom walls, my grandmother's voice and my mother's, the two of them arguing ferociously in the kitchen. Then a door slammed, and the whole building shuddered around me.

I don't know where my mother went that night, but she was there again in the morning when I woke up. Her hair was still up and pinned, as it had been for the theater the night before, but her face was pale, stripped of makeup. She made me breakfast, and we ate in silence at the small table in the kitchen. I knew better than to ask any questions.

There was no sign of my grandmother. I hadn't realized it at the time, but I could see now that they must have worked out some kind of agreement, the terms of which had been settled on for my sake, a cease-fire that allowed them to share a living space without acknowledging each other's presence.

After breakfast, my mother got her violin, and we walked together to my school on the rue Huvelin. Before saying goodbye and catching her bus to the American University, she stopped and set her violin case down on the sidewalk.

"This has nothing to do with you," she said, putting her hand on my shoulder, crouching until our faces met. "You understand that, don't you?"

I nodded, but I could tell she didn't believe me.

"That man you saw last night was an old friend of mine. We went to the university together a long time ago." She hesitated before going on. "He's a Shiite. That's why your grandmother didn't want me talking to him. Do you understand why that's wrong?"

"Yes," I said, though at the time, I couldn't have possibly understood. I knew only what I heard, that the war had been fought between us but that the Palestinians were the real culprits.

"Good," my mother said. "I love you." Then she kissed me on the head, picked up her violin, and headed off down the rue Huvelin.

■　■　■

I woke before dawn, slipped into my shoes and coat, and let myself out of the apartment, leaving Graça and the cat asleep together on the cot. I wasn't sure what my next move would be, but I knew I worked better and faster on my own and that the last thing I needed was to hold Graça's hand. She'd told me everything she could; now it was up to her to get herself out of whatever mess she'd made.

I stopped beneath the cracked gaze of the milkmaid and lit a cigarette, babying the flame between my hands. I believed what Graça had told me the night before, believed she didn't know anything beyond the original job she'd agreed to do. The real question was why Rahim had gone to al-Rashidi in the first place.

Shaking the match to the ground, I started off again, laying out the possible answers in my mind as I headed for the river. It didn't surprise me that Rahim had agreed to help Graça. It was easy to be a sucker for youth, even easier when youth looked like Graça Morais. But there was more, much more, that didn't make sense. Like the picture of Rahim and al-Rashidi at Brasileira, and the fact that Rahim had stayed in Lisbon at all. For if he'd known, as Valsamis had insisted, that someone was looking for him, there were plenty of places he could have gone.

Then there was the matter of the invoice itself, that last document left in Rahim's printer. Carelessness, I'd told myself at the time, but the explanation had rung hollow even then. Rahim had never been a careless person. None of us was. Our profession was one that required a religious attention to detail, and I couldn't see Rahim overlooking something so important. My gut told me there was a reason that printer and invoice had been left behind.

Youth and beauty, I reminded myself, the two qualities Rahim had appreciated the most. Though above all this, there was one other thing, something he would not have been able to turn away from. Not Graça Morais, for there were others like her, as there had been others like me. No, if Rahim had chosen to stay, it would have been for one thing only: money. And not the ten thousand euros al-Rashidi had already doled out. True, it was a lot for such an easy job, but it wasn't enough to risk one's life for.

No, Rahim had seen something funny in that invoice. What Sergei had seen, or something else altogether, something that told him he could get more than just Graça's ten thousand euros out of al-Rashidi. That was why the two men had met at Brasileira. It was why Rahim had kept a copy of the invoice in his printer. And in the end, it was what had gotten him killed.

None of this explained the bigger problem, the original invoice and the cargo it described, the five Alazan rockets that had slipped quietly out of Odessa harbor. *Worse than Nairobi.* Valsamis's warning repeated itself in my head, the only thing so far that made sense. I thought of Beirut, the Alazan's invisible and deadly cloud spreading out over the city. Through Hamra and the narrow alleyways of Ras Beirut and out onto the crowded Corniche. It would be the same no matter where it happened, in the mosques and markets of Tehran or the beehive of ancient Jerusalem. Worse than Nairobi, I told myself, so much worse.

I was rounding the corner toward the waterfront when I heard footsteps behind me, a woman's gait, quick and light. Graça, I thought, glancing back to see her coming toward me.

By the time she overtook me, she was panting, her breath thick and tangled in the cold morning air.

"You shouldn't have followed me," I told her, picking up my pace, making her jog to keep stride with me. "It's not safe."

"I'm coming with you," she insisted.

"If I were you," I told her, not breaking my stride, "I'd disappear for a while. Get out of Lisbon. Maybe even leave Europe. I'm sure you'll have no problem getting a passport."

She shook her head. "I'm not going back to the dairy."

"Do what you like, but you're not coming with me."

We'd reached the waterfront, and I could see the ferry coming in, its lights reflected in the river's oily surface. Above us on the dark hillside, the great Cristo Rei hung like a hacked sliver of moon.

"You're going to need a translator," Graça said.

"My Portuguese is fine," I told her.

"I've heard your Portuguese." She hesitated. "Look, Gomes had an apartment in Campo de Ourique. I can take you there."

I stopped walking and turned to look at her. Scared, I thought, and yet she wouldn't back down.

"You'll do what I tell you," I said. "Understood?"

Graça nodded.

"Understood?" I repeated.

"Understood."

■ ■ ■

Sabri Kanj raised his head and looked up at his interrogator. The man walked to the crude sink in the corner of the cell and rinsed his hands, then rolled down his sleeves and carefully buttoned the cuffs, as if these smallest of gestures could somehow civilize him. Kanj had come to recognize this as a sign that they were done for now, and he let his weight relax slightly against the ropes that held him. The day before, two other men had beaten his hands with electrical cords until every bone in his fingers was broken. The pain now was so intense that he found himself slipping in and out of consciousness, struggling to hold on.

He'd once thought this was the worst of all possibilities. When they'd read *1984* in his first-year literature class at the American University, Kanj had told Mina afterward that they could do anything else to him but this. For if they broke his fingers, he would never be able to play the violin again.

Mina had thought him naive, had laughed, even. "There are so many worse things," she'd said at the time, the two of them in the little coffee shop on the rue Bliss that they liked to frequent after class, "things more terrible than death." Kanj could still remember the earnestness of her face, how he'd leaned across the table and kissed her, partly to hide the fact that he didn't believe her. But he believed her now, had seen these things himself, had been both witness and perpetrator. It had been years since he'd played the violin, decades, his last instrument destroyed along with his parents' house during the Israeli siege of Beirut in the summer of 1982.

The cell door swung wide, and Kanj forced his eyes open. There was a man in the corridor, a silent figure in a pair of light khakis and a crisp cotton dress shirt. He nodded to Kanj's interrogator, and the Jordanian stepped aside, relinquishing his turf. An American, Kanj thought, and the physical sensation of relief was so powerful that he had to fight to keep from crying.

He steadied himself, then looked up into the man's blue eyes. "I want to see Richard Morrow," Kanj said.

■ ■ ■

Under the cover of darkness, and after half a dozen drinks, the nightclub on the rua do Sol ao Rato in Lisbon's immigrant Campo de Ourique neighborhood might have looked like a place to go to have a good time. But in the morning's gray light, it was hard to imagine why anyone would go there willingly. The walls were peppered with African graffiti, the black door streaked with piss stains. Someone had vomited in the gutter the night before, and you could make out the contents of the person's last meal: chicken and rice, the vivid blue of a neon cocktail. The sign above the door read ENCLAVE, the script a flourish of pink on black.

"Vitor's apartment is upstairs," Graça said, nodding to a doorway several meters to the left of the club's entrance. "Third floor."

"You've been inside?" I asked.

Graça nodded.

"What's the layout?"

"Front entryway, with a living room off to the right. That's as far as I've been. The kitchen's in the back. And there's at least one bedroom in the back as well."

"Any idea how many people to expect?"

Graça shook her head. "He's usually got at least one girl up there."

I looked up at the third-floor window. Someone had put cardboard across the panes, so it was impossible to tell whether the lights were on. Early as it was, I figured we would catch Gomes either asleep or at the tail end of his evening.

"Let's go," I told Graça, heading for the door, letting myself into the building's foyer.

There was a stink to the place, stale beer and the ammonia tinge of urine. We made our way up the stairs and stopped on the third-floor landing. There was a barrage of Afro-techno music coming from behind Gomes's closed door.

"You wait out here," I said, slipping the FEG from my pocket and engaging the clip.

Graça blinked at the sight of the gun. "Why don't I go first? At least he knows me."

I shook my head and pointed to a spot near the stair rail. "Wait right there," I told her, then tucked my hand and the FEG behind my back, took a step toward Gomes's door, and knocked.

The music stopped, and I could hear rustling and bumping within, someone fumbling with the bolt. The door swung open to reveal an African woman in a leather skirt and a bright yellow tube top. She was a good six inches taller than I, her eyelids a shimmering blue, her lips stained a muddy purple, the color of young red wine. She looked down at me, wavering drowsily on her tall platform shoes. Half gone, I thought, plummeting toward her own sweet opiate oblivion.

"I'm here to see Gomes," I said.

She blinked once and nodded, moving in slow motion as she swung her head toward the interior of the apartment. "Vitor!" she called lazily. "Vitor! Baby!"

An irritated male voice shouted from inside the apartment. "What?"

"There's a woman," she yelled in reply, her head drooping between her bare shoulders as she reached out to steady herself on the wall. Then she turned and staggered off, disappearing through a doorway.

There was a brief and hostile exchange between the two voices, then a man emerged from the same door. He was smaller than I'd expected, pale and wiry, with all the nervous energy the woman lacked.

"Vitor Gomes?" I asked.

Gomes nodded and started warily toward me. "Yes?"

I smiled. "I've been told you're the man to see for a certain kind of entertainment."

"Who told you that?" he asked, stopping just inside the doorway.

I shrugged. "A friend."

Gomes's eyes narrowed. "I don't do dykes," he sneered. He took a step forward, backing me away, and peered out into the hall.

His gaze lit on Graça and stopped there for a split second. "Shit!"

he muttered. He put his hand on the door and moved to close it, but I caught him just below the chin with the FEG.

"Inside!" I pushed him back into the apartment, motioning for Graça to follow. "Get the door," I told her.

"Fucking bitch!" Gomes spat.

"Any other girlfriends here?" I asked, nodding to the doorway where the woman in the tube top stood, mouth open, eyes half closed, calmly watching the scene go down.

Gomes shook his head, and I shoved the pistol harder into his jaw. "Don't lie to me," I warned him. He looked scared, for real, like a man who would say anything to keep from getting shot.

"What do you want?" he asked.

I turned to Graça. "Ask him how he knows al-Rashidi."

Graça relayed my question.

"I don't know . . ." I heard Gomes say, the words picked from his rapid torrent of Portuguese.

"Bullshit," I said. I snapped off the FEG's safety and moved my finger toward the trigger.

"Please," Gomes pleaded, in English now. He turned his frantic eyes to mine. "I don't know al-Rashidi."

Graça shook her head. "I don't think he's lying."

"Then ask him who exactly he recommended your services to."

Graça began to translate, but Gomes cut her off before she finished, his answer spilling out of him, too fast for me to follow.

"He says it was someone he met through one of his contacts in the Public Security Police," Graça explained. "A foreigner, he keeps saying."

"And does this foreigner have a name?"

Graça conveyed my question and waited for an answer. "They met only once," she said. "At a café in the Alfama."

"The man was an Arab?" I asked.

Gomes shook his head. "No," he said in English. "No Arab. American." Then he turned to Graça and let out another frantic flood of Portuguese.

"Apparently he told Gomes he needed some shipping documents. He wanted someone without a lot of experience. Someone who could do the work but didn't know much about the business . . ." Graça trailed off, her face sagging. "An amateur," she translated.

I took my finger slowly from the trigger, eased the FEG's safety back on, and released the barrel from Gomes's jaw.

Gomes exhaled audibly. I could smell the fear on his breath, the rancid odor of old cigarettes and metabolized alcohol. His face, already pale, had blanched a milky green.

"This American," I said. "Ask him what he looked like."

Gomes glanced up at Graça, nodding while she relayed my words, then he put his hand slightly below the top of his head.

"His height," Graça said, speaking for Gomes. "Maybe a few centimeters shorter. But bigger . . ." She stopped, searching for the right word. "Wider," she tried finally.

Gomes motioned to his face.

"Ugly," Graça explained. "Like a rock, he keeps saying."

"And his clothes?" I asked. "How was he dressed?"

Gomes shrugged at the question. "Como turisto," he said.

Graça looked at me, but I didn't need her to translate. I knew exactly what Gomes had meant.

"Like a tourist," I said, before Graça had a chance to. Valsamis.

NINETEEN

■ ■ ■

RICHARD MORROW ROLLED OUT OF BED and slid his feet into his slippers. Three A.M. and the phone in his office was ringing. Nine rings, ten, each tone echoing insistently through the house. Someone who wasn't going to give up.

Morrow's wife stirred slightly, put her hand on his back. "Christ, Dick," she mumbled. "You'd think the goddamn sky was falling."

He rose and shuffled out of the room and down the hallway, shrugging off the ghost of sleep as he set his hand on the receiver.

"Morrow here."

"Dick, it's Charlie Fairweather, in Amman."

"Do you know what time it is?" Morrow asked.

"Yes, sir. But I thought you'd want to know right away—it's Kanj."

Morrow ran his thumb and forefinger across his eyes and sat down in the armchair opposite his desk. Not just tired but weary, the last thirty years catching up with him. Thirty years of chasing a shadow. Lebanon, Cyprus, Iran, Algeria, Afghanistan, Pakistan. And now that they'd caught up with Kanj, Morrow didn't know quite what to think. "He's talking?"

"Not exactly, sir." Fairweather's voice was like a child's, a little boy afraid of being scolded.

"What's that supposed to mean?"

"He wants to talk to you, sir."

"That's impossible. You know that. Tell him it's impossible."

"We've made that very clear, sir. He's had it pretty bad—you know how it is. I'm sure he's just playing us. But he's very insistent. He claims it's about the '83 embassy bombing. In Beirut, sir. Something about a mole."

Morrow felt his chest seize up and every muscle in his body tighten. "What does he want?" he snapped, rising from his chair.

"I believe he wants to make a deal, sir. But it's hard to know exactly. Like I said, he claims he won't talk to anyone but you. He must know you were the DO for Mid-East back then."

A handful of people, Morrow thought. A handful of people who knew about what had happened in Beirut, and most of them dead. Kanj was not supposed to have been one of them. He could have been bluffing. Push hard enough, and people will say anything. Whatever they think you want to hear. Whatever they imagine will buy them a way out. But this, this didn't make sense.

"Sir?" Fairweather asked.

"Keep him comfortable," Morrow told the man. "I'm coming over."

■ ■ ■

"You were lovers, weren't you?" Graça asked, though there was little question in her voice.

I slid a cigarette from her pack and tapped it against the bar, hesitating before pressing the filter to my lips. I had more questions for Sergei, but my better judgment told me not to go back to the Largo do Picadeiro, so Graça and I had taken the train from Gomes's place to the Rossio instead. I had a hunch there would be a cybercafé near the train station, and I was right. We'd found a busy storefront on the Praça dos Restauradores and settled in at the bar to wait for a free computer.

I struck a match, then touched the flame to the cigarette, lifted my face upward, and exhaled. "Yes," I said.

"What happened?" Graça asked.

I shrugged. "It was a long time ago."

"But you loved him?"

I thought about the question, the answer I expected myself to give. "I don't know," I told her finally. "Did you?"

"Yes," she said easily. Her eyes held mine, then she reached forward and picked up her cigarettes.

Had I ever been that sure? I wondered. Those first days in Marseille? The months on the Travessa da Laranjeira? From where I sat, such faith seemed impossible, and yet there was a time when my answer would have been the same as Graça's. In the end, though, I hadn't even said goodbye. I'd packed what little I had while Rahim was out one afternoon and taken a taxi to Santa Apolonia Station. From there, a train north to my father's house in Collioure.

"Who was he?" Graça asked, and initially I thought she meant Rahim. "The man at my grandfather's," she elaborated.

"I don't know. He's an American. With the government."

"He's the one who killed Rahim, isn't he?"

I nodded.

"But why?"

Because I betrayed him, I thought. Because I was afraid. Because you took al-Rashidi's job. But I didn't say any of this. "That's what we need to find out," I told her.

She lit her cigarette and looked across the table at me. Stony, as she had been that first day on her grandfather's doorstep, her dark eyes reflecting the café windows, the steady stream of passersby on the sidewalk outside.

"Did you know Rahim was blackmailing al-Rashidi?" I asked.

Graça looked up at me, and I could tell immediately that she'd been telling the truth all along, that Rahim hadn't told her about the invoice. "What do you mean?"

"The invoice," I said. "It was a fake."

"Of course it was a fake."

I shook my head. "I don't just mean the forgery. The whole document's wrong. The cargo. The destination. That's why whoever hired you through Gomes wanted an amateur. It's the only thing that makes sense. They figured you wouldn't see it. What they didn't bank on was you bringing Rahim in to help."

"I don't understand."

"Neither do I. But Rahim did, and whatever he knew, he must have guessed it was worth more than what al-Rashidi had already paid."

"How can you be so sure?"

"I'm not sure of anything. But he met with al-Rashidi. I'm sure of that. And I can't think of any other reason why Rahim would have stayed in Lisbon, knowing it wasn't safe for him here. Can you?"

Graça's face darkened. I realized then that she must have thought Rahim had stayed because of her. She was quiet, then she shook her head.

The barman came over and gathered our empty cups, then pointed toward the back of the café.

"Looks like it's our turn," I said, following the man's finger to a computer that had just come open. I crushed my cigarette in the cheap tin ashtray and slid off my stool. "We'll get out of this," I told Graça. "Don't worry."

I wove back through the rows of desks and slid in behind the keyboard, then logged on to my Hotmail account. There was nothing from Sergei, no new information, just a handful of spam e-mails sitting in my in-box. I deleted them, then addressed a new message to Fernando76. *Need info on John Valsamis,* I wrote. *Showed me U.S. Defense Department credentials.*

I hit SEND and waited, checking my watch, making a mental note of the time. Sergei was a night owl, but the time difference made it close to four in the morning in the Islands. I'd give him half an hour, and if I hadn't heard anything by then, I'd check back later.

Showed U.S. Defense Department credentials, I thought. But Valsamis hadn't really, had he? What he'd shown me had been a business card, ink on paper. Something even Graça Morais could have done. There'd been the photographs as well, and more than that, there had been everything Valsamis knew. My story at his fingertips.

You can't just act the part, my father had told me once, early on. *You have to be the part.*

I drummed my fingers on the desk and sat back in my chair, glancing around the café. Graça had found a free computer and was hunched intently over the keyboard. Stupid, I thought, cursing her silently. I got up and shrugged out of my coat, then laid it on my chair to keep my place and made my way toward Graça.

"What the fuck do you think you're doing?" I asked.

She looked up at me and blinked, then motioned to the screen. "I did a search for al-Rashidi," she said.

"Well?"

"I found an Ibrahim al-Rashidi, but he's not exactly the one we're looking for."

"What do you mean, 'not exactly'?"

"Evidently his son is quite popular. He's an orthopedic surgeon in the U.S."

I looked at her quizzically, and she moved aside to give me a better look at the monitor. "See for yourself."

I bent down and peered at the article on the screen. It was a puff piece from *The Seattle Times,* a Sunday feature on the city's most eligible bachelors. An architect, a chef, a football player, and an orthopedic surgeon, Ibrahim al-Rashidi. There were pictures of the men, each well groomed and likable-looking, each smiling his flawless smile. Each a perfect combination of looks and ambition, the marrying type. I skimmed through the text, the cursor passing the first three stories, slowing at al-Rashidi's.

"Here," Graça said, setting her finger against the screen.

Dr. al-Rashidi was born in Iraq, the sentence she'd picked out began, *where his father was a high-ranking member of Saddam Hussein's government. Al-Rashidi lived a privileged life, his childhood split between homes in Beirut and Baghdad.*

Beirut, I thought, my neck prickling as I stopped on the word. Iraq and Lebanon were close neighbors, had been allies for a long time. If the elder al-Rashidi had been an intelligence man, he could have been sent there under diplomatic cover.

In the early 1980s, the article continued, *both he and his sister were sent to the United States to study at the prestigious Phillips Exeter Academy in Exeter, New Hampshire. Dr. al-Rashidi went on to attend Princeton University and the University of Washington's medical school . . .*

There was no further mention of the sister or any of al-Rashidi's other family members, nor of the turbulent times that must have followed, a family split by war and distance. And yet somehow the younger Ibrahim al-Rashidi had found a way to stay in the United States. Or his father had found a way for him.

I scrolled back to the picture of al-Rashidi's face, trying to match the square jaw and dark eyes with the photograph Valsamis had shown me, the older al-Rashidi in his uniform, and later, at Brasileira with Rahim.

"Close out of this," I told Graça, straightening up, heading back to my computer. Coincidence, I reminded myself, and yet nothing seemed coincidental anymore.

There was an answer from Sergei waiting in my mailbox. Working late, though at this hour Sergei was more likely cruising his favorite adult websites. What was it about the Russians that made them such suckers for big hair, fake tits, and too much makeup?

Give me twelve hours and I'll see what I can find out, Sergei had written.

Not the answer I'd been hoping for, but one I could live with. I closed out of my account, then crossed back to the bar, where Graça was waiting for me. "I'm sorry I yelled at you before," I apologized. "That was smart, looking for al-Rashidi like that."

Her face softened slightly. She shuffled her feet and craned her neck, peering toward the door. "What next?" she asked.

Just killing time, I thought, waiting for Sergei's answer, hoping for something on Valsamis that would make all the pieces fall into place. "I want you to take me to Rahim's apartment."

■ ■ ■

"You don't really believe in all that Kissinger bullshit, do you?" Andy Sproul had asked, dividing the last of the Ksarak among their three glasses.

Morrow was visiting Beirut on his annual tour of the Mid-East stations. He and Sproul and Valsamis had gone out to a late dinner at one of the cafés near the embassy.

The golden boy, they called Sproul at the Beirut station, but Morrow wasn't impressed. Foolish, he thought, hopelessly naive. Though not a threat, not yet. Sproul was like the white kid who went into the ghetto speaking jive, and Morrow figured the Arabs would see right through him. Though of course they never did.

"What I believe," Morrow said, "is that we have to look out for our own best interests."

"And by 'best interests,'" Sproul countered, "I assume you mean the seven-hundred-billion-plus barrels of oil our neighbors in the Gulf are sitting on right now."

Morrow smiled. "Perhaps you'd like to phone the folks back in Wichita and tell them to start chopping wood for this winter."

Sproul sat back in his chair and lifted the Ksarak as if in a toast. "Touché," he said, but there was the faintest hint of mockery in his tone.

"Everything in this world has a price," Morrow reminded him fiercely. "It's easy to forget that, but it's true."

Sproul touched the glass to his lips and drained it, then set it back on the table. "You know," he said, "there are a lot of Lebanese who think we want the Syrians here. That it's all part of some scheme to get the Palestinians out of Israel and give them Lebanon instead."

Morrow shrugged. "They're entitled to their opinion, aren't they?"

He turned to Valsamis, hoping to shift the conversation his way. "I hear you've picked up an asset in Amal. A true believer, from what people are saying."

"Peace and country and all that," Valsamis agreed.

Morrow nodded. "It's the true believers that are the most useful."

"Or the most dangerous," Sproul added.

■　■　■

Dick Morrow sat awake in the darkness and listened to the sounds of his house, the whir of the furnace, the patter of rain on the eaves. *They're all here,* he could hear his father saying, the old man's last words, death already scrabbling at the back of his throat. *They're all here.*

Morrow's mother had reached out and put her hand on his father's papery wrist, smiled her detached smile, whispered, *Yes, dear, we're all here.* But this wasn't what he'd meant, and Morrow had known it, could see the ghosts waiting in the room's dark corners: the German kid his father had bayoneted at Belleau Wood; his best friend, Jack Harrison, who'd died in agony in a little church near St. Mihiel, his legs blown to pulp by a German mortar.

Yes, Morrow thought, this is how it happens: At the end you are alone with them. And his own ghosts? Still gathered at their usual table at the Commodore. Bryce and Wilson and Valsamis. Andy Sproul in the ridiculous keffiyeh he'd taken to wearing at the end, catching the waiters off guard with his easy Arabic.

There were footsteps in the hallway, and Morrow's wife appeared, her hair sleep-tousled, silhouetted in the doorway. "Can't this keep until morning?"

Morrow shook his head. "Go back to bed."

■　■　■

The peace to which my mother and I returned was quick to fail. In March the fedayeen attacked Tel Aviv, and the Israelis responded by crossing the border into southern Lebanon, sending tens of thousands of refugees streaming north to Beirut. After Tony Franjieh, son of the Syrian-backed president, was assassinated, old rivalries flared, and by the summer of 1978, the city was once again a war zone.

My grandparents and I were among the flood of prosperous Beirutis to seek refuge at their weekend homes up the coast in Jounieh. The port town was barely thirty kilometers from Beirut, but it was another world entirely, untouched by the raging destruction of the conflict and the homeless squatters who had swamped the city.

My mother had long since made the decision to stay. She would not leave this time, would not watch the war from afar, as she had those years in Paris. My grandmother knew better than to cross her daughter, but my grandfather fought her tooth and claw.

In the end, my mother won. Like many of the other Beirutis who stayed behind, she believed in the heroism of daily and modest defiances, of teaching her classes and feeding herself amid the car bombs and rockets. At least this was what she told us at the time. And what, I suppose, she believed.

Even then I think she understood that there was more than duty that compelled her to remain in Beirut. She'd been gone often that spring, coming in late from her classes and leaving at night, reappearing for breakfast as she had the morning after we'd gone to see *Petra*. She and my grandmother maintained their truce, but in the evenings after I went to bed, I could hear my grandparents arguing.

We finally left for Jounieh in July, the three of us packed into my grandparents' Mercedes with the good china and the family photos, sepia prints of my mother and her sister in their school uniforms, of picnics in the cedars, and of elegant women in long slim gowns. Snapshots of another time. On the steps of the Achrafiye apartment building, my mother stood in a stylish Parisian pantsuit, waving goodbye.

■ ■ ■

Everything I knew about the way Rahim worked told me not to expect much from the apartment, that anything of interest most likely would have been at the Cacilhas workshop. But I'd wanted to come, had held out hope that I might find something that would help me understand. I'd wanted something else as well, some physical reminder of our life on the Travessa da Laranjeira, the old green chair or the knife-scarred kitchen table, remnants of who we had been.

Rahim's apartment had already been ransacked by the time Graça and I got there. The drawers had been emptied, the mattress and pillows sliced open, the cabinets searched in a way that suggested both carelessness and attention to detail, as if whoever had been here had known Rahim wouldn't be coming back and had taken his time.

I paused in the bedroom and glanced at the chaos around me: shattered glass, a heap of sheets on the floor. The window had been left open and several rainfalls had poured in, leaving a dark wash of mildew on the curtains. There was a musty smell to the room, the rotten stink of waterlogged fabric. Gone, I thought, the old iron bed frame and the mahogany dressing table, the chair with its green tapestry, a worn Eden of flowers and vines.

It was raining now, not rain so much as mist driven in from the Atlantic. I walked to the window and peered across the Travessa da Água de Flor and out over the rooftops of the Bairro Alto, letting the rain settle on my face and in my hair. I could hear Graça in the living room, stumbling through the clutter.

They would have made love here, I thought, turning back to face the bed, not ours but theirs, Graça and Rahim's. I closed my eyes and tried to imagine the dissolution of his body, the marks of time and age that my own body mirrored back to me. And yet for all my effort, I could see him only as he'd been that night many years earlier on the train from Marseille. Young, as we'd both been, and flawless.

An amateur, I heard Graça say, her translation of Gomes's words catching her like a fierce and unexpected slap. The humiliation of youth and inexperience, the loss of everything she'd imagined herself to be.

Fumbling in my coat pocket, I took out the copy of the shipping invoice and unfolded it. BSW AIR CARGO, I read, skimming the letterhead, the United Arab Emirates address, letting my eyes wander down the page, trying to see what Rahim had seen. Fishy, I thought, remembering the word Sergei had used in his e-mail. Not just the dimensions but the itinerary as well, the question I'd asked myself still nagging at me: If the Alazans were headed for embargoed Iraq, as the invoice said, why broadcast that fact by listing Basra as the cargo's destination? Especially if the shipment was going by way of Sharjah. And if the Iraqis were buying dirty bombs from the former Soviet stockpile, then why wouldn't the Americans want the world to know?

No, I thought, working the problem over and over in my mind, each answer like a square block in a round hole. There was something I was missing.

Graça appeared in the doorway. Her eyes were red, as if she'd been crying. "Find anything?"

I shook my head. There was nothing left for us to find. Nothing left for me, either.

TWENTY

■ ■ ■

JOHN VALSAMIS HADN'T WANTED TO RETIRE. Barely fifty, he hadn't thought of him-self as old, though his father hadn't been much older when he'd left the smelter, and Valsamis had regarded him as ancient at the time. But things had been different then. That kind of work and the weight of so many children took their toll on a person's body.

In the end, it hadn't been Valsamis's choice to make. In his last eight years at the Agency, the world had easily outpaced him, along with so many others who'd done their jobs just a little too well. Men and women like Valsamis who, through a combination of their own efficiency and blind luck, had been rendered obsolete.

As much as he didn't want to leave, Valsamis was a man who knew how to make a graceful exit, and he was gracious in defeat. He had smiled placidly through the retirement party Morrow presided over for him in Near East, careful not to drink himself into a bitter nostalgia, as he'd seen too many of his colleagues do. At the cere-mony in the Bubble, he'd gritted his teeth and returned the admiring and slightly patronizing handshakes of the twentysomethings who had come to take his place, nodding at their talk of tropical beaches and beautiful women, a paradise built from Gauguin paintings and Club Med ads.

But Valsamis had other plans for himself. Five days after his re-lease from the Agency, he'd cleaned out his already spare apartment and boarded a plane. A tourist this time, heading not south but east, to a country he'd known intimately for so many years, for which he'd given so much, though he'd never once set foot within its borders.

It was January when he arrived in St. Petersburg, and he was un-characteristically nervous as he handed his brand-new passport and tourist visa to a bored customs agent. Half an hour later, he was out on the airport breezeway with his one small bag, his teeth chattering, his back turned to a wind he hadn't felt since he was a boy, the same punishing cold that battered the Montana plains. But Valsamis hadn't gone to Russia for the weather.

The next morning he took a tram to the Hermitage and wandered among the masterpieces that had been denied him for so long. Titian's *Danae*, Leonardo's *Madonna and Child*, Rembrandt's *Return of the Prodigal Son*. In the afternoon he went up onto the roof and looked out over the palace's weathered copper gables toward the frozen Neva and the snowy expanse of Vasilyevsky Island, the towering rostral columns and the Exchange Building like some icy, arctic Parthenon.

The new Russia, Valsamis had thought, his Russia, as cold and broken as it still was. And then, alone on the windy rooftop balcony, with all of St. Petersburg at his feet, he'd broken down and wept.

■ ■ ■

Another e-mail, Valsamis told himself as he took a seat at the nearly empty bar. Another message, and now Nicole was asking about him. They'd been slow this time. It had taken Kostecky's man a good half hour to get the call through, and by then Nicole was long gone. But they would be ready when she went to pick up the Russian's reply. Until then all he could do was wait.

Valsamis ordered a whiskey and soda, the cheap stuff, what he preferred, the taste that reminded him of somewhere else. Early morning in the Pintlers, Hank Williams on the truck's old AM radio and his father singing along in broken English. Outside, in the head-lights, snow and more snow, flakes the size of a man's fist, downy and friable, as if the clouds themselves had broken apart and were falling. Inside, the rattle of the Ford's ancient heater, the bottle of Ten High sloshing on the seat between them. The truck such meager shelter from the wilderness around them, the dark miles of snow and ice, the mountains echoing back and back, all the way to the Idaho border and beyond.

It was early still, but out on the dance floor, two young men were moving in ecstatic synchronicity. They had taken off their shirts, and their bare skin flashed in the club's colored lights, chest and shoulders, the curve of a well-crafted back. Youth on display.

The music stopped abruptly, and the two men lingered for a moment, then headed for the bar. Valsamis huddled around his drink, his eye on the darker of the two. He was taller than Valsamis by a good six inches, his hair long and straight, swept languorously across his face, but he was slight of build, his arms and chest frail as a young girl's.

The boy caught Valsamis's stare and held it, then glanced nervously at his empty hands. This one, Valsamis thought, imagining how it would happen, the boy's slender hips beneath his. Valsamis felt his stomach contract, felt the hot rush of blood to his groin, repulsion and desire at the same time.

He could hear Dick Morrow all those years earlier, the last thing he'd said before disappearing into the crowd at the L.A. airport. *These are your choices, John: to be the stronger or the weaker, to be the ruler or the ruled, to be the powerful or the powerless.*

Valsamis took a sip of his whiskey and watched the young man come toward him.

■ ■ ▨

In the end, the choice is made for me. Rahim and I have gone out to a dinner party at a friend's house in Belém. It's a pleasant evening. Our host, a Frenchman, has made real coq au vin, and for dessert tiny pots de crèmes peppered with lemon zest and orange-scented muscat. Gifts of edible sunshine in the midst of gray winter.

It's the usual suspects, a ragtag conglomerate of drifters and crooks. Two Russians, the Frenchman's Hungarian girlfriend, an Italian con man. A week and a half since the first attack on Iraq, and already people here are weary of talking about it, tired of the Americans' relentless prowess and their own anger, the nightly films of precision killing. "A clean war," one of the Russians snorts, "there is no such thing." And then, as if by silent pact, we move on to other subjects.

It feels good to be free of it for a few hours, such a surprising return to normalcy. In the cab on the way home, Rahim kisses me, and I can taste the sweet muscat in his mouth, orange blossoms and honey and lavender. Back at the apartment, we barely make it up the stairs. We stumble over each other in the darkness, fingers fumbling with buttons and clasps, key clawing at the lock. So desperate that I am momentarily afraid, acutely aware of his physical power, so much greater than mine, and the fierceness of what brought us together.

Inside, coats still on, we make love on the living room floor. For the first time, though I still haven't told him, I am certain he knows about the baby. Hungry as we are, there is a tentativeness between us, a sense of deliberation, our bodies slow and cautious. When we are finished, we lie together for a long time, silent and still, hearts hammering against each other.

It isn't until I pull away and feel Rahim slide out from inside me that I realize what has happened. On his stomach and my thighs is a dark stain, my own blood, musky and rich.

Rahim sees it as well, and a look of involuntary disgust crosses his face. Here is the one great taboo between us. This prohibition that is part of his faith and that has become my monthly humiliation. By the time he understands and recovers himself, it is too late.

For a moment, more than anything, I am deeply relieved, then a wave of loss hits me, a feeling of grief that I couldn't have expected. Suddenly I know, with utter certainty, that I cannot stay.

■ ■ ■

It was just shy of Sergei's twelve hours when Graça and I stepped into the cybercafé on the rua Diário de Notícias. The café was packed, pulsing to the angry rhythms of Goth rock, the crowd mostly pale faces and black hair. Trying to ignore the high-decibel screams ricocheting off the brick walls and concrete floor, I left Graça at the bar, found a free computer, and logged in to my Hotmail account. There was nothing from Sergei in my account yet, no messages except for a few spams, come-ons for breast enhancement and penis enlargement, the usual stray detritus of the Internet. Still a good half hour to Sergei's promised deadline, I reminded myself, checking my watch. Time for the Russian to come through with something tonight, and I'd give him every minute.

Wiping the spam from my in-box, I followed Graça's earlier lead and typed Valsamis's name into the search engine. A list of websites flooded the screen: a marine engineer in Houston, Texas, a wedding announcement from a small-town newspaper in upstate New York, a teenager's home page. Nothing even remotely related to the John Valsamis I was after. Killing time, I typed in the address for a different search engine and entered Valsamis's name once again.

■ ■ ■

Valsamis had thought the young man pretty when he'd first seen him at the bar, but here, against the shabby surroundings of the apartment, he was almost beautiful. Valsamis reached up and touched the sleeping boy's shoulder, ran his finger lightly along the hollow of his collarbone. His hair smelled of cedar and cigarette smoke, of sweat and faded cologne. His chest was smooth and delicate, his skin luminously pale.

There had been something slightly off about the young man, something passive and yet powerful about the way he carried himself, the demeanor of an untrained whore. Offering his body and yet not, and the combination had made Valsamis want him even more.

Leaving the boy to sleep, Valsamis rolled out of bed, dressed quietly, and set two twenty-euro notes on the hall table. Then he let
himself out through the apartment's front door and took the stairs
down to the street.

The night had barely begun, and the cramped neighborhood
around the Praça do Principe Real was just finding its rhythm.
Groups of men paraded up and down the narrow streets. Like an
Arab city, Valsamis thought, reminded of the cafés in Cairo or
Damascus, men walking arm in arm and the smell of knocked-off
European cologne. The freedom of a world unburdened by the com-
plications of gender.

A young man crossed the street in his direction and Valsamis felt
his heart catch, remembering the apartment he'd just left behind,
the stale smell and the shared bathroom on the landing, the boy's obvious embarrassment at all of it.

The cell phone in Valsamis's right breast pocket rang. He drew it
out and flipped it open. "Yes?"

"We've just recorded a hit, sir." A woman this time, young, with a
slightly Southern twang. Never the same person twice. How did they
do it? Twelve-hour days at some basement computer, and the other
twelve, sir, trying to forget everything they'd heard or seen. On the
weekends, backyard barbecues where everyone knew better than to
ask about work.

"What's the location?" Valsamis asked.

"It's coming in now, sir. Are you ready?"

"Go ahead."

"One-twenty-six rua Diário de Notícias. Looks like a public
server."

The café above São Roque, Valsamis thought. A fifteen-minute
walk at most. "She's still online?"

The woman paused, then, "Yes, sir. Is there anything else, sir?"

"No, nothing else," Valsamis told her.

■ ■ ■

Once more my search came up bust. The engineer, the newlywed, and now a Greek musician. Again, nothing on John Valsamis. I logged back in to my Hotmail account, and this time there was a message waiting for me.

Where Sergei got his information, I didn't know, and I didn't want to ask. What I did know was that my friend had a network to rival that of the best small-town gossip, an electronic web of contacts, old and new, that seemed to know where every body, from Minsk to Mexico City, was buried.

John Valsamis, Sergei had written, his answer characteristically brief. *U.S. Central Intelligence Agency. Mid-East division. Field officer, Istanbul, Cairo, Beirut. Retired, 1997.*

There it was again, I thought, an electric chill coursing up my back. Beirut. Not coincidence, then, this city that connected us all, Valsamis and al-Rashidi and me. *A car bomb,* I heard Valsamis say that night in my kitchen, his finger on the picture of the girl and her mother. Later, on his way out, his thin smile. He'd known about my mother, known before I did that I would agree to find Rahim. Known just what I'd need to justify my choice, to let myself think it wasn't fear or anger driving me but something else.

What was it my father liked to say? *You can't con an honest man.*

I glanced up and saw Graça slide off her bar stool. She waved at me, pointed back through the café, toward the alcove marked wc.

■ ■ ■

Valsamis flipped the collar of his coat up around his neck and turned down the rua da Rosa, powering forward past the clubs and fado houses, the steamy overflow of bodies outside Play Bar and Nova. On the narrow sidewalk in front of O Forcado was a less sophisticated clientele. Obvious tourists huddled against the rain, fighting for the few taxis that had wandered into the hilltop neighborhood.

Close now, Valsamis thought, just a few more blocks. He crossed the street to avoid the crowd, his gait almost a jog, then he turned onto the Travessa da Boa Hora and the quieter rua Diário de Notícias. He could hear the Internet café from a good block away, the thump of electronic music pounding out into the narrow lane. A group of kids in makeshift costumes eyed him with unchecked suspicion as he opened the door and let himself inside.

Valsamis stood near the door, getting his bearings. Then he elbowed his way into the crush of bodies, starting for the back of the café and the monitors he'd glimpsed through the crowd.

A hand caught the sleeve of his coat, and Valsamis turned to see a young woman glaring at him with unvarnished contempt. She couldn't have been over twenty, her pale face bristling with a dozen different piercings. Her body was slightly too doughy for her black vinyl corset and zippered miniskirt, her arms stippled with goose bumps, her white stomach bulging over her waistband. "There's a wait for the computers," she snarled in Portuguese. "You need to get in line."

Valsamis shook off her hand and started forward again, scanning the crowd for Nicole's dark hair and narrow face. But the girl wouldn't let him go.

"Hey, asshole!" she snarled. "Are you deaf?"

■ ■ ■

There was some kind of disturbance at the front of the café, a woman's voice shouting angry Portuguese. A clutch of bodies at the counter shielded my view, customers waiting to pay and others loitering, gawking at the uproar. I couldn't tell exactly what was going on, but I could see one of the counter girls through the crowd, the same surly young woman who'd assigned me my computer. Some poor soul had crossed her and was paying for it.

I ducked into the stairwell that led down to the restrooms, years of prison instinct telling me it was best to lie low.

A man's voice answered the young woman's, the Portuguese a broken growl. There was a slight movement in the crowd, and then I heard the girl gasp, her breath high and tight, caught against her throat. The sound a puppy might make when kicked.

"Hey!" someone shouted. And another voice: "Get your hands off her!"

The crowd fell silent. Over the music I heard the unmistakable click of a bullet being chambered, the sound itself warning enough. The ring of people fell away, and I could see the gun, the metal glinting in the café's halogen spotlights, and the man's hand on the girl's wrist, her arm turning uncomfortably purple beneath his grasp.

He pushed her aside, then pivoted, his eyes raking over the café, toward the alcove where I stood, pressed up against the wall. I could see his face and the look of disgust on it, the same contempt I'd seen that morning in my kitchen in Paziols.

Ducking farther into the alcove, I slid the FEG from my pocket and took the stairs down to the basement landing, where Graça was waiting outside the women's room.

"He's here," I told her, taking a split-second inventory of my surroundings. There were three doors off the landing, the men's and women's bathrooms, and a third, unmarked door.

"Who?" Graça asked.

"The American," I answered, pushing the men's room door open with my foot, peering in at the stained walls and filthy floor toilet.

I tried the unmarked door next, revealing a cramped utility closet, a mop and broom, a shelf stocked with spare paper and cleaning supplies, a stack of cardboard boxes.

Graça nodded to the women's room. "There's someone in there."

There was the sound of a toilet flushing. The door opened and a young woman stepped out, another of the café's counter girls. She glanced down at the gun and froze.

"Is there a way out of here?" I asked in my broken Portuguese.

The girl blinked back at me, uncomprehending.

"Ask her!" I told Graça.

Graça quickly translated, and the girl blinked again, then raised her hand and pointed to the closet. Her fingers were trembling, her black nails chipped where she'd chewed off the polish. She spoke rapidly, and Graça nodded. Then Graça stepped into the narrow space and shoved aside one of the boxes, revealing not a wall but the beginning of what looked like endless darkness, a passageway stretching back into the rock, a relic of the ancient city.

"She says she's heard it goes all the way to the Largo Trindade Coelho," Graça explained.

I looked back at the girl, and she nodded at me. "Yes!" she insisted. "Yes!"

Graça shrugged. "I believe her."

The girl's eyes were glassy with fear. "You're coming with us," I told her, grabbing her arm with my free hand.

■ ■ ■

The rear of the café was divided into two churchlike columns, with five straight rows of tables and monitors laid out along a center aisle. Drawn by the woman's protests, most of the clientele had congregated near the front counter, but there were a few stray customers still at their workstations and a handful more huddled beneath the tables.

There's nothing like a gun to get people's attention, and Valsamis's Ruger, though not flashy, commanded definite respect. As he made his way toward the back of the café, Valsamis listened with satisfaction to the numbed silence, the perfection of it broken only by the girl's sobs. By the time he reached the second row of tables, even those had begun to fade. The door whooshed open behind him, and Valsamis swung around in time to see a trio of figures escaping into the night. Three potential heroes, Valsamis thought, watching the boys disappear. He would have to work quickly.

Valsamis swept forward again, scanning the hunched forms on the floor. A young man with jet-black hair. A blond girl in a dark velvet cape, her incisors capped with two long fangs. And then, at the far end of the very last row, Valsamis caught a glimpse of cropped brown hair, a woman's long lean back, her knees bent tight against her chest, her face buried between them.

Valsamis skirted the tables and came up behind the woman. She was crying, not sobbing like the girl at the front, but just quietly weeping, her whole body racked by the force of her fear.

"Get up," Valsamis told her, setting the Ruger's barrel against the back of her neck. "Get up now."

"Please," she whispered, unfolding slowly toward him, arms and head and face. Not Nicole, not even close. "Please," she repeated, but Valsamis was already turning from her, his eyes scanning the café, lighting on the stairwell that led down to the restrooms.

■ ■ ■

None of us spoke. From time to time I could hear the counter girl choking back a sob, a rat scrambling by, cockroaches rustling. But mostly there was silence, the sound of my own heart, the blood hammering in my ears.

Graça went first and we followed behind, groping our way along the wall, feeling the old pipes and stones with our fingertips, stumbling over hazards whose real shapes we could only guess at, loose mortar and piles of rags, bits of metal that rang against the soles of our shoes. Or worse, what we wouldn't let ourselves imagine. The detritus of some three thousand years of fear and occupations. The Romans and the Visigoths, the Moors and the Spaniards. And later, the assassination of Don Carlos and the rise of Salazar. Centuries of siege and plague and inquisition. The whole violent history of a continent borne by the ghosts of thousands of fleeing souls huddled around us.

It wasn't far to the Largo Trindade Coelho, a five-minute walk aboveground. It couldn't have taken us over thirty minutes to navigate the tunnel, but it seemed like hours. Near the end there was a rancid odor, the unmistakable stench of death, and I thought I might be sick. Then the walls opened up, and I could smell the rain.

Graça stumbled, and I heard her catch herself. "Stairs," she warned, her voice moving upward.

My foot found the first step and the second, and then I could see Graça's shadow above me, her head and shoulders silhouetted against the night sky.

■ ■ ■

Nicole was here, Valsamis thought, contemplating the landing, the two empty restrooms, and the closet. No windows and no way out. He turned and started back up the stairs, then stopped himself. He should have had her, and yet somehow she was gone.

He stepped back toward the closet and paused in the doorway, his gaze moving across the little room, taking in the cluttered shelves, the boxes stacked slightly askew. Nothing, he told himself. Or something? He moved forward and then froze. From somewhere far in the distance came the tinny wail of sirens, the sound moving louder and closer.

No, he told himself, he'd been right the first time. There was nothing to see, no way out. And no way out for him if he stayed. He glanced at the boxes again, the dark shadow where the ceiling met the wall. Then he turned and headed back up the stairs, back through the café, and out onto the rua Diário de Notícias.

TWENTY-ONE

■ ■ ■

WARM WATER AND WHITE SAND and a sky so blue you could have dived into it. My first bikini, two canary-yellow swatches of fabric sent from France by my aunt. The saltwater smell of my skin after a day at the beach. This is what I remember of Jounieh. Among my friends there was an adolescent cynicism bred from the combination of privilege and war. A sense that everything was cheap and that nothing much mattered.

Our life continued much as it had in Beirut, my grandfather fighting to keep his shipping business alive, my grandmother determined to salvage the tattered remnants of Beirut society, each believing that the war would end sometime soon. There were dinner parties and ladies' lunches, polished silver and crystal, and the same bone china that had traveled with me from Beirut.

My mother came on the weekends when she could, and we would take the *téléphérique* to Harissa or drive up the coast to Byblos and have lunch on the beach. For the first few months, she and my grandfather argued, but as the war dragged on and it became clear that my mother would not join us, even he gave in.

Nothing is simple in the Middle East, especially not war, and the Lebanese civil war was no exception. The roots of the conflict reached far beyond the country's borders, into neighboring Syria and Israel, and further, even, toward the Western colonial powers upon whose shoulders the shaky dream of a unified Lebanon had been built.

The Syrians, fearful of a Christian-Israeli alliance, had involved themselves directly almost from the beginning, while the Israelis, alarmed at the prospect of a Palestinian stronghold to the north, had chosen a more covert path. After their attack on Palestinian bases in southern Lebanon in the spring of 1978 drew the ire of the United Nations Security Council, the Israelis withdrew from Lebanon, but not before establishing the pro-Israel South Lebanon Army to take their place. It was a well-managed alliance, and for the first few years, the SLA partnership, coupled with the Israelis' Phalange allies in the north, were enough to satisfy Israeli interests. But in the spring of 1982, all that would change when the Israeli army marched into Lebanon, sweeping through the Bekaa Valley and northward until they reached Beirut.

Even then my mother stayed. Through the worst of it, we thought at the time: the Israeli siege of West Beirut and the bombing that left some twenty thousand dead in its wake; the horrific events at the Sabra and Shatila refugee camps; the assassination of the young Phalange leader, Bachir Gemayel, and the chaos that followed.

Later, much later, I would come to better understand what had happened during those years. But at the time, what I knew was only what I heard from those around me, snippets of dinner conversation, the sound of Gemayel's voice on the radio while my grandmother and her friends played 41 in the living room. Another crisis in the south. Another massacre by the Palestinians. These people, these terrorists, who had already taken too much and would take our country if we didn't stop them.

Beirut was only twenty-one kilometers away, but from my bedroom in Jounieh, with its crisp sheets and lemon-yellow walls, its posters of adolescent longing, the war seemed a faint and hollow thing. What I remember most clearly from that time is neither fear nor grief but my own shameless anger. Hating neither the Israelis nor the Palestinians, nor the outsiders who had taken our country hostage, but my mother for having chosen to stay, for having chosen him instead of me.

By then I knew his name, had heard it through the walls of my bedroom after my grandparents thought I had gone to sleep. Sabri Kanj. And my grandmother's voice, an angry whisper now: *She will wind up dead because of this man.*

■ ■ ■

"How did he know where to find us?" Graça asked.

I exhaled, long and slow, and looked out through the smeared windows of the dockside café at the ferry sliding toward us across the Tagus, the black gap of the river laced with twin wings of foam.

I shook my head, thinking of Sergei's messages, always some bait to come back for. And yet my heart and my gut told me without doubt that the Russian would not have set me up, that if anything, Sergei was in danger now because of me. "Valsamis must have been tapping into my e-mails."

"But how—" She started and stopped herself, alarm registering on her face as she answered her own question. Not only had Valsamis been reading the e-mails, he'd known where they were coming from.

A gust of wind slammed the windows and knocked free a few stray drops of rain. A storm was pushing inland, Adamastor and his furies. We had lost the girl from the cybercafé not long after emerging from the tunnel. Now it was just me and Graça and a few night-owl stragglers waiting for the late ferry. A man in a janitor's outfit. A drunk sleeping uncomfortably in his seat. A young couple kissing desperately, bodies interlocked beneath their coats. And on the bar, the day's flotsam of discarded newspapers. The ubiquitous *A Bola* and *Correio da Manhã*, respective authorities on sports and gossip, and the relatively staid headlines of *Diário de Notícias* and *Público*.

On the front page of the latter was a photograph of a beleaguered United Nations weapons inspector, a tired Swede whose face betrayed his own inevitable defeat. One of Amadeo's mongrels, I thought sadly, glancing at the headline: YES OR NO? All at once the wrongness of the shipping invoice made perfect sense, the poorly disguised missiles and their destination. The question so simple I'd overlooked it all this time.

No, I thought, there were no rockets. The Americans had arranged the forgery through al-Rashidi to make it look as if the Iraqis were buying the Alazans from Trans-Dniester. In fact there were no Alazans, no dirty bombs headed for Basra. It was the invoice itself that mattered, the invoice that would provide the proof the weapons inspectors had failed to find, the proof the Americans needed to go to war.

The forgery had to be done in such a way that the cargo's dimensions would be a red flag to anyone who knew better, so it would seem obvious that the cargo wasn't really steel cables but Alazans. But the forger himself couldn't know or the lie would be blown. That was why Valsamis had asked for an amateur when he went to Vitor Gomes. That was why he'd hired Graça Morais. He hadn't counted on her bringing in Rahim.

All of it was part of whatever deal al-Rashidi had made with the Americans, with his old friend Valsamis. His loyalty in return for a new country for his son. And more, no doubt, once Saddam was defeated.

Shivering, I slid my hand into my pocket and fingered the FEG. Though if I was right about the invoice, the gun could do little to protect us now.

"What is it?" Graça asked.

Her face was drawn, her eyes hollowed by the café's fluorescent lights. So delicate, I thought, as Rahim must have seen her, here in this same place, perhaps, in this same shadow. So vulnerable, as we all were.

I shook my head, wishing I didn't know. "We have to get out of here," I said, pulling a handful of coins from my pocket, piling them onto the bar.

Graça nodded out the windows toward the river. "The ferry's got a good ten minutes, at least."

"No," I told her. I grabbed her arm and pulled her off her stool. "We've got to get out of Lisbon."

■ ■ ■

A goddamned wasteland, Richard Morrow thought as the Gulfstream banked into its final turn and the lights of Amman rolled into view beneath them, the crooked cross of the runway, and the city's minarets piercing the night sky. All those years in Near East, and he still preferred the landscape of his childhood, green hills, trees and more trees, a smudge of mist on a wet spring morning, the forest laced with dogwoods. There was something so utterly vulnerable about the desert, the land naked and scarred, like a scalp freshly shaved. Exposed, even under the cover of darkness.

The engines whined, and the Gulfstream eased its belly down onto the runway, then rolled to a stop on the outskirts of the airfield, near an empty hangar. In the distance, Morrow could see the orange lights of the Queen Alia Airport, the low-slung terminal building with its humped windows and hulking control tower. Closer, near the open mouth of the hangar, a single black SUV was parked on the tarmac: Morrow's welcoming committee.

The SUV's driver door opened, and a figure emerged from behind the tinted windows, a young man in light pants and a white oxford shirt. It was Charlie Fairweather, but for a moment, seeing his blond hair and easy gait, his quarterback's physicality, Morrow was again reminded of Andy Sproul and of his father's words: *They're all here.*

The copilot emerged from the cabin and opened the hatch. Warm night air filled the plane, the smells of jet fuel and baked asphalt. Morrow gathered his briefcase and bag and made his way through the cabin and down the folding stairs to where Fairweather was waiting to meet him.

"Welcome to Amman, sir," the young man said, extending his

hand for Morrow's overnight bag, hefting it easily. "There's a room ready for you at the InterContinental, if you'd like to get some rest."

But Morrow shook his head. "I want to see Kanj."

■ ■ ■

"What's going on?" Graça asked as we ducked out of the rain and into the underground parking garage on the southern edge of the Praça dos Restauradores. The concrete steps were slick beneath our feet, the landing off the square flooded with a good inch of rainwater.

I stopped beneath the lip of the garage's first level and caught my breath. "Is there somewhere you can go?" I asked. "Somewhere safe?"

Graça thought. "I have an aunt and uncle," she said, "on Madeira."

I shook my head. "No relatives. Somewhere no one would think to look."

"What's going on?" she asked again, scared now. She was shivering slightly, her long hair soaked, her coat steaming in the sudden warmth of the garage.

"You're going to have to disappear for a while," I said. "We're both going to have to disappear. We'll go to France first, to my house. I can make us documents there. Passports. Papers. Do you understand?"

She hesitated, then nodded.

"Good. Now, do you have a place?"

"Yes—"

"Don't tell me," I said. "It's better that way."

She nodded again.

"And money?" I asked. "You're going to need money."

"In my grandfather's safe. Back at the house."

I shook my head. We wouldn't be going back to Morais's. "I'll take care of it," I told her. I started forward into the garage, heading down toward where I'd left the Renault.

TWENTY-TWO

■ ■ ■

Y OU KNOW," CHARLIE FAIRWEATHER REMARKED, motioning tour-guide fashion to the claustrophobic darkness outside the windows of the SUV, "Lawrence holed up out here during the Arab revolt."

They'd been driving for a good two hours. East through the steppe, with its sad, stunted attempts at flora, toward the black basalt desert and the Saudi Arabian border. There was nothing to see but what their headlights illuminated—the road before them and a relentless hail of bugs swirling toward their deaths.

Morrow had been here once before, years earlier, on a bizarre courtesy trip to which he'd been subjected for unknown reasons. A pair of obsequious Jordanians from the ministry of culture had taken him to the Azraq Oasis, which had been nothing but mud and stink at the time, and then to the crumbling basalt fortress Fairweather had alluded to, the one made famous by Lawrence of Arabia. But this was not where they were headed tonight.

As if out of nowhere, a dirt road appeared on their left. Fairweather slowed the giant SUV, then turned onto the pocked and rutted track. In the distance—it was impossible to tell how far—Morrow could see a single yellow light.

"We'll go in together, sir," Fairweather said. "He should be pretty talkative by now." The qualities that made the young man handsome, cut jaw and square features, deep-set eyes, were ugly in the un-earthly light of the dash, exaggerated so that they verged on macabre.

"No," Morrow told him. "I'll talk to Kanj alone."

Fairweather paused, and Morrow could tell he was torn, wondering whether to contradict him or not. In the end, he didn't object.

It took them a good twenty minutes to reach the light. For some time it seemed to grow no closer, but then they were upon it, the headlights washing in through the walls of a courtyard, across a squat and windowless building. Fairweather cut the engine and drew his key from the ignition, then popped the door and climbed out, his city shoes raising clouds of powdery dust.

Lunar, Morrow thought, climbing out himself, taking a breath of the dry air, its odor not even a smell but an utter absence of smell. No trees, no grass, just the desert stretching for miles around them. Morrow felt a desperate and primal urge to stay with the SUV, as if leaving it would mean relinquishing his one thin connection to the living world. But Fairweather was ahead of him, already halfway across the courtyard, and Morrow forced himself to follow.

There was no one there to greet them. They entered the building through a single steel door, then descended a narrow concrete staircase into the desert earth. Underground, the interior seemed boundless, a dizzying, bunkerlike maze of subterranean corridors and empty rooms.

In a big, open room off one of the hallways, a half-dozen men in plain clothes were playing cards around a rickety folding table. Mukhabarat, Morrow thought as he followed Fairweather inside. The men looked up, bored Jordanian secret police. They were unshaven and dirty, the arms of their shirts discolored by old sweat stains. In the far corner was an old propane stove, the remnants of a meal. Half-eaten flatbread and something that looked like meat stew. Grimy glasses with the dregs of mint tea.

"We're here to see Kanj," Fairweather announced ridiculously. As if there could be some other purpose for their visit.

One of the men grunted and said something in Arabic. Fairweather nodded and turned back into the corridor, motioning for Morrow to follow.

They continued on for a few yards, then stopped in front of a windowless door. Morrow knocked, and eventually a man cracked the door and glared out at them. He was dressed like the others, yet Morrow could tell at once that he was in charge. After a moment of appraisal, he ushered them inside, where a second, shirtless man was seated in a metal chair, smoking.

There was a famous picture of Sabri Kanj, taken in Afghanistan, during his time with the mujahideen. By all accounts, it was the last picture made of Kanj, and it was this image that Morrow had harbored all these years. Kanj in a flak jacket and bandolier, like a modern-day Zapata, his beard nearly obscuring his dark face, his eyes staring angrily at the camera.

It had not occurred to Morrow that Sabri Kanj might have changed; it had not crossed his mind to think of Kanj in any other way. Looking at the gray-haired man in the chair in front of him, Morrow didn't recognize him at first, just as, more and more often, he failed to recognize himself in the mirror in the morning. Then the man dropped his cigarette to the floor and looked up, and suddenly Morrow understood.

"Leave us," Morrow said to Fairweather and the Jordanian.

Fairweather nodded reluctantly. "I'll be in the corridor, sir."

"Go," Morrow snapped. He waited for the two men to leave and the door to close, then took a step toward Kanj. "What do you want?" he asked.

Kanj smiled, showing a mouthful of broken teeth. The Jordanians had cleaned him up some, and he looked almost relaxed, sure of himself. Morrow didn't understand why, didn't quite see what Kanj thought he had to gain. Surely Kanj knew that he wouldn't be allowed to leave here alive, not knowing what he knew. Perhaps it was relief, then.

"Justice," Kanj said.

Morrow laughed despite himself, but Kanj was not amused. Painfully, he spread his swollen hands out on his knees and regarded them.

"I don't know what you think I can do for you," Morrow said. "But we're not the only ones involved here. There are the Israelis, for instance."

Kanj shook his head. "Don't underestimate yourself," he said. "Everyone knows that there is very little you can't do. But I'm not asking for your help."

"No?" Morrow observed. It was hard to say whether Kanj was bluffing or not.

"What is it you like to say?" Kanj asked. "Something about the truth setting you free?"

"Don't patronize me," Morrow said.

Kanj looked down at his hands again, then back at Morrow. "You didn't spend much time in Beirut, did you?" he asked wearily.

Morrow didn't move. He met Kanj's gaze and held it. "What do you want?"

Kanj sat back in his chair and closed his eyes, as if conjuring a mental picture of the past. "You recall, of course, that one of your agents had a man in Amal during the early years of the civil war."

Morrow nodded. The asset in Amal had been John Valsamis's greatest coup, a case that, all these years later, was still taught to rookie agents.

"I believe his name for me was Hassan," Kanj said. His gaze was on Morrow's face, his eyes carefully taking in the other man's reaction to this piece of information.

All these years and Valsamis had never revealed the man's identity. Now Morrow understood why. It was Kanj who had been Valsamis's contact in Amal.

"I heard Valsamis bought you cheap," Morrow said. It was a lie. "Hassan" had been the kind of asset agents dreamed about. To Morrow's knowledge, there had been no money involved in the cooperation.

Kanj shrugged off the comment. "You must have known that in the months following the Israeli invasion, there were people within the movement who believed the time had come to do more to advance our cause."

Morrow nodded. He knew all about the schism within Amal out of which Hezbollah had emerged.

"In the summer of 1982," Kanj continued, "there were rumors that the Syrians had brought an American to meet with some of these people."

"I've heard the rumors," Morrow conceded, his right hand tensing involuntarily.

"At the time we didn't understand what this meant." Kanj coughed, and his whole body flinched with the pain. "We went to Valsamis," he announced when he'd recovered himself. "Two days before the embassy bombing, we went to Valsamis." Kanj looked up at Morrow, waiting for him to follow. "He knew," he said insistently. "Don't you see? He knew the day, the time, even. And yet he did nothing."

Yes, Morrow thought, I do see. Valsamis was the mole Kanj was fingering. Kanj was telling him that Valsamis was the American who'd gone to Hezbollah. That Valsamis had had a hand in the embassy bombing. It made sense, since Valsamis was the only member of the Mid-East contingent to have missed the meeting that day, the only one to have survived.

"Who else knows this?" Morrow asked.

Kanj shook his head. "There was a woman in Beirut, an old friend of mine, a Christian. It was through her that I communicated with Valsamis. She knew everything I did."

"She had a name?" Morrow asked.

Kanj shifted in his chair.

All these years, Morrow thought, and the man still felt an urge to protect her. They would have been more than just friends.

"Mina LeClerc," Kanj said finally.

"She's still in Beirut?" Morrow asked. The name was familiar, though he couldn't quite remember how.

Kanj shook his head. "She was killed by a car bomb. Two days after the embassy bombing."

Morrow saw why Kanj had asked for him and what he'd meant earlier. Kanj thought Valsamis had killed Mina LeClerc, that he'd arranged for the car bomb to cover up his own role in the embassy bombing. All these years, Kanj had been waiting to see Valsamis brought to justice.

Morrow was struck by a deep sense of pity for Kanj, for all he thought he knew yet didn't. "So you are the only one who knows, then," he said.

A second passed and then another, the silence ticking off around them. Morrow could hear Kanj breathing, his lungs wheezing like rusty bellows, his body laboring against what had been done to it.

Kanj looked up at Morrow and shook his head. "There are letters," he said.

■ ■ ■

The only confession you need to make is to Allah, Sabri Kanj's father had told him once. Kanj had been twelve at the time, earnest in his belief, and he had not been satisfied by his father's advice. He could not remember now what he had done wrong, only that he'd wanted concrete absolution for it, some form of humiliation or punishment to set the score straight. His father had refused to indulge him. Now, watching the door close behind Richard Morrow, Kanj understood for the first time what his father had meant. He felt physically changed, as if he'd been scoured clean by the truth.

Kanj was not naive enough to believe there was anything left for him but the inevitable. He would die here, in this place, or out in the desert. Once they no longer needed him, they would kill him without ceremony.

But he had done what he had not been brave enough to do all those years earlier. Morrow knew now about the bombing, that it was Valsamis who had betrayed the others and killed Mina. Because of what she knew. Because of what Kanj had told her. No one could abide a traitor, he told himself. Surely, now, Valsamis would pay.

For the first time since he'd boarded the ship at the Jounieh aquamarina all those years earlier, Kanj allowed himself to think of Mina without guilt. He closed his eyes and thought back to that last morning in Beirut. From the beginning, they'd agreed on a meeting place, a deserted building off the rue de Mazraa where they would rendezvous in the event that something went wrong. Mina's job at the American University gave her a legitimate reason to travel to West Beirut, so she would be the one to come to him.

Kanj had gotten there before dawn the day after the bombing. There had been a skirmish near the museum crossing that morning, and Mina had been held up getting across the Green Line. It was nearly noon when she finally arrived, and Kanj had almost given up. She was flustered, her hair slipping from beneath the black scarf she always wore to their meetings. For the first time since he'd known her, Kanj could tell she was afraid. By then they both understood it was not coincidence that Valsamis had escaped the embassy bombing, that he had never intended to share the information they'd given him. Both knew just how much danger they were in.

Mina had driven from her parents' house in Jounieh earlier that morning. She was leaving, she explained. The whole family would be heading to France the next evening on one of her father's ships.

The building they were in had housed apartments at one time. As Mina spoke, Kanj realized that they were sitting in the shell of someone's living room. In one corner, half buried in rubble, was what was left of a couch. And next to the couch, listing on three broken legs, was a child's table and a small chair. For the first time, Kanj could see clearly the perversion of war. He thought of *Petra* and that night at the Piccadilly, Fairuz weeping over the body of her dead child. Though even this, he realized, was wrong, for in the end, any attempt at finding a moral in war, tragic or not, seemed like an indulgence.

"There will be someone waiting for you," Mina told him then. "On the rue Said Khadige at the Green Line, before dawn. They will take you across and on to Jounieh and the aquamarina. There is a freighter leaving for Cyprus in the afternoon that will take you on. My father has arranged everything."

Kanj bristled. "Your father hates me."

Mina shook her head. Nothing was this simple.

She put her fingers on his face, and he could feel her hand shaking. "You can't stay here," she said, and she was right about this as well.

■ ■ ■

"We're leaving," Morrow told Fairweather. "Go to the truck and wait for me."

A wounded look crossed the young man's face. He shoved his hands into his pockets and glared at Morrow like a petulant teenager, then turned and started down the corridor.

Morrow waited until Fairweather was out of earshot, then lowered his voice and addressed the Jordanian. "You will get nothing more from him," he said, motioning toward the door of Kanj's cell.

The Jordanian nodded. He was a man, Morrow thought, who knew how these kinds of things worked. He had been waiting for just this authorization, relishing it. Still, he did not like being told what to do.

He curled his lip and leered at Morrow, his tone acerbic, half mocking: "Whatever you say, sir."

TWENTY-THREE

■ ■ ■

OUR DECISION TO LEAVE LEBANON was a hasty one. I came home from school on a Monday afternoon in April to find my mother and grandparents sitting together in the kitchen of my grandparents' villa. My mother had been up that weekend and had returned to Beirut only the night before, so when I came through the door and saw her, I knew immediately that something was wrong.

The radio was tuned to the Voice of Lebanon, and I could hear the familiar patter of the announcer, the bland voice of tragedy that had become the background noise of our lives. The news that afternoon was no different from what it usually was: an explosion in Beirut, a truck bomb. This time, however, the American embassy had been the target.

"What's going on?" I asked, setting my books down on the counter.

For a long time no one answered, then my grandmother looked up at me. "Go pack your things," she said.

I turned to my mother for an explanation, for some harbor from the insanity that seemed to have gripped the three of them, but she just nodded her assent. "Do what your grandmother tells you."

My grandmother seemed to know she would never see Beirut again. This time she packed for a permanent exile, the furniture padded and crated, the silver and china carefully wrapped for the trip. In the morning my grandmother drove me down to school so I could say goodbye to my friends, and when we got back, my mother was standing in the driveway with her keys in her hand.

"I have to go back to the city," she said as we climbed out of the car.

My grandmother shook her head, but my mother was insistent. "I'll be back by noon," she promised.

She walked to where I was standing, put her arms around me, and kissed the top of my head. "Don't worry," she told me. Then she pulled her head back and smiled broadly, hopefully, this smile her greatest lie.

■ ■ ■

It was noon by the time we reached the French border and headed the last few miles up the coast, past Banyuls sur Mer and Port-Vendres. Graça had driven part of the night shift, across the Spanish plains, and she was still sleeping when I nudged the Renault off the main road and down into Collioure.

It was a perfect spring day, clear light dazzling the sea, the water a deep sapphire, the waves cresting white in the distance. Along the waterfront, a line of palms waved like cabaret girls. On the gray pebble beach, where the surf came and went almost imperceptibly, a handful of pastel fishing boats languished in the sun.

This was the tourist's France, a place of manufactured charm, of waterfront restaurants selling overpriced pizzas and cheap Matisse reproductions in the souvenir shops. Even the boats were waiting not for fishermen but for the perfect photo opportunity.

I turned onto one of the old town's narrow streets, and Graça stirred.

"Where are we?" she asked, opening her eyes, glancing out the window at the unfamiliar surroundings.

"Collioure," I explained. "My father has a place here."

Turning down another lane, I pulled the Renault to the curb in front of a pale green building with a weather-faded sign that read HOTEL DERAIN.

"Wait out here," I said. "I won't be long."

Graça nodded, and I cut the engine and climbed out.

It had been nearly a decade since I'd visited my father, six years in Marseille and another four in the mountains, yet the hotel seemed unchanged. Even the planters on either side of the doorway were untouched, the dead geraniums just as withered as they'd been on my last visit, another of Ed's misguided attempts at beautification.

A sign on the door, printed in five different languages, advertised clean rooms and harbor views. One of my father's cons, for the rooms, at my last visit, had been dirty at best, and the water views had been obscured several centuries earlier by neighboring buildings. "The sea is there," he would tell his guests, the ones who had the cheek to complain. "It's on the other side of that rooftop."

There was a woman behind the small front desk, a fat Catalonian with transvestite's makeup and thinning hair the color of eggplant. She looked up and scowled at me, her smudged eyebrows arching painfully.

"I'm looking for Ed," I said when she failed to offer assistance.

She pursed her lips, and I could see the tiny red fissures where her lipstick had run. Her scalp was white beneath the tinted curls.

"What do you want?" she asked contemptuously.

"I'm his daughter."

It hadn't occurred to me that the woman and my father might be a couple, but I could tell immediately by her expression that this was the case, and that Ed hadn't told her about me. Without saying a word, she got up from her chair, opened the door behind the desk, the one I knew led to Ed's living quarters, and disappeared.

There was silence, then the sound of a quarrel, the voices intelligible only in their anger. Then, suddenly, the door opened and my father appeared.

He had aged, though not as much as someone else might have, for he had done much of his aging earlier on and possessed the same static quality Valsamis did. He looked at me and smiled, and it was as if he'd been expecting me, as if it had been one year instead of ten.

"Nic!" He stepped forward to greet me, but I took an instinctive step back.

"I need to talk to you," I said.

He lifted his arms out from his sides, as if trying to show me he was unarmed. "What's going on?"

I looked at him, trying, as I had in the past, to see him as my mother had. He was still handsome, though in a dissolute sort of way. Like a bum you might pass on the street and recognize some element of yourself and your own humanity in.

"I need money," I told him.

He didn't flinch, just kept smiling, the same smile I'd seen him use a thousand times. "Whatever you need, sweetheart." He took out his billfold and started to open it.

I shook my head. "No," I said, "real money. I'm going to have to disappear for a while."

Not just the money, I thought, though I needed it—Graça and I needed it—but something else, some other reason why I'd come. As if the request were a gift in itself, this one last chance for my father to redeem himself.

"Of course," he answered, suddenly serious. "I'll do what I can. It'll take me a day or two to round up that kind of cash. You can stay here."

I shook my head again. "I need to go home first, pick up some things." I didn't say where home was, though I had a hunch that he knew, that perhaps he had lied to Valsamis, or Valsamis had lied to me when he'd said my father hadn't known where I was. Ed had a way of finding things out when he wanted to.

"Sure, baby. Whatever." Years, decades now, living in Europe, and Ed still talked like a character in a bad American movie. "When will you be back?"

"Tomorrow." I shrugged. "I'm not sure."

"Okay," he said.

He reached out his hand, and this time I let him touch me.

■ ■ ■

"There's a plane on the way now," Charlie Fairweather said, slipping his cell phone back into his pocket, signaling to a passing waiter. He grinned over at Morrow, then lowered his voice conspiratorily. "I know you won't believe it, but these are the best margaritas outside of Texas."

The waiter approached their table and peered out from under the brim of his spangled sombrero. Filipino, Morrow thought, as were most of those who did the actual work in this part of the world. But he'd been outfitted to look the part, as had the restaurant, all of it made to conform to some rich Arab's idea of a Mexican cantina.

Fairweather ordered a round of drinks, and Morrow let him. If the Gulfstream had stayed put, as he'd been told it would, he would have been gone by now, instead of drinking overpriced margaritas in the lounge at the Amman InterContinental. But the plane had been summoned elsewhere, and there was nothing to do except wait. For some reason, Morrow didn't particularly want to be alone.

Fairweather picked a corn chip from the basket on their table and scooped up some salsa. "So what did Kanj have to say?" he asked, popping the chip into his mouth, brushing the salt from his hands. "Any meat to his story?"

Again Morrow thought of Andy Sproul. Something about Fairweather's gesture and the ease with which he asked the question, his obliviousness to its audacity.

Morrow shook his head. "Nothing but bluster," he answered. "A waste of my time and yours."

Fairweather shook his head in sympathetic agreement. "They'll say anything, won't they?"

The waiter returned with their drinks, two fishbowl-sized glasses filled with green slush. He set them ceremoniously in front of the two men before retreating to his discreet post near the bar.

How did they teach the waiters to serve so perfectly? Morrow wondered. Without judgment. Without reason. Without regard for anything other than the needs and comfort of the few privileged men passing through this place.

Morrow raised his finger just slightly, and the waiter, ever vigilant, hustled across the room.

"You can take this," Morrow told him, motioning to his drink. "I'll have a martini instead. Tanqueray, no ice."

■ ■ ■

A *different kind of project,* Valsamis could hear Morrow saying, his voice grainy and distant on the battered black telephone in his landlady's kitchen. Though it was the only call Valsamis had gotten in the six months he'd spent on Crete, he hadn't been surprised by the predawn knock on his door, the widow's husky voice in the corridor. A woman who didn't mind waking people up. "Mr. Valsamis, there's a phone call for you. Very urgent." Valsamis hadn't asked how Morrow had found him.

Six in the morning in Hania, and in Washington it was still the night before. September 11 and the Pentagon smoldering, the remnants of the towers still in flames. And Morrow himself on the line. "It's the kind of thing we've been trying to get okayed for years. On the high side," Morrow said. "Our money comes straight from the secretary of defense. Christ, the Agency won't even know we exist." Not an apology, not even close, but an acknowledgment that they needed him.

No matter what they thought, they still needed him.

Valsamis hunched his shoulders and shuffled north along the Avenida da Liberdade, trying not to think about Nicole. He would find her, he reminded himself. Kostecky's people were still listening. For now it was just a matter of waiting it out, of trying to keep his nerves in check until the next call came in.

It was far too early for the real showgirls to be out, but there were a few desperate early birds peddling their wares. On the opposite side of the street, a tall transvestite in a denim miniskirt clung to her doorway, watching the traffic go by. Down the block, a fat woman in a fishnet halter top tottered on eight-inch heels, her arms stippled with dark vines of needle tracks, her scarred stomach stretched like a deflated balloon.

Valsamis was reminded of the central panel of Bosch's *Garden of Earthly Delights*. All the grotesque compulsions of man on display, Valsamis's very much among them.

A boy stepped out of a doorway up ahead of Valsamis, and their eyes met briefly. The boy's head was bare, his slight frame lost beneath the folds of a thick wool coat. A coat that had fit him once, Valsamis told himself. A coat a mother or a grandmother would have bought, a gift of warmth.

The young man was smoking, the smell of the tobacco heightened by the cold air, the smoke wreathing his face like a mourning veil. He looked slightly unwell. In need of something, of whatever it was that had brought him to this life in the first place.

Valsamis slowed his pace and angled himself in the boy's direction. He lifted his head and tried to think of something to say. This was always the hardest part, the stilted attempt at conversation, the meager gestures at fantasy. What was the point? After all, they both understood why they were here.

The boy smiled uneasily, and at the same moment Valsamis's phone rang, flooding him with a profound sense of relief. He turned away and picked up his pace again, slipping the phone from his pocket, pressing it to his ear as if for salvation.

Kostecky, he thought, but the voice on the other end was one he didn't immediately recognize.

"You told me to call," the man said. Then there was a hesitant silence, the caller waiting for Valsamis to understand.

"She's there?" Valsamis asked.

"She left about ten minutes ago," Ed Blake replied calmly. He didn't sound like a man who was giving up his own daughter. "She's on her way home, but she's coming back here. She asked for money, and I stalled her."

"Did she say when?"

"Tomorrow, I think. She's not sure."

Valsamis thought. "Was she alone?"

"There was another woman in the car. She didn't come in, but I saw her when they were leaving. Young. Pretty. Long dark hair."

Graça Morais, Valsamis told himself. The two of them heading for Paziols together.

"It's good?" Ed asked. "I called, just like you wanted."

"Yes," Valsamis assured him, "it's good." Even he was awestruck by the coldness of the man, the ease with which he had betrayed Nicole. "You'll get your money."

■ ■ ■

Kanj had not been able to bring himself to go to the rue Said Khadige. That last night in Beirut, he'd lain awake sorting through his options, fully aware of what his choice to stay would mean. In the end, he could not accept the help of the man whose pride had kept him from Mina all those years earlier, whose scorn kept them apart still. Kanj had watched dawn come and go from his window over-looking the ravaged southern slums, then finally fallen asleep.

It was midmorning when he heard the knock on his door. Khalid or one of the others from Amal, Kanj thought. Come to check up on him, for he had been uncharacteristically absent the last few days. But when he opened the door, he saw Mina standing in the hallway.

She had been to the apartment several times before, in the earlier days, before Valsamis, when their affair was just that, but even then they had been aware of how dangerous it was for her to come. Now it seemed inconceivable that she would have navigated the neighbor-hood alone.

"My friends called to say you hadn't come," she said as Kanj pulled her inside and shut the door.

"I can't," Kanj told her, but she wasn't listening.

"You can still catch the freighter," she insisted. "It doesn't leave until three. You can take our old fishing boat. It's at the yacht club. The *Patxi*. You'll find it easily. I can't imagine there will be anyone there to stop you. The key is under the captain's chair."

Kanj shook his head, but Mina persisted. "Don't you see? They're not here to help us. None of them are. This isn't their country."

She was right, of course. They had all known it for some time now. The Americans would leave as soon as their presence in Lebanon no longer suited them, as would the Russians and the Syrians and the Israelis, as the French had done before. Still, Kanj could not bring himself to accept that the sacrifices of the last few years, the deaths and betrayals, had all been in vain.

Mina ducked her head to avoid his gaze. "I'm scared, Sabri," she said. "I've written my sister. In case something were to happen. I've told her everything."

Kanj wanted to lie, to tell her that nothing would happen, but he couldn't. He reached out to touch her, but she turned away.

"I can't stay here," she said, opening the door, stepping into the hallway. "Three o'clock," she reminded him. "The ship is the *Akilina*."

She moved her hand to her face, as if to adjust her head scarf, but Kanj could see that she was crying, and that the motion was one of camouflage.

It was this final gesture that Kanj would carry with him for the next twenty years, to Cyprus, Algeria, Afghanistan, and Pakistan. Through war and rage and flight. This gesture and what Mina had said to him. *They're not here to help us.*

This and the knowledge that it was his own indecision that had killed her. That if he had left in the morning, if she had not returned to Beirut to find him, she would not have been stuck in traffic on the rue Huvelin later that morning when a black Mercedes pulled up beside her car and the driver leaped out and sprinted to the far side of the street. Not before triggering the explosion that would kill Mina and five others.

■ ■ ■

Kanj took a deep breath and pulled the desert air into his lungs. At least he wouldn't die in some concrete cell beneath the sand. The moon had not yet risen, and the sky was thick with stars, an endless field reaching back and back toward the moment of creation. It was a sight both beautiful and frightening, and it was all Kanj could do to keep himself from turning away.

And we have adorned the lower heaven with lamps; and set them to pelt the devils with; and we have prepared for them the torment of the blaze! Kanj repeated the words from the Sixty-seventh Sura to himself in his dream. *Blessed be He in whose hand is the kingdom, for He is mighty over all!*

In the distance he could hear the scrape of a key in a lock, the sound of a door clanging wide. When he opened his eyes, the face of his jailer hovered above him in the semidarkness. An Arab face, Kanj thought, so much like his own, his skin the color of goat hide, desert skin, tanned and beaten by centuries of sun. Abraham's skin, and Isaac's. The skin of the Prophet. The skin of Kanj's mother, of his sister.

"It's time," the man said, and Kanj nodded.

TWENTY-FOUR

■ ■ ■

I T HAD SNOWED IN THE MOUNTAINS, a late-season storm, heavy and wet. The road to my house was still unplowed, the snow soft beneath the wheels of the Renault. I didn't stop at my driveway but drove past it, turning off the road before I reached the Hernots' driveway, pulling the Renault onto an overgrown fire road. Better, I reasoned, not to advertise our presence.

"We'll walk from here," I told Graça, cutting the engine, stepping out into the snow. It was deeper in the woods than it had been on the road, cold against my ankles.

We crossed the road on foot and skirted my yard, coming up through the back garden. The sun was out, and the sky was shockingly blue against the bleached valley below, the mountains etched in sharp relief, black crags against white slopes. The house itself was dark and still.

I unlocked the patio door and stepped inside, waiting for Graça to follow. It was only a matter of days that I'd been in Lisbon, and yet I felt like a traveler returning to a place from which I had been absent for a long time. It was cold in the house, frost on the windows, our breath frosty in the air. I made my way to the kitchen and piled some kindling in the old woodstove, then lit a fire.

"I'm going to get started on the passports," I told Graça. I motioned to the wicker basket that hung on the back wall. "There should be eggs in the coop, if you're hungry. And there's a spare bedroom upstairs. Second door on the left."

Graça nodded. She had asked thankfully little since our last night in Lisbon, and I was grateful for whatever held her back now. The less she knew, the better off she would be.

"Don't worry," I told her, "I'll wake you if I need you."

■ ■ ■

"I told you they would come," Andy Sproul said.

It was a Saturday afternoon in September 1982, the last one either of them would spend in Beirut. Sproul and Valsamis were standing on the roof of the embassy watching the Israeli jets pummeling the Palestinian camps. The entire south of the city seemed to be on fire. Black smoke choked the sky around the airport and the Sports City. The bombings had been going on for some time now, and Valsamis was surprised that there was still anything left to burn.

Sproul bent down and picked up one of the thousands of yellow leaflets that had descended on West Beirut that morning, a polite warning of annihilation to Colonel Halal and the Syrian forces on the ground from the advancing Israelis: *We shall capture the city in a short period . . . As an experienced general who lacks no wisdom, you surely know that any attempt to throw your forces against the Defense Force would be suicide.*

From the beginning, Andy Sproul had predicted that the Israelis would not stop at the Litani River, as they had promised, but would push north into the heart of the country and on to Beirut. To everyone at the embassy, Valsamis included, Sproul's prediction had seemed ill informed at best; such aggression on the part of the Israelis could only be construed as political suicide.

One of the jets dropped its payload, and the entire city shuddered. There was a sound like the violent ripping of fabric, then a giant ball of flame and smoke blossomed from what remained of the Sabra camp.

"Looks like you were right," Valsamis said.

Sproul folded the leaflet into neat quarters and slipped it in his pocket. He didn't look like a man who had just won an argument.

■ ■ ■

Valsamis nudged the dial on his car radio up the band, catching nothing but static. Behind him, the parched land rose and fell toward the horizon, the highway cutting a malignant swath through wheat fields and scrub. Like Montana driving, Valsamis thought. Numb hours along Highway 2, through the northern reservations and the mammoth dryland farms. Wrecked lives and radio silence, the occasional staticky interruption of some local Christian station broadcasting redemption.

A blast of pop music crackled through the Twingo's tinny speakers, and Valsamis lingered on the station. Zaragoza coming in, he told himself, moving once more through the band, more slowly this time, hoping to catch a Spanish news station, maybe even the BBC. Hoping for any voice besides the one in his head.

There was more music, flamenco and bad European pop, and then, out of the broadcast haze, a man's voice, the news from RNE1. Valsamis stopped to listen.

The station was broadcasting an excerpt from the secretary of state's speech to the United Nations Security Council. Valsamis could hear Powell's voice beneath that of the translator: "The material I will present to you comes from a variety of sources."

He sounds so sure of himself, Valsamis thought, so confident in his certainty. ". . . People who have risked their lives to let the world know what Saddam Hussein is really up to," the secretary continued.

Powell was good, though Valsamis knew it was his naïveté that made him so, his ability to be duplicitous without knowing it, so that what he said was never actually a lie.

"I cannot tell you everything that we know," Powell went on. "But what I can share with you, when combined with what all of us have learned over the years, is deeply troubling."

Valsamis moved to turn down the radio, then caught himself, his finger settling lightly on the knob. The piece on Powell's speech had ended, and a Spanish commentator had broken in with a critique of American foreign policy.

"Take this incident in Jordan today," the woman said, speaking in almost hysterical Spanish. She was making a point about secrecy, but it was her next question that caught Valsamis's attention. "Are we to believe the official reports that Sabri Kanj was killed while trying to evade arrest?" Valsamis turned up the radio another notch, but the woman had already moved on to her next point.

So Kanj was dead, Valsamis thought, though he wasn't quite sure what this meant. If Kanj had managed to find a sympathetic ear, then his death made little sense. The Jordanians certainly wouldn't have killed him without an American okay. The Americans wouldn't have killed him without first consulting the Israelis. That was the way things worked with men like Kanj. Beirut or no, Kanj was far more useful alive than he was dead.

Valsamis fed the Twingo more gas, then glanced quickly over his shoulder and swung out into the passing lane. No, he told himself, something didn't make sense.

■ ■ ■

From our earliest days, we have lived in a world obsessed with identity. Think of Chronicles and the descendants of Israel, or Moses' numbering of the tribes, our story written back through the blood of all those generations, all the way to the first womb. There were stories then to help us remember. Later, paper and wax, seals ripe for tampering. And the body's proof, birthmarks and fingerprints and scars, signs of the indisputable, of name and class and country, and all those other immutable truths to which each of us is born.

Yet, from the beginning, there were also those who tried to invent themselves anew. Fugitives and con men and thieves. People seeking sanctuary from their own existence. And there were those, like me, who learned the alchemy of identity.

It is not an easy practice. There is so much attached to the individual today, an encumbrance of proof. Paper and ether, the delicate helices of the genome. Our entire being in a single strand of hair or a cluster of cells on a Q-Tip. So much that one can never change, and so I, at least, have learned to concentrate on the possible.

I had no intention of giving Graça or myself a whole new life. A project like that would have taken weeks, and not all of it would have been work I could do. What I wanted was a quick fix, traveling papers, a passport for each of us. After this, Graça would have to find her own way.

Graça's passport would be easy. I'd done some work on the new Brazilian passport just a few months earlier, and I'd been given several documents to tamper with. Most of them were mangled beyond repair, but there was at least one I knew could be modified to work for Graça.

My own passport was a different matter. There were several possibilities in the collection of castoffs I kept in my filing cabinet. Belgian and Swiss and Canadian, all of which would have worked. But I could not pick any of them.

I stood there for a good twenty minutes, trying to reason with myself, knowing each moment was one I couldn't afford to waste. I am a person who has lived my life with very little proof of self, without the comforts of inheritance or parentage, and I simply could not bring myself to forsake the one thing my mother had intended for me. Finally, it was the familiar blue cover that I chose. An American passport.

Just a document, I told myself, though even I could see this wasn't true. I had chosen it this time, taken it for myself, not just a name and a place but citizenship and all that went with it.

The laminate facings on both of the passports were intact; my first priority was to peel them away without mangling the paper beneath. Everyone has his or her own style with laminates, and my preferred method has always been a combination of cold and adhesive remover. In this case, cold would mean an hour or two in my kitchen freezer.

Taking my digital camera, I went downstairs to the kitchen and stowed the passports in the freezer, then made my way out into the living room. The television was on, the satellite tuned to CNN, but Graça wasn't watching it. She had fallen asleep on the couch.

I moved to turn off the TV but stopped myself, my eyes catching the ticker at the bottom of the screen. The information was frustratingly brief, gone before I had a chance to get a handle on it, leaving me to sports scores, and on the main screen the day's weather forecast, though the words were clear enough. Punching the remote, I flipped fruitlessly through the other news channels, LCI, EuroNews, and BBC World, then back to CNN, waiting for the ticker to scrawl through its cycle again.

Too many coincidences, I thought as I read the words for the second time. SABRI KANJ, #4 ON THE INTERNATIONAL TERROR WATCH LIST, KILLED DURING A RAID BY JORDANIAN SECURITY FORCES.

Valsamis and now Kanj. Beirut's ghosts. My mother's ghosts. Of all the people Valsamis could have used to get to Rahim, he'd chosen me. There was something more at stake here than the invoice.

From up the hill at the Hernots' came the low, mournful sound of a dog howling. Lucifer, I thought, recognizing the throatiness of his voice immediately. My skin prickling, I turned instinctively from the television to the glass patio doors. Down at the far edge of the garden, a slender shadow moved across the drifts. A pine marten or a stoat sniffing out a meal.

Old business, I told myself, watching the animal nose its way across the yard. I was finally beginning to understand. Old business, and yet Valsamis had come to me.

Graça stirred, then lifted her head and blinked sleepily up at me. "What is it?" she asked.

"Nothing." I shook my head, then motioned to the camera in my hand. "I need to get a picture."

■ ■ ■

Morrow leaned forward in his seat and peered down at the farmland patchwork of the Jordan River valley far below. To the west, the fortifications of the Israeli border lay like an ugly scar against the Jordan's banks, miles of concertina wire and electric fence, long, dusty gashes where patrol roads had been hacked into the valley floor. To the south, a dry canal bed, a remnant of good American intentions left to rot, spurred back toward Amman, its concrete sluiceway tinted green with scrub and grass from decades of disuse. Yet another failure, Morrow thought, watching the canal disappear beneath the plane, a physical reminder of all that they had squandered.

It was nearly dusk, the sun wild and red, plunging toward the horizon of the sea. In the distance, beyond the Judean Hills, the lights of Jerusalem were beginning to wink. Morrow allowed himself a glimpse of the world as it could have been if they had stayed the course. The shanty camps of Gaza and the West Bank gone and Israel restored. The Syrian border stretching across the Bekaa Valley and over Mount Lebanon to the Mediterranean shore. The world as it might still be.

Not peace but something bigger than peace. The fruit of war. The beginning of the end. This was what Andy Sproul hadn't been able to understand.

Twelve years, Morrow told himself, for the chance to finish what they'd started in Iraq. Twelve years, and this time there would be no leaving until things were set right.

The cockpit door opened, and the copilot ducked out of the cabin to make his way toward Morrow's seat.

"Satellite call, sir," he said, passing Morrow the handset, then starting back toward the front of the plane.

Morrow pressed the receiver to his ear. "Yes."

"I've found the sister," the voice said. "Emilie Delon, deceased."

"Any relatives?" Morrow asked. Even if the sister was dead, the letters were somewhere.

"Husband, Olivier, still living. Two children, Antoine and Marie, also still living. Antoine's in Paris, and Marie is in London. There's also a third child, a niece, I believe, raised by the Delons after her mother died. Name's Nicole Blake. Spent six years in prison in

France on forgery charges. Currently living in the French Pyrenees, a little town called Paziols."

Morrow felt his heart catch. Valsamis had known, he thought. He must have heard something when Kanj was first apprehended in Pakistan, must have figured Kanj was about to finger him. It was why he'd been so insistent on using Nicole Blake to find Rahim Ali.

"Sir?" The voice crackled back at him through the static of space.

"Yes." Morrow recovered himself. "I'll need an exact location on the Blake woman."

■ ■ ■

In the twenty-year-old photograph on my computer screen, the destruction looked almost elegant. Where the front of the American embassy had been, there was a waterfall of rubble, the seven floors sheared perfectly away, pancaked onto one another. The picture had been taken at night, and there was an element of theater to it, the bulldozers toiling away beneath the lights like actors on a set.

Nighttime clearing operations at the American embassy in Beirut, April 1983, the caption read. *Sixty-three people were killed in the bombing, seventeen of them Americans.* Citizens even in death.

Working on a hunch, I perused one of the websites turned up by my Internet search for information on the Beirut embassy bombing. The site was a memorial, an online tribute created by one of the victims' children.

Just a hunch, and probably a misguided one at that. Still, it had been this act that had convinced my mother it was time to get out.

I clicked on a link marked FACTS and waited while the new screen loaded. It was crazy to be online, and I knew it, but I was hoping Valsamis's surveillance extended only to my e-mails. Besides, even if people were listening, I planned to be long gone by the time they traced the computer and found the house.

A bulleted list appeared, the basics of time and means, another breakdown of the dead by rank and nationality. Seventeen Americans. One marine guard. One journalist. Several army trainers. Three USAID employees. Near the bottom of the list, one piece of information caught my eye.

The entire U.S. Central Intelligence Agency Middle East contingent was killed in the bombing. But of course this wasn't quite accurate. John Valsamis was still very much alive.

■ ■ ■

Valsamis pulled the Twingo to the side of the road and cut the engine. It was snowing again, winter's final, flimsy pronouncement skittering down through the trees and into the barrels of the headlights. Ahead, the road curved up and away, the last quarter-mile climb to Nicole's driveway vanishing into the woods.

Valsamis turned off the lights, then opened the door and stepped out, his shoes punching through the snow's thin crust of ice. It was dusk already, and the sky and the snow were the same cool shade of blue, the trees stark and bare.

Valsamis's cell phone rang, cutting through the twilight stillness. He jumped at the sound and fumbled the phone from his coat pocket to his ear.

"Yes?" he answered quietly.

"John?" It was Kostecky.

Work hours, Valsamis thought, counting back to D.C. time. "Yes," he said. Something was wrong.

"Rumor is, someone else has been asking about your girl." Kostecky cleared his throat.

"Who is it?" Valsamis asked. He could tell Kostecky didn't want to be the one to tell him.

There was a long pause, and Valsamis thought he had lost the connection. Then Kostecky's voice came back to him.

"Morrow," he said.

TWENTY-FIVE

■ ■ ■

WHEN, BY MIDAFTERNOON, MY MOTHER still had not returned, my grandfather drove down to the city to find her. We were to sail at six, and aside from our suitcases, everything we were taking had already been loaded on board the freighter. It was too hot to sit in the garden, so my grandmother and I waited together in the empty villa, and she paced the hollow rooms.

It was a forty-kilometer round trip, down the coast and back, but my grandfather was gone for several hours before we heard anything. It was after six when he finally called, and by then my grandmother and I both knew something was terribly wrong and we would not be leaving Jounieh that night. They spoke only briefly, just long enough for my grandfather to tell her what had happened. He did not have it in himself to console her: There was too much to be done still. The business of the body. He would need all his strength.

It was nearly midnight by the time he returned, the lights of his Mercedes sweeping up the hill, then pulling to a slow stop in the drive while I watched from the veranda. The car sat for some time, the engine softly cooling in the darkness. I could see the silhouette of his head through the window, his shoulders bobbing and shaking. Ten minutes, fifteen, before he steeled himself and climbed out of the car.

My grandfather was the only one of us to see my mother, to witness what had been done to her. But my grandmother would have her own, weightier burden to bear. It was she who had let my mother go that morning, and she carried the guilt of it until she died, just as my mother had carried her own guilt all those years earlier. Her choice then, to sacrifice everything for me. And later, as if in penance, her choice to stay.

It was another week until we could leave, until what remained of my mother was buried in the family cemetery in Achrafiye and all the other chores of death were attended to. Kanj was not at the funeral. He could not have come even if he had wanted to. The war had segregated us even in mourning. And yet I could not help but look for him at the church that day. After all, he had been her lover.

It would be some time before I would learn what had become of him and who he had become. Who he had been even then. It seems somehow fitting, a testament to the utter gracelessness of war, that he should have escaped Beirut while my mother died there.

■ ■ ■

I put my flashlight in my mouth and squeezed my hips through the narrow trapdoor above the second-floor landing, ducking low to avoid the attic rafters. It was dark and close in the cramped space, the air thick with centuries of must, the floor littered with other people's castoffs, most of them mysteries in themselves. A legless doll, a case of empty bottles, a leather suitcase, a box of rations from World War I. And other things, indistinguishable in their dustiness, bits of machinery and mounds of fabric, home now to the mice I shared the house with.

Pushing aside a cobweb, I reached down, opened the battered footlocker that held the remnants of my life, and ran the flashlight beam across the contents. It was a meager collection. A few stray photographs, my discharge papers from the Maison des Baumettes, some things my aunt had left me before she'd died: a brown paper satchel that held family pictures and a white shoe box with gilt letters that read DIOR, PARIS.

I lifted the lid and set it aside, then pulled the last letter from the box, put my face to the envelope, and inhaled deeply. Expecting what? Sea air and rosemary and geranium, the rock terraces of Jounieh baking in the afternoon sun. What I smelled was merely the taint of time, mildew and mothballs, the chest's fading cedar perfume, and the faintest hint of the rose sachets my aunt put in her closets each fall. Someone—my grandmother, I assume—must have hand-carried the letter to France, for there was no postmark, just my aunt's address and a hastily affixed stamp.

Carefully, I pulled the paper from its sheath, unfolded its two yellow creases, and held it up to the light.

Jounieh

April 20, 1983

Dear Emilie,

I have been thinking about that night all those years ago when we went swimming off the beach here and got caught in the undertow. Do you remember how I panicked and you had to keep me from drowning? I thought we were going to die, so I confessed to all sorts of things. How I'd let Marc Nazal kiss me by the tennis courts at the Summerland, even though I knew you liked him. How it was me, and not the housekeeper, who stole the bottle of Chanel that Nana Sophie sent you from France for your sixteenth birthday. I've never been good at keeping secrets from you.

There was so much I wanted to tell you on the phone the other night but couldn't. I promise to tell you everything when we get to France. Maybe you've known all along what was happening. Like you knew about me and Marc Nazal but never said anything. You always were smarter than I am.

I'm sorry I've lied to you. I know it's a poor excuse, but I've meant well. Sabri and I have both meant well.

I guess I should say it's for the best that we are leaving Lebanon, but I can't. It would be a lie on my part. Leaving is the only choice for me now. I have convinced Papa to get Sabri onto one of his ships, and Sabri has agreed to go.

It's hard to believe the Americans will protect us if they are willing to destroy themselves. And it seems as if this is what happened, that the bombing was allowed to happen. This makes no sense, of course, but then there isn't much about this war that does.

I called the French embassy yesterday to tell them what I knew. Hardly a heroic gesture, but it was the best I could do. There is no getting through to the Americans at this point, and the sad truth is that I trust the French more than I trust the Lebanese.

Honestly, I think they thought I was insane. I didn't even have a name to give them, but the man I talked to promised to get my information into the right hands, whatever those might be.

I have never been so scared in my life. I am afraid of dying in pain or alone. I am afraid of dying for someone else's cause, for something I don't believe in. I am afraid of the obscurity of death here. That horrible woman on the Voice of Lebanon each night with her tallies of the dead. Not even names anymore. I am afraid of not dying, of being taken by the Syrians or the Hezbollah instead, whoever this man was working for. I have seen what they do to people.

I want you to promise to take care of Nicole if I die. She may find out everything one day, but I don't want you to tell her. Maybe someday I will be able to tell them both the truth, but now, more than ever, I know I made the right decision. The powerful have the advantage in this world. I can only hope Nicole will understand and forgive me. I hope someday Sabri will forgive me, too.

It's hard to believe that in a matter of hours we'll be gone. Maman has driven Nicole to her school to see her friends, and Papa's men have taken the furniture and boxes and gone. It is strange to think that this place and the war will go on without us.

I wish you were here. We could walk down to the promenade one last time, or take the car up into the mountains. Maybe I will go myself. There is plenty of time, and it would be better than sitting in this empty house. I will say goodbye for you, too.

All my love,

Mina

Of course, my mother had not gone down to the promenade or driven up into the mountains. Somewhere between the moment when she'd licked the envelope closed and when we'd caught her in the driveway, she'd made other plans. She had gone to see Kanj; of this I had never had any doubt. But what had made her go in spite of her fear was a mystery with which I would have to reconcile myself, since there was no one left to answer that question.

For an instant I could see her again, her smile blooming up at me. And later, what I could only imagine: that long drive down the coast, her windows open to the sea, the water stretching dark to the horizon. Twenty kilometers to Beirut, twenty kilometers in which she could have pulled the car over, could have turned around and headed back. Twenty kilometers in which to unmake her decision, and yet she hadn't.

I tried to concentrate on the puzzle at hand, Valsamis and Kanj and my mother, what she had said about the Americans and the Syrians. But there were other, darker questions clamoring for my attention.

Forgive her for what? I wondered as I set the letter aside and picked up the next one from the box.

Beirut

April 14, 1983

Emilie,

There was a massive evacuation in West Beirut today. French soldiers found an unexploded Israeli bomb buried next to an apartment building in Hamra. It took me forever to make the crossing.

Sabri was very upset. There has been talk of attacking the Americans for some time now. And then, just yesterday, he heard that Hezbollah has prepared two martyrs for a car bombing of the embassy next Monday.

I'm sure this is all just panic on our part. This city is so full of rumors. But Sabri feels the Americans should be told all the same. It would be a disaster for the country if they were to leave now. Though I'm starting to believe disaster is what some people want.

I will see our American friend tomorrow if I can. Though I'm sure they already know. According to Sabri, they have their own contact within the new movement.

Do you remember old Mrs. Wazzan from the first floor? I forgot to tell you in my last letter that she died. Her nephew found her in her apartment with the cats last week. It's been so long since anyone we knew died of natural causes that everyone is stunned.

I promised Papa that I will go up to Jounieh this weekend. Sometimes I think they are the crazy ones, living there as if nothing has happened. But I am grateful every day for Nicole's safety.

I will write to you next week.

Mina

Our American friend. The shadowed eye of my flashlight stuttered back over the three words. It was such a strange thing to have written, as if somehow she and Sabri had shared this person. And then, later, *Sabri feels the Americans should be told all the same.*

What else had Kanj told them? It was a strange alliance, Amal and the Americans. Though in Beirut at that time, all sorts of unlikely friendships had flourished.

A car bomb. I heard Valsamis again, what he'd said to me that first night suddenly clear. He had known, I thought. My mother had gone to him with Sabri's warnings, and he had done nothing to stop the embassy attack. This was why she had been so afraid in her final letter. And her fear had been well-founded. Valsamis could not have allowed her to live with that kind of information.

I remembered that first afternoon, how I'd known even then that Valsamis was a con. *According to Sabri,* my mother had written, *they have their own contact within the new movement.* My mother hadn't seen it, and neither had Kanj, but Valsamis had been playing them all.

■ ■ ■

With the exception of that night five years earlier at the Piccadilly, when he had first noticed her and Kanj together, Valsamis had never seen Mina LeClerc outside the little bookstore on the rue Achrafiye where they met faithfully every second Monday of the month. So when she came to him that last time, Valsamis almost didn't recognize her.

It was a Saturday night. Most of Mid-East was in town already for the meeting on Monday, and everyone was gathering at the Commodore for dinner and drinks, but Valsamis was headed home. He had realized early that his place in the Agency would always be separate from the others, and he knew better than to pretend that wasn't the case.

Mina was standing in the doorway of the building across the street from the embassy; he saw her as soon as he turned onto the street. Her hair was pinned neatly in a head scarf, and she was dressed in the modest, smocklike attire that was the uniform of so many of the city's young Shia women. An attempt at disguise, Valsamis had thought, though a poor one, for here in the northern part of the city, the costume made her stand out more.

Valsamis didn't approach her. He made sure she'd seen him, then kept walking, listening for her footsteps on the sidewalk behind him. Though they had talked about this kind of thing before, this was not one of the scenarios they had agreed upon, and Valsamis wasn't sure how to proceed or what she wanted from him. Eventually he ducked into a café on the rue Clémenceau.

Their previous meetings had all been on her territory, and Valsamis could tell she was nervous as soon as she stepped inside. Her eyes ranged across the café as she made her way toward him. She sat down at the next table, ordered a coffee, and drank it quickly and without looking at him. When she was finished, she stood as if to leave, then glanced hastily back at Valsamis.

Without saying anything, she reached into her smock, pulled out a folded piece of paper, and set it on the table next to Valsamis's coffee cup. Her hand was shaking, and her face was pale beneath the scarf. She had taken a huge risk coming here, and she knew it. Valsamis knew it as well.

"Sabri wanted you to have this," she said. Then she turned and made her way out of the café and back onto the dark street.

■ ■ ■

Valsamis stopped at the edge of the garden and let his shoes sink into the snow. He was panting from the walk, and his own ragged breath was all he could hear, his old lungs working against the cold. His father's lungs, he thought, and he was back in the Pintlers again, tailing the old man up into some godforsaken draw. Even handicapped by forty years of Lucky Strikes, Valsamis's father had always been able to outwalk him.

There was no car in Nicole's driveway, but the downstairs lights were on, the windows of the kitchen and living room shining out onto the snow. At the back of the garden, where the hump of the stone wall rose up like a surfacing whale, two neat sets of footprints, now partially obscured, emerged from the woods and crossed the yard toward the house.

Valsamis slid the Ruger from inside his coat and checked the clip one last time, then fitted the silencer on the barrel. Still as the evening was, a gunshot here would be heard all the way down in the valley. He scanned the garden, then started walking again, hugging the wall as he went. From somewhere in the distance, past the dark fringe of the trees, came the sound of a dog barking, lonely and wild.

There would be Nicole's dog to contend with, Valsamis reminded himself, angling toward the front of the house and the driveway, and the kitchen door, which he remembered as being slightly blind. Nicole's dog, and the two women, and the twelve-gauge he'd seen in the hallway on his first visit.

Valsamis stepped into the side garden, then stopped himself and drew back. It was dark here, the windows on this side of the house all black, but in the meager illumination the snow threw up, Valsamis could just make out the silhouette of a figure moving through the snow. Not Nicole.

It was Graça Morais, her long hair loose down her back. She was carrying a basket in one hand, and in the other, something Valsamis couldn't see. She made her way to the fence that surrounded the chicken coop, then pulled the gate open against the snow and slipped through it.

■ ■ ■

It was surprisingly warm inside the small house, the hens tucked into their nests, the rooster perched on one of the upper rafters, his lizard eyes glistening like crushed glass. Graça closed the door behind her and switched on the camp lantern she'd taken from Nicole's kitchen, then set it on one of the empty roosts and took a step into the coop. There was a general disquiet at her presence, the rustling of feathers, the birds' cosmic dialect of fear and warning playing on their throats' crude flutes.

It's better this way, Graça heard Nicole say. Better for each woman to know only what she needed to survive. Yet Graça understood more than she would have liked, could see clearly now the price of what she'd taken from Rahim.

She closed her eyes and thought of her grandfather's house in the Alfama, the place to which she would not be going back, the chipped face of Saint Vincent above the front door, the tiny garden in the back, the patio where she'd first seen Rahim, where she'd first seen Nicole as well. And later, through the window of the front room, the two of them embracing beneath one of the gas lamps. Rahim's hand beneath Nicole's shirt. Nicole's mouth on his ear. Then something whispered and they were gone again, slipping off down the hill. She'd thought Nicole sophisticated at the time, and she had been, mysterious as Eduardo's workshop, the jars of ink and acetone, the shelves of tools Graça was forbidden to touch.

It was in this same way that Graça had come to fall in love with Rahim, wanting not him but the idea of him, the place he came from and the mystery of it. The medina, with its secret alleyways and hidden gardens, women swaying behind dark veils.

Ten years later, with Eduardo asleep inside, trundled off early to bed after too much wine, they'd found themselves awkwardly alone together for the first time. Nothing happened between them, but when Rahim got up to leave, he put his hand on Graça's arm, and she understood that it was just a matter of time.

It was two months before they ran into each other outside the Café da Ponte down at the Santo Amaro docks. Both of them had been dragged there by friends, and both were looking for an early exit and a cab ride home. In the end, they'd taken the train together and walked up into the Alfama. Not to Eduardo's house but to Rahim's apartment in the tumbledown neighborhood on the hill's western flank.

What she hadn't told him then, what she had never told him: This had been her first time. There in the dark foyer of his apartment, her legs failing, her hands shaking so hard he'd had to undress them both.

Graça reached her hand into the nest of one of the Marans, and the bird rose up from the touch, fluttering her wings like a bony, feathered angel. The straw was hot where she'd lain, the egg red, dark as blood.

Better not to know, she told herself again, slipping the egg into the basket, moving on like the robber she was. Then the coop's door flung open, and for an instant she felt the breath knocked from her body, felt herself a vessel filled entirely with fear.

■　■　■

There was one scream, high and quick, and then there was nothing. Graça, I told myself, setting the next letter back in the box unread, straining to hear across the silence. In the garden, though I couldn't be sure, fleeting as the sound had been, muffled by the attic's rafters, the stone walls of the house.

Grabbing the shoe box and the letters, I peered out through the open trapdoor, then carefully lowered my body down. It was a house full of creaks—the loose board in the front foyer, the groaning hinges on the kitchen door—but I could hear nothing.

Sliding the FEG from the back of my pants with my free hand, I ducked into my office and peered out the window at the driveway below. The outside light was on, the snow churned and muddled where tracks led from the kitchen door and disappeared around the side of the house toward the garden and the chicken coop.

Stupid. Silently cursing myself for having used the computer, I moved back out to the hallway, then into the dark spare bedroom. I could see the continuation of Graça's tracks from the window, her footprints veering across the yard and in through the door of the chicken coop. I could see another set of prints as well, this one emerging from the woods, joining Graça's at the hut.

I turned out of the office and went downstairs to the kitchen, switching off the lights behind me. It was a calculated sacrifice on my part, for it meant Valsamis would know I had heard something, but the advantage of the darkness was worth the trade. I set the letters on the kitchen counter and made my way carefully into the living room.

I've often wondered, driving past the old Cathar refuges on the Perpignan-Quillan road, what my choice would have been had I been one of the unlucky inhabitants when the soldiers of the pope came riding across the valley. There was hardly any hope for salvation, for those who stayed faced certain slaughter, and those who fled were almost invariably captured and burned as heretics.

Standing alone, staring out through the glass patio doors toward the back garden, I thought of the Cathar women in the stone coffins of their fortresses, and I felt a desperate urge to run.

Steady, I told myself, taking a deep breath, feeling the FEG against my palm. Silently, I slid the door open and stepped outside. It was snowing again, the flakes fine as pastry flour, settling on my bare arms and in my hair, veiling the woods and the valley below, the meager lights of the town. I took a step forward and another, hugging the house with my left shoulder, picking my way through the drifts.

As I rounded the corner of the house, I could see that the door to the chicken coop was open, and there was a light on inside. My camp lantern, I thought, the one I kept by the back door. Graça must have found it, but there was no sign of her now and no sign of Valsamis. Only the breathy warnings of the hens, and the rooster squawking excitedly.

Then, through the tattered scrim of the snow, I saw two dark silhouettes hobbling together toward the driveway like a pair of drunks. Valsamis had his arm around Graça's shoulder, but the gesture wasn't a friendly one. In his other hand he held a gun, the barrel obscenely distended by the silencer that had been fitted to it, the muzzle pressed against the back of Graça's neck.

Crouching close to the house, I lifted the FEG and sighted at their retreating backs. Easy, I reminded myself. I tried to get a bead on Valsamis, but it was impossible to distinguish him from her. My finger caught against the trigger, and I could hear the rush of my own heart.

The duo reached the far corner of the house and stopped suddenly. At first I thought Valsamis had heard me, but he turned toward the woods instead, his gaze resting on the dark fringe of the trees. The marten again, I told myself, or an owl cruising for its dinner. In trees this thick with snow, the slightest movement was catastrophic.

And then, out past the garden wall, I saw the humped back of a creature moving through the underbrush. Lucifer.

"Luce!" I whispered fiercely. "No!" But it was too late.

The dog burst forth into the yard, his front legs churning through the drifts, his neck bristling, his lips pulled back against his teeth. He lunged forward, then stopped in front of Valsamis and crouched down, snarling and barking.

Valsamis regarded the dog, then lifted the gun from Graça's neck and pointed it at Lucifer's head. It was a swift and easy motion, Valsamis's hand and arm sweeping out in perfect alignment, as if the gun were an extension of him, as if it always had been. There was one shot and then another, the muzzle flaring with each round, and Lucifer collapsed into the snow.

As if from some unrecognizable source came the sound of a third gunshot. Valsamis spun around, and I fired again, my hands steady on the FEG's grip, the gun suddenly my own. The second round caught Valsamis's forearm, and his pistol leaped from his hand.

"Go!" I yelled to Graça. "Get inside!"

She wrenched herself free and staggered forward, her boots kicking up snow as she disappeared around the corner of the house.

I pointed the gun at Valsamis's head but didn't fire. "Get down!" I shouted. "On your knees!"

He hesitated, looking back at me, cradling his injured arm. Slowly, he lowered himself into the snow.

TWENTY-SIX

THE FESTIVITIES WERE IN FULL SWING by the time Valsamis got to the Commodore. There was a sense of overblown joviality among the crowd, the locals wanting to show their guests an authentic Beirut good time, and the visitors hungry for a taste of wartime camaraderie.

The hotel was no one's first pick. Too many journalists were there, for one thing, too many other Westerners hanging around the bar drinking Scotch and sodas. But since the siege and the attacks on the Multinational Force a month earlier, there was really nowhere else to go, so everyone was making the best of it. There were two female journalists at the bar, a Swedish AP photographer and a young reporter from *The Irish Times,* and both were enjoying unlimited free drinks.

Valsamis ordered a bourbon and found Kip Bryce in a corner booth opposite the bar. Bryce was a good Mormon kid who'd just transferred in from Cairo, and he appeared to be the only sober one in the bunch. "You seen the chief?" Valsamis asked. He needed to let the station chief know about his meeting with Mina as soon as possible.

Bryce shook his head. "He and Sproul went up to the Chouf."

"You know when they'll be back?"

The kid shrugged. "Sometime tonight. They must have gotten stuck at a checkpoint." His eyes wandered across the room and lingered on the Irish girl.

Siobhan, Valsamis thought, digging deep to remember her name. Sproul had introduced her to him once at the Summerland. Valsamis had given him a hard time about it later. Sleeping with the enemy, he'd said when he saw Sproul the next morning at the embassy. He'd been joking, but Sproul hadn't been amused.

"For fuck's sake," he'd shot back, then hastily apologized. "I mean, we all want the same thing for this place, don't we?"

Valsamis had laughed. It wasn't intentional, and he'd immediately felt bad about it, seeing the hurt look in Sproul's eyes and realizing for the first time that the younger man really meant all of it.

Valsamis left Bryce and crossed to the bar, fingering the note in his pocket. *Islamic Holy War.* Valsamis repeated the words to himself, what Kanj had called this new group. It was a name none of them had heard before, though they'd known it was coming for months, since the siege, since rumors of a split within Amal had begun to circulate. A new, more frightening face to the Shiite militia, financed by the Iranians.

"Why do Arab girls carry a fish in each pocket?" Valsamis overheard one of the agents, a man named Jack Bentley, say to Siobhan and the other woman. Bentley had been in Beirut when Valsamis had first arrived in Lebanon; he worked out of the Damascus office now.

Bentley's drink sloshed precariously against the lip of his glass as he leaned in toward the two journalists. Valsamis could see the looks of horror on the women's faces as they waited for the inevitable punch line. They'd heard the joke, or variations of it, too many times, and not one of them had been funny.

Bentley caught Valsamis looking and leered back drunkenly, his face a mixture of warning and contempt.

Yes, Valsamis thought, he knew his place, but still, he hated to be reminded of it. Just as he hated being forced to work their scrap pile. Five years, he told himself. Five years of an asset so plum they were teaching it at the Farm, and Valsamis was still picking the shit out of other people's shoes.

"So they can smell like their mothers," Bentley said, turning back to the women and laughing proudly.

■ ■ ■

"Get up."

Valsamis turned his head just slightly so that he could see my face, and I moved the barrel of the gun with him.

"Get the fuck up," I repeated.

This time Valsamis struggled to rise. His right arm was bleeding badly. Worse than I had expected from the Makarov round. The flesh and bone were shattered where the bullet had hit. He staggered to his feet, and I pushed him forward, then bent down and picked up his Ruger.

I could see Lucifer in the snow, his body caved in on itself, what was left of his head twisted to one side. There was no sense in going to him, nothing I could do to help him.

"Inside!" I nudged Valsamis again with the pistol, and we moved together across the yard and the driveway, in through the back door, into the kitchen, where Graça was waiting.

I pulled a chair out from the table and pushed Valsamis into it, then handed the Ruger to Graça. "Watch him," I told her. Then I opened the upper cabinet above the sink and took down a first-aid kit and two pill bottles. "Here." I shook two pills from each into my palm. "Vicodin and amoxicillin."

Valsamis watched as I set them on the table just beyond his reach.

"How much was it worth?" I asked, opening the first-aid kit, taking out a package of hemostat sponges. "Did Hezbollah pay you off, or was there something else?" If Valsamis wanted to live, he would have to work for it. I looked down at his arm and the growing red stain on the floor. "Talk soon," I told him, "or you're not going to be able to talk at all."

He lifted his head and blinked up at me. "I don't know what you're talking about."

Here he was, I thought, after all these years. Here was the man who had murdered my mother. I closed my eyes briefly and thought of Lucifer, the way his legs had buckled beneath him, of Rahim in the doorway, his hand on mine.

Valsamis shook his head wearily and glanced at the gilt Dior box on the counter.

"Is this what you came for?" I asked angrily. I lifted the lid, took out the last two letters, and laid them on the table in front of Valsamis. "Here," I told him.

■ ■ ■

The pain was like a living being, singular in its purpose. When Valsamis moved, the pain consumed him. To be aware of much more than this was difficult, and yet he knew he had to try. Valsamis read the letters, then read them again, trying to find a way around the pain, trying to make sense of it all.

According to Sabri, Mina had written, *they have their own contact within the new movement.* If this had been true, if someone in the Beirut office had managed to cultivate an asset in Hezbollah, then it seemed almost impossible that Valsamis hadn't known. And yet there had been someone: Kanj had said so.

"This is why you came after me to find Rahim," Valsamis heard Nicole say. "Not because I could give you Rahim but because of the letters. It's why you had Kanj killed. It's why you had my mother killed: because she knew."

Valsamis shook his head, trying to focus on the letters. *I called the French embassy yesterday,* Mina had written. And what had she told them? That she'd passed a note to a man in a café on the rue Clémenceau. Or had she simply said that there was someone, an American, who had known in advance about the bombing, when it would happen, and had done nothing to stop it? She hadn't known his name, and neither had Kanj: Valsamis had been careful about this.

The man I talked to promised to get my information into the right hands, whatever those might be. Two days after the bombing, Valsamis reasoned, the Beirut station still in chaos, and where would the

French have gone? To Langley, to the next man up, the Mid-East DO, and yet clearly they hadn't, for the next man up at the time had been Dick Morrow.

The truth was so simple that Valsamis was ashamed of himself for having missed it. *Rumor is, someone else has been asking about your girl,* he heard Kostecky say.

There had been a contact in Hezbollah, someone else who'd known about the bombing and had survived it. Someone who had his own reasons to be afraid of Sabri Kanj and the secrets he'd carried from Beirut. Someone with access to Kanj in Jordan.

All these years Valsamis had thought the LeClerc woman's death a coincidence, but Nicole was right: It hadn't been. The French had gone to Morrow, and Morrow had assumed Mina was fingering him, just as Valsamis had assumed the same about Kanj all these years later.

■ ■ ■

A game of chicken, I thought, watching the blood drip from Valsamis's hand as he lowered his head and scanned the papers, what I wanted from him and what he was willing to give me. A secret so long and tightly held that it seemed inconceivable he would release it now. A log settled in the stove, and I could hear the fire rearrange itself around it, the crack and hiss of sparks and sap, of water forced from the wood.

Valsamis finished reading and lifted his eyes, then looked from me to Graça and back again. He hadn't shaved for some time, and his face was gray beneath gray stubble, though his eyes were disturbing in their lucidity.

"It was Morrow," he said.

I hesitated before taking the bait. "Who's Morrow?"

"Dick Morrow," Valsamis answered.

I shook my head. "You knew about the bombing," I insisted. "No one else survived."

Valsamis nodded. "You're right, but Morrow knew, too. Look." He gritted his teeth against the pain, then motioned to the letters. "He was director of operations at the time. The French would have gone to him. He would have known what your mother told them."

A con, I reminded myself, but I still felt a cold flush across my body, as at the mention of a ghost in a dark house.

"He's coming here, Nicole." Valsamis motioned to the letters. "He's been to see Kanj, and he knows you have these."

I moved as if to step forward, then stopped myself. "You're lying."

Valsamis closed his eyes, and I thought he might pass out. Then he opened them again and looked right at me. "How do you think I knew you were here?" he asked.

I shrugged. There hadn't been enough time since I'd used the computer for Valsamis to have driven from Lisbon, so I figured he must have already been on his way. "You came for the letters," I said. "You didn't care if I was here."

"But I knew," Valsamis said. "How do you think I knew?"

I moved away from him, pressing my back against the counter.

"Did you really think Ed wouldn't sell you out again?" Valsamis asked. "Did you really think you could trust him?"

I shook my head. I could hear Valsamis that first morning. *Even your father doesn't know where you are.* They must have struck a deal, I thought, the terms of which I didn't want to know. Ed must have agreed then to let Valsamis know if I came to him.

"He called me after you left the hotel," Valsamis offered, as if Ed's deception were proof of something larger, as if this were all the corroboration he needed. "He told me you were heading up here."

"What does this have to do with Beirut?" I asked.

"Nothing," he said.

But I could see this wasn't quite true, either, and when he lunged for the pills, I didn't stop him.

TWENTY-SEVEN

■ ■ ■

IT DIDN'T MATTER WHAT I BELIEVED, whether Valsamis was telling the truth or not, or if Morrow was really on his way. Graça and I had already stayed too long at the house. What mattered now was that we get out, but before we could, I needed to finish our passports.

I dressed Valsamis's wound as best I could, packing it with coagulant and wrapping his arm in a compression bandage. Then I left him with Graça, took the passports from the freezer, and climbed up to my office.

I figured these documents would be a breeze, as far as forgeries went. There were no tricky stamps or inkless images to deal with. All I really needed to do was peel away the laminates and switch out the photographs, then put everything back as I'd found it.

The passports were brittle from the freezer, and the plastic on both documents came away easily. Still, it was meticulous work, and it took me a good hour to coax the laminates off and slip the new photographs into place. It was delicate work as well, for I had to line up the original guilloches perfectly before I could reapply the laminates.

My aunt Emilie always used to say that the first crepe out of the pan is for the dog. As anyone who has ever made crepes will attest, rarely does the first attempt turn out the way you hope. The pan is either too hot or not hot enough, or there's too much grease or too little.

Sadly, my aunt's rule too often proves true for laminates as well. Add too much heat, and the plastic bubbles. Add too little, and your one chance at making a perfect seal is squandered. Though unfortunately, where passports are concerned, there is little room for waste.

Knowing how tricky this first attempt would be, I'd chosen to finish my passport before Graça's. If one of the documents had to fail, I figured it was best that it was mine. There were plenty of places on the continent where I could go without papers these days, plenty of old friends who'd be willing to get me what I needed. Graça, on the other hand, needed a good fresh identity, as she would be on her own from now on.

Saying a quick prayer, I laid my passport out flat on my worktable, covered it with a cotton pillowcase, and pressed the preheated iron over the page. I counted out a full minute, then pulled the pillowcase back. It wasn't perfect, but as far as I could tell, it looked like an adequate job. The print was clear, the fibers and seals well matched. If the name was not my own, it would be soon. Satisfied, I set the document aside, then turned the iron up just a notch and readied Graça's passport.

We would be gone, I told myself, and this was all that mattered. But there was the question of what to do with Valsamis. I'm not a vengeful person. I've seen too often and too clearly the consequences of retribution and the inadequacy of justice.

Valsamis had killed Rahim and he had killed Lucifer, and I hated him for this, as I hated what he'd done to my mother. Whether he'd known about her murder or not, he was responsible for it all the same. Just as Kanj was. Just as she was. And yet I could not bring myself to condemn him. He would have to do that himself.

I laid the iron across Graça's passport, pressing all my weight into it, and counted out the seconds. Yes, I told myself, the best we could ever hope for was to reconcile our own choices.

■ ■ ■

The group had moved from the bar to the Commodore's dining room by the time Sproul finally arrived. He was freshly showered, his hair still damp, his face clean-shaven, but he looked pale and tired. Slightly off his game, Valsamis thought, disappointed to see that Sproul was alone. Kanj's note was like a weight in Valsamis's pocket, and he desperately wanted to pass off the information and head home.

Sproul took the last empty seat, at the far end of the table from Valsamis, and one of the waiters hustled over to greet him as if he were an old friend. Sproul was a minor celebrity with the staff at the Commodore, as he was nearly everywhere in the city. He knew all the waiters by name, as well as their wives and children. Every really good agent worked this way, but there was something about Sproul that made his efforts seem entirely without guile. The two talked easily for a moment, then the waiter headed off to get Sproul's drink.

"It's the goddamn Arabs," Jack Bentley said. He was sitting next to Valsamis now, close enough so that Valsamis could smell the gin on his breath. "Give them a gun and they'll shoot themselves in the foot."

Talk around the table had turned to the dissolution, just a week earlier, of the U.S.-brokered plan to establish a new Palestinian homeland in Jordan. Predictably, it was the divisions between Arafat and Hussein that had scuttled the plan in the end.

It was a discussion they'd had many times, in one form or another; Valsamis hadn't been paying much attention. He hadn't seen much sense in moving the Palestinians from Lebanon to Jordan. It seemed like a temporary solution at best. Now he was focused on Sproul, trying to catch his eye to ask if the chief was on his way.

"At least with the Israelis, we know exactly what we're getting," a rookie agent from Istanbul interjected.

There was a murmur of general agreement, but Valsamis saw Sproul's gaze shift uneasily toward the young man. He was a prep school kid, fresh off the Farm, and he must not have known who Sproul was.

"What?" the rookie challenged, looking back at Sproul.

Sproul didn't say anything, but the kid must have known what he was thinking. He stammered something about the benefits of regional stability and responsibility to our allies, as if he felt the need to explain himself.

Sproul was quiet, and Valsamis thought he was going to let it go. Then he leaned forward over the table, as he always did when he wanted to make a point. "You think he gives a fuck about your goddamn New World Order?" he asked, motioning to a passing waiter. "Do you think any of them do? All he's thinking about is feeding his kids tomorrow."

The waiter stopped, then scuttled away, anxious at having been singled out.

Sproul was stone sober, but his voice was just a notch too loud for the room. "The Israelis don't give a damn about this place, and neither do we. They're slaughtering each other up in the mountains. Did you know that? They're killing each other like fucking animals. And when the Israelis leave, it's going to be a bloodbath."

The kid bristled like a little dog trying to make itself look larger than it was. But Sproul was finished. He pushed himself away from the table and walked out of the dining room, heading toward the bar.

No one spoke. The kid looked around nervously. Then Bentley started laughing, as he had earlier when he'd told the joke to the two journalists, and the others joined in.

Valsamis finished his drink, then pushed his chair back and started to get up.

"What's the matter?" Bentley put his hand on Valsamis's elbow. "Your boyfriend get his feelings hurt?"

There was another round of laughter. Valsamis tugged his arm free and looked down at Bentley, trying to gauge the depth of the remark. "Fuck you," he said under his breath.

"Whoa!" Bentley threw his hands up and glanced around the table, then turned back to Valsamis. "What's your fucking problem?"

he asked. "It's no secret you've been trying to get your cock up Sproul's ass since you first got to Beirut."

Valsamis clenched his fists and for a moment was back in his father's old station wagon, watching the empty highway fade away behind them, the silhouette of the bar growing dimmer and dimmer in the snow, the Indian kid in Valsamis's coat and boots. And on his face, the sting of his father's palm, the bruise that would take a good week to fade.

Bentley sniggered. "Seems like Sproul's the only one who doesn't know."

"Go to hell," Valsamis said stupidly, then turned and made his way out of the dining room and into the bar.

The two journalists were gone, and the place was uncomfortably quiet. Sproul motioned for Valsamis to join him, then ordered two beers.

"I'm sorry," he said when the bartender had gone, and Valsamis thought Sproul had overheard Bentley. But if he had, he didn't let on.

"I didn't mean to lose my temper like that," Sproul said. "I made a bit of a fool of myself, didn't I?"

"No." Valsamis shook his head. Behind him, in the dining room, raucous laughter erupted from the table.

"What's up with them?" Sproul asked, looking past Valsamis.

Valsamis turned and followed Sproul's gaze. Bentley had gotten up and was doing an obscene pantomime, a caricature Valsamis recognized immediately as himself.

"Idiots," Sproul murmured. He took a sip of his beer and turned to Valsamis. "I forgot," he said suddenly. "You must be wondering about the chief. I saw Bryce in the lobby on the way in, and he mentioned you were looking for him. Is something wrong?"

Valsamis put his hand in his pocket and fingered the note. The choice, then, between country and self. Between everything he believed in and everything he believed himself to be.

"No," Valsamis said, watching Bentley. "It's nothing." He drew his hand from his pocket.

Feeling awkward, he said to Sproul, "I was thinking we could drive up into the Chouf on Monday morning. You could show me around."

"There's the big meeting," Sproul reminded him absently. "Wouldn't want to miss it."

"We'll leave early," Valsamis persisted. "Before dawn. I'll have you back by noon."

Sproul hesitated, his gaze still fixed on the dining room, on Bentley. "Yes," he said, as if the decision were an afterthought. "Yeah, sure, Monday."

■ ■ ■

There was a noise on the stairs, and Graça and Valsamis both turned their heads. Nearly two hours had gone by since Nicole had left them, and it was the first real movement either of them had made.

Nicole appeared in the doorway. She held a small travel bag, enough room for the most meager basics. She stood there without saying anything, then ducked from view again. Valsamis could hear her footsteps on the hallway tiles as she made her way to the front door and back. When she returned, she was holding the shotgun in her free hand.

"You ready?" she asked, turning to Graça.

Graça nodded silently.

Nicole looked briefly at Valsamis, crossed the room, and propped the gun against the kitchen counter.

The end, Valsamis thought, watching her take the FEG from Graça and move toward him. Then he heard the click of the safety reengaging.

Nicole leaned across him and reached for the letters. She folded them carefully, put them back into the shoe box, and slipped the box and the FEG into her bag.

■ ■ ■

Gone to seed, I thought, closing my eyes, letting my garden lay itself out in my mind. Rafts of yellow and purple and white where I'd dug the crocuses in the previous autumn. And in the tiny cups, against the black stamens, the season's first bees, hungry as newborns, drunk on the nectar. In the borders, the promise of lilies and liatris, the old hedge roses I'd salvaged from the grip of weeds. By the old stone wall, the green jungle where I'd left the spearmint to go wild.

"You'll never get rid of it," Elodie Hernot had warned me in my first summer at the house, shaking her head as I tipped the plants from their pots and set the roots into the soil I'd tilled for an herb garden. She'd been right. After three summers, there was nothing left but the mint, a whole fragrant field of it, marching forward into the lawn and up toward the house.

I knelt in the snow next to Lucifer and put my hand on his flank. It was snowing still, and the dog's body was cold already, dissolving into the drifts where he'd fallen, as if the grave had come to him. Another hour and there would be no more trace of his passage through the world.

For the best; I could not have taken him with me, and it would have broken his heart to stay. But still, every greedy part of me wanted him alive, wanted the love-worn nub of his soul restored, if only to allow me a goodbye.

Graça shifted in the snow behind me, and I lifted my hand away and forced myself to stand. Yes, I thought, taking one last look at the garden before starting for the woods, some of what I'd planted would survive, as the roses had through all the years of neglect, but mostly there would be wild daisies and clover, and the pale orange poppies that sowed themselves each spring. Not my garden but a garden nonetheless.

TWENTY-EIGHT

■ ■ ■

"Valsamis?" Kip Bryce's voice was groggy over the intercom. "Gosh, John. It's five in the morning."

Three years Bryce had been in Beirut. Three years of the worst of it, Israeli phosphorous bombs and Syrian mortars, the slaughters at Sabra and Shatila, and Bryce still couldn't bring himself to use the word "god."

Valsamis pushed the speaker button. "Where's Sproul?" he asked. "We were supposed to go up to the mountains."

Valsamis had been heading reluctantly back to his car after buzzing Sproul's apartment for a good ten minutes when it had occurred to him that Bryce lived in the same building and might know where Sproul was. Now, standing in the dark foyer, listening to the breathy crackle of the intercom, he felt like an idiot.

"I saw him at the Commodore last night with that Irish woman," Bryce said. "I think they've been seeing each other."

"Fucking each other," Valsamis said cruelly, then felt bad for having said it. But there was a part of him that wanted Bryce to be shocked.

He thought briefly about asking Bryce if he knew where the Irish woman lived, but his pride won out, and he headed back to his car.

It was a strikingly beautiful morning, the sky luminous along the coast, almost as if it and the sea were extensions of each other. For much of the drive south, Valsamis was able to convince himself that what he had done meant less than it did.

There was a part of him that didn't expect the attack to succeed.

After all, the embassy was American soil. Everyone knew the consequences of such an act. Besides, there was nothing to confirm Mina's fourth-hand information. These kind of reports were not uncommon. Just the previous summer, after a van was stolen from the embassy pool, there had been talk of an attack, and it had never materialized.

The Israelis had taken the Chouf some months earlier, but their hold was fragile. They had not only the Syrians to contend with, but the rivalry between the Druze and Phalange villagers as well. There were a thousand unforeseen hazards in the mountains, roadblocks and checkpoints and unexpected skirmishes. But Valsamis had not waited for fate to intervene. Outside of Beiteddine, he'd pulled off the road, taken out his pocketknife, and carved a crude gash into his tire. Then he'd waited for an Israeli tank to come along and flashed his AID card, explaining how the embassy pool had neglected to furnish him with a spare.

The Chouf was an unlucky assignment for the kids from Tel Aviv and Jerusalem who should have been home chasing girls instead of manning tanks on the road to the cedars. They were happy to take in the hapless American, sharing their tea and cigarettes, passing him from one vehicle to another.

Valsamis was outside of Damour when he heard the first news of the bombing. It wasn't until evening that he made it back to Beirut and could see for himself what had happened. It was dark when he got to the embassy, and giant banks of light had been set up around the blast site, giving the rubble an unearthly clarity. Several mammoth dirt movers had been brought in and were pawing clumsily through the rubble.

After so many wars, the destruction was not unfamiliar. Valsamis had witnessed this before, and worse. He'd been at the American University hospital once, after the Israelis had dropped a phosphorous bomb on Hamra, and had seen a child on fire, a little girl drenched in so much phosphorus that even after the nurses had submerged her in a tub of water, she had continued to burn.

Yet there was something about the embassy that sickened him as even that had not. Somewhere deep inside the rubble, a fire was burning. The air was thick with the reek of it, and it wasn't flesh or hair or bone but something entirely inhuman.

Maybe Sproul hadn't made it to work, Valsamis told himself. Maybe he was still at Siobhan's place, getting his dick sucked, nursing his Commodore hangover. Maybe she was such a good fuck that he hadn't heard yet, or if he had, he didn't care.

One of the marine guards, a squat-faced kid with a thick Okie accent, recognized Valsamis in the crowd of onlookers and came toward him. "Jesus," he said, "I didn't think any of you guys got out."

Valsamis didn't say anything, just stared at him uncomprehending, so the kid motioned to the rubble. "The conference room," he explained, referring to the meeting space that had once occupied the front of the building, the room where that afternoon's meeting was to have been held, "it's fucking gone. Blasted clean away. Fuck, a couple of those AID guys got blown all the way to the Corniche."

■ ■ ■

Eight kids and a wife, years and then decades notched into the basement rafters, each mark a symbol of his longing, and Valsamis's father had never once been back to Greece. Right up until the end, he'd talked about it as if it were inevitable that he would return, as if Greece, not the winter-stricken mountains where he'd lived out the better portion of his life, were his real home. If Valsamis had believed in God or an afterlife, he would have wished his father there now, drinking muddy coffee in a waterfront taverna, staring out across the sea.

It was snowing hard, six inches since Nicole and Graça had left, and no end in sight. A Montana snow, as in the springs of his childhood. Valsamis had a vision of his father, cursing in the June darkness as he struggled to protect his tomato plants from a late blizzard.

And his mother leaning from the doorway, yelling at him for ruining her sheets.

There was no leaving now, Valsamis thought, staring out the window at the driveway. Even if he wanted to, there was no way the Twingo would make it through this snow. Though Valsamis had little doubt Morrow would find a way up the mountain.

Valsamis turned from the window and rattled another Vicodin from the bottle. Just one, he told himself, bargaining with the pain. Just enough to see him through, for it seemed of the utmost importance that he be lucid when Morrow arrived.

The shotgun was still propped where Nicole had left it. Valsamis had thought it a strange offering at first, but he could see now that she'd meant it as a way out, a gesture not quite of forgiveness but of reconciliation. This, his final choice to make.

■   ■   ■

Dick Morrow hit the defrost button and ran his glove across the inside of the Range Rover's windshield. The road stretched up and away from him like the barrel of a gun, a tunnel of white trees and white snow against the night's utter darkness. The snow was soft and wet, heavy as concrete, and Morrow could feel the Rover's tires struggling against it.

Just about here, Morrow thought, searching the trees for a light, any sign of habitation. From what he'd been able to see on the satellite maps, Nicole's house should be just past the next bend.

A stoat darted into the Rover's headlights, its slender body stippled with snow, and Morrow tapped the brakes, felt his wheels sliding out from underneath him and his heart with them. He was too old for this sort of thing. Then, on his right, the trees parted, and he could see a driveway curving downward.

He stopped the Rover and squinted through the falling snow at the unbroken expanse of the drive. The snow was like a fresh duvet, quilted here and there by a neat herringbone of stitches where a chiffchaff or a blackcap had crossed. The house's bulk was visible at the bottom of the slope, the windows all dark.

Morrow nosed the Rover down the driveway, set the brake, and climbed out, scanning the woods and the yard, letting his senses adjust to the stillness of the place. The air was heavy with wood smoke. The fire from the farmhouse up the hill, Morrow thought, remembering the satellite map once again as he made his way toward the house. He'd been good at this kind of thing once, but all that had been years earlier, and Morrow was relieved when the door swung open without a fight.

He stepped inside and hesitated, then started into the darkness. It was warm in the house, hot even. Ahead, where a doorway opened off the hall, Morrow could see the reflection of a dim fire.

Cautiously, he moved toward the doorway and peered inside. There was a woodstove burning in the far corner of the room, its grate shivering pale light across what Morrow could now see was a kitchen. There was a range and a refrigerator, a long row of cabinets against the far wall, and in the middle of the room, a table and three chairs.

It took a moment for Morrow to find Valsamis. He was sitting just inside the doorway, in the darkest part of the room, and it wasn't until Morrow saw his eyes that he realized the other man was there.

"John?" he asked. He could smell Valsamis now, the vaguely animal odor of the wounded. Valsamis shifted, and Morrow could see the bandage on his arm, the dark stain on the fringes where he'd bled through. There was a shotgun resting against the wall next to him, its barrels catching the light.

"Jesus, John. You scared the hell out of me." Morrow laughed gently, then slipped his hand into the pocket of his coat and rested his palm on the stock of his Browning.

■ ■ ■

"There's nothing left," Valsamis said, nodding to the woodstove. "I've burned them all."

Morrow was quiet. Valsamis could see him fingering the gun in his pocket. "And the women?" he asked finally.

"Out past Forte do Bugio by now, I would think," Valsamis replied, referring to the old lighthouse at the mouth of the Tagus. It was a weak lie, and Valsamis was almost surprised at the ease with which Morrow believed him.

Morrow smiled slightly, as if he'd been proved right about something, as if Valsamis's final act of brutality was merely confirmation of what he'd known all along. Valsamis thought of the boy on the Avenida da Liberdade, the look in his eyes when he'd seen Valsamis watching him. Yes, he thought, there was no point in pretending they didn't both know what was going to happen.

"I've taken care of the invoice as well," Valsamis added, but Morrow waved away this news.

"Haven't you heard?" he said. "The *Guardian* broke the Niger uranium documents this morning. ElBaradei and those pricks at the IAEA are screaming forgery." As always, the obscenity sounded wrong coming from Morrow, the word awkward in his mouth.

Valsamis didn't say anything. The Niger documents were big, far bigger than the Lisbon invoice, a chronicle of Iraqi efforts to buy enriched uranium from the African nation. They were a British effort, first acquired by MI6, but the Americans had leaned on the documents heavily in their case for war.

Morrow shrugged. "It's not as bad as it seems. Don't get me wrong, it'll be ugly for a while. But we're committed now."

He glanced at the fire, as if looking for the remnants of the letters there. "You understand, don't you? You understand why it had to happen. There was no other way to make people see. Sproul was just a part of it."

Valsamis shook his head, trying to clear away the Vicodin haze. *We all want the best for this place,* he heard Sproul say again, though of course that hadn't been true. "You arranged for the theft of the van," Valsamis said. "You were there that summer. You arranged it all through the Syrians."

Morrow nodded. "You do see, don't you?" he asked again, as if looking for absolution, though Valsamis knew this wasn't the case. "This is bigger than any of us."

Valsamis closed his eyes and was back on that footpath in the Annam highlands. He could see the girl again, her feet bare in the moonlight, her sandals clutched in her right hand. Sneaking out to visit her lover, Valsamis had thought after the adrenaline of fear had subsided and he'd had time to think. Gone shoeless so that no one would hear.

"Yes," he said. "I see."

"Sproul was right, you know," Morrow added. "The true believers are the most dangerous."

There was a click then, the sound of a safety disengaging, and Valsamis looked up to see Morrow's gun, the barrel's vacant eye staring back at him.

"I'm sorry," Morrow said.

Valsamis shook his head. "No, you're not."

Then Morrow's finger found the trigger and there was nothing left to say.

■ ■ ■

"Two coffees, please." I set a five-euro note on the counter, lit a cigarette, and watched Graça make her way back through the café toward the bathrooms.

The bartender turned to the espresso machine, and I could see her scowl reflected in the bar's back mirror. Behind her was the glare of the Perpignan train station's main concourse, the ceiling arching upward and out of sight. Midnight, moving into the wee hours, and the woman would have rather been anywhere but here. The television flickered silently over the dusty bottles. The weather on Euro-News.

Several bedraggled newspapers were heaped together at the far end of the bar, and I helped myself to the pile, salvaging a copy of *Le Monde* and part of a *Guardian*. The story of the day was the U.S. secretary of state's speech to the United Nations, and both papers had devoted a fair amount of copy to it. But there was a second, smaller article in the *Guardian* that caught my eye. UK NUCLEAR EVIDENCE A FAKE, the small headline announced.

British intelligence claims that Saddam Hussein has been trying to import uranium for a bomb are unfounded and based on deliberately fabricated evidence, I read, skimming quickly through the text. *"Close scrutiny and cross-checking of the documents led us to conclude with absolute certainty that they were false," an official with the International Atomic Energy Agency said. . . . The fabrication was transparently obvious and quickly established, the sources added, suggesting that British intelligence was either easily hoodwinked or a knowing party to the deceit.*

The bartender set down our coffees, and I moved the paper aside and looked up into her impassive face. On the TV screen behind her, the day's sports recap was playing, a football player rushing toward the goal. Late in the day, I thought, glancing down at the article one more time, and already none of this mattered. Or if it did, there was a collective sense that nothing could be done, that the machinery of war had already overtaken us.

"Is something wrong?" Graça slid onto the stool next to mine.

I shook my head. "Ten minutes," I reminded her. "You don't want to miss your train." I opened my bag, took out a large manila envelope, and handed it to her. "You can't come back here. You understand that? Not here. Not Lisbon. At least not for a long time."

Graça lifted the flap on the envelope and peered inside. "I can't take it," she said, shaking her head at the stack of euros I'd crammed inside along with her Brazilian passport. "It's yours."

"Don't worry," I told her. "I've set aside some for myself. Besides, it's not much. Enough for a plane ticket, I hope. I wouldn't hang around Paris, if I were you."

She dropped a lump of sugar into the tiny cup and stirred it in. "What about you?"

"You'd better get going," I said.

She looked at me for a moment, then drank the coffee in one gulp and slid off her stool. It seemed as if I should say something, as if we should both say something, but neither of us knew what.

I watched her walk away, then reached into my jacket and pulled out Rahim's invoice. It was tattered and creased, the paper frayed from having spent so much time in my pocket. Yes, I thought, I had been played. We all had been played, and good.

I set the invoice on the bar, took my passport from my bag, and opened it to the front page, to my own face staring up at me from beneath the cracked plastic. I'd been right; it had been a less than perfect job, and the laminate hadn't held. As it was, the document would be worse than useless, but I still couldn't bring myself to leave it behind.

Slipping the passport into my pocket, I finished my coffee and walked out onto the concourse. At the far end of the deserted hall, the massive departure board leered down at me, destinations in digital neon. PARIS ST.-LAZARE, the top line read, Graça's train. And beneath that, the next train out, the sleeper to Barcelona. The coast train, through Elne and Argelès-sur-Mer.

Through Collioure, I thought, pausing before taking a step toward the ticket booth. *Did you really think Ed wouldn't sell you out again?* I heard Valsamis say, though the real question was not this but why I had given him the chance.

No, I had been there and back already. I would wait for the next train out.

■ ■ ■

TWENTY-NINE

AT FIRST IT'S JUST A FEELING, nothing more, the internal knowledge that something has changed. Two weeks later, I know for sure. Rahim has gone out, and I'm standing in our chilly bathroom, bare feet on the cold tiles. In the silvered mirror above the sink, my own face stares back at me, all my physical imperfections magnified by the room's unforgiving overhead light. On the rim of the sink, balanced carefully on the curve of white porcelain, is a slender finger of plastic.

Outside, on the rua da Moeda, the Bica funicular groans up the hill. Ninety-nine, ninety-eight . . . I start a long count backward from one hundred, listening to the car fade slowly into the distance, teeth grinding at the worn rails. Never before has my life felt so precarious, the whole of it sliding away. And what's left, ravaged and raw.

I think of my mother, alone in her room in my grandparents' apartment in Achrafiye, packing a suitcase with clothes she will soon be unable to wear. For the first time in my life, it's almost possible for me to imagine what she felt. What amazes me is her conviction, her certainty, even amid such raging fear, that she would keep me. At least this was the way she always told the story. No doubts, not even a moment's cringing desire to give me up.

Eighteen, I count, seventeen . . . Suddenly I am ashamed of myself, embarrassed by my own wavering, my panic. What I've known all along now confirmed for me: that I will never be as strong as she was. On the sink, in the tiny window, a thin blue bar has appeared. No question, no doubt, except for the choice waiting to be made.

The front door opens, much earlier than I had expected it would, and I hear two voices in the living room, the guttural reverberations of Arabic. Rahim and one of his Moroccan friends. I take a deep breath and gather myself, pressing my palms against the sink's cool porcelain. Out in the living room, the radio comes on, Europe 1, from France. I will have to tell him, I think. If he hasn't guessed already, he will.

I tuck the plastic stick in my pocket, open the door, and start down the hall. Rahim is in the kitchen making tea.

"I'm going out," I say, and he nods silently, spooning dried mint into the ornate teapot his brother, Driss, brought as a gift a few weeks earlier.

Rahim's friend Mustapha shouts something from the living room, and Rahim answers back, his tone angry. This is their new nightly ritual. Mint tea and the news and, later in the evening, a bottle of cheap port. The long slow countdown to January 15. The long final breath before war.

In the living room, Mustapha lights a cigarette, one of his shaggy roll-your-owns. The smell of the tobacco makes me gag.

Rahim looks up at me. "What's wrong?" he asks, and I am beside myself, undone by love, mine and his. We can do this, I think, looking down at his hand on the old silver spoon, his fingers so graceful at even the simplest task. I can do this.

Of course I can't. I want to tell him, but I don't.

The real story, then. Not the one I've told myself all these years but the truth, the way it actually happened. The first betrayal of how many? Not for country. Not for God, even.

And what would it take now? Not to go back but to go forward. To be forgiven.

Nice

January 6, 1969

Dear Emilie,

I've done it. I know you thought I wouldn't go through with this. The truth is, I didn't think I would, either. But there's no way I can give her up. And yes, she is a girl. Everyone says you can't know these things, but I do.

It wasn't hard to find Ed. The Côte d'Azur is such a small world. He and his friends had docked in St. Tropez, just like Papa said. But by the time I got there, they had moved up the coast to St. Raphael.

He didn't want anything to do with me or the baby at first, but I told him I would go to his hosts if he didn't sign the papers. I could have made life difficult for him if I had.

I felt bad at first, lying to him. He really believes the baby is his. But there is Papa's check, much more than what Ed's name and nationality on a piece of paper are worth. I don't think he's a bad person, but I think he would do just about anything for money.

I know you. I'm sure you think I was wrong to do this. But I hope you understand why. And if you can't understand, I hope you will at least forgive me. There's no other way I can keep her.

Even you have to admit I'm right about this. The attack in Athens and the bombing of the airport are proof of what I've said all along. This tug-of-war between the Israelis and the Palestinians has just started, and there is no place for us in it, no future for a girl with a Christian mother and a Muslim father. Just as there is no future for Sabri and me.

Please tell Maman I love her. She doesn't know anything, and I'm trusting you not to tell her. Respectability is so important to her. My choice will be hard enough for her to bear. Not to mention how angry she would be at Papa if she were to find out that he helped me.

I'm leaving for Paris in the morning. Please don't worry. Marie Haziz is there—you remember her, she played fifth chair at AUB—and I can stay with her until I get on my feet. I will write again soon.

Love,
Mina

The first letter, then. The first one written and the last one read. All these years and they had known, my grandfather and my aunt. All this time they had collaborated to keep this secret.

And what had my father said? His second rule: It's always the marks who think they're too smart to be played who are the easiest to con.

I set the letter aside and fingered the frayed passport in my pocket, even this, even my failure, telling me what I should have known all along: that Ed Blake was not my father.

The bartender approached me and for a moment I struggled to remember where I was, in which language I would be expected to communicate. A month on the road, a day or two before moving on, and I was no longer fluent in anything.

On the television screen, ragged palm trees spanned the fortress bulk of the presidential palace. The lights in the high-rises along the Tigris were still on, and even from the camera's distance, it was possible to make out people moving behind the windows of their apartments. *They should all be forced to do this,* my mother had written in one of her later letters, after she'd spent a sleepless night helping her downstairs neighbor console her four small children while mortars fell all around them. *To hold a child in your arms. There is no other way to understand.*

Yes, I thought, it's one thing to expect war from afar, to wait, as we all have these last days, our televisions tuned to the Baghdad skyline, to the silhouette of Saddam's great palace, the roads scarred by the green glow of headlights. It's one thing to watch the quiet city, cars moving toward their wee-hours destinations. Sick children, women in labor, men heading home from the late shift.

To those of us watching, there's a sense of relief when the fighting comes, a feeling that something finally has happened. There's also the spectacle, the glare and chatter of death, the beauty of it. Like the vulture with its onyx wings.

But to be there, to be engulfed by those great wings, is something else entirely.

I am grateful every day for Nicole's safety. How many times had my mother written this? How many versions of the same prayer? How could I possibly understand what it meant, how I had informed her every decision? From the beginning she had known something we hadn't. The price of war, perhaps, or something else.

The city was so quiet that for a while I was convinced nothing would happen. Then the first Tomahawk hit, and the television screen exploded into a fluorescent glare. The blast echoed across Baghdad, the thunderous force of the concussion followed by a moment of profound silence. And then, from somewhere in the distance, came the sound of sirens, the wail plaintive and powerless.

ACKNOWLEDGMENTS

■ ■ ■

The author wishes to thank the following people for their invaluable help, counsel, and encouragement: Simon Lipskar, Mark Tavani, Jane Wood, Jack Macrae, and Dan Conaway. The debts owed can never possibly be fully repaid. Thanks also to all the talented people involved in the production and design of this book, especially Beth Thomas for her superhuman skills as a copy editor, and to the author's family for their extraordinary patience.

DOSSIER

An Accidental American

ALEX CARR

MORTALIS

ON APRIL 18, 1983, at one o'clock in the afternoon, a van carrying two thousand pounds of explosives blew up outside the American embassy in Beirut, killing sixty-three people. Among the victims were seventeen Americans, eight of whom represented the Central Intelligence Agency's entire Middle East contingent. In the years preceding the bombing, an increasing number of attacks on Western and Israeli interests had been carried out by Palestinian and Muslim extremists, but the Beirut bombing was widely seen as a watershed event for American policies in the region. With the exception of the seizure of the American embassy in Tehran four years earlier, an act that was carried out within the framework of Iran's Islamic revolution, the embassy bombing represented the first time America had been so directly and bloodily targeted by Islamic terrorists for its military involvement in the Middle East.

It's impossible to see why the United States was such an unwelcome force without an understanding of the history of Lebanon and the surrounding region, and of American and Western involvement in the politics of the Middle East in general. Though Lebanon has existed in one form or another since the ninth century B.C., the modern country of Lebanon was not established until 1920, when it was granted to the French as part of a system of mandates established for the administration of former Turkish and German territories following World War I and the collapse of the Ottoman Empire. In fact, almost all of what we think of as the modern Middle East was shaped by these mandates.

America's first direct intervention in Lebanese politics came in 1946. During World War II, Lebanon had been declared a free state in order to liberate it from Vichy control. But when, after the war, Lebanon eventually moved toward full independence, the French balked, and the United States, Britain, and several Arab governments stepped in to support Lebanese independence. It was at this time that Lebanon's system of political power sharing was devised. Well aware of the country's shaky precolonial past and determined to keep Lebanon intact, the fledgling nationalist government agreed to split power along sectarian lines, based on the numbers of the 1932 census. It was a well-intentioned plan, but one that inadvertently set the stage for decades of strife and civil war.

The power-sharing government's first major stumbling block came with the partitioning of the British Mandate of Palestine in the wake of World War II, and the 1948 Arab-Israeli war that followed. The ensuing influx of some 100,000 Palestinian refugees into Lebanon proved a strain on the carefully crafted power-sharing system. Tensions were further exacerbated in 1956, when Egyptian president Gamal Abdel Nasser nationalized the Suez Canal, provoking the United States, along with Britain, France, and Israel, to respond with military force. While Lebanese Muslims wanted the government to back the newly created United Arab Republic, Christians fought to keep the nation allied with the West. In 1958, with the country teetering on the brink of civil war, the United States sent marines into Lebanon to support the government of President Camille Chamoun, thus inextricably linking itself with Christian forces.

It was an alliance that would be tested when, nearly two decades later, sectarian rivalries finally erupted into full-scale civil war. While Lebanon had enjoyed a period of relative peace and prosperity, tensions between the United States and the Soviet Union, and between the United States and Iran, had escalated significantly, as had tensions between the Israelis and the Palestinians. By the spring of 1975—when gunmen from the Christian Phalange militia attacked a bus in the suburbs of Beirut and massacred twenty-seven Palestinians on board in what is widely agreed to have been the first act of the civil war—the forces at work in Lebanon were not merely internal ones. The Cold War, as well as the larger Arab-Israeli conflict, were both being played out in Lebanon, and would be throughout the course of the war, as international players funneled weapons and money to the various Christian, Muslim, and Druze militias.

The United States was a major player in the civil war from the beginning, providing mainly covert support for the Christian government, with whom it had traditionally been allied. But it wasn't until 1982, after the Israeli siege of Beirut, the assassination of Phalange leader Bachir Gemayel, and the horrific massacres at the Palestinian refugee camps of Sabra and Shatila, that U.S. troops, along with other members of a multinational peacekeeping force, formally intervened in the conflict. The United Nations–backed coalition was meant as a neutral presence, but the complications of Cold War allegiances and the United States' traditionally close ties to Israel and Lebanon's Christian government meant that the Americans were inevitably viewed by Muslim and Druze factions as anything but impartial. It was in this environment, less than six months after the Americans arrived as peacekeepers, that the embassy bombing took place.

There can be no doubt that the main goal of the bombing was to intimidate the United States into pulling its forces from Lebanon. But there were other, less obvious but no less significant reasons behind the attack. Responsibility for the bombing, and the subsequent bombing of the marine barracks, was claimed by a radical wing of the Iranian-backed Hezbollah. In the years leading up to these attacks, Iran had taken an increasingly aggressive role in its support of Lebanese Muslim militias, most of which were traditionally Shiite, transforming what had once been a mainly political fight into a religious and moral one. Not only did Muslim radicals want American troops gone, but they wanted to rid the country of Western cultural influence—which they saw as mainly American—as well. In the bloody years to follow, the American University of Beirut, as well as American and Western journalists, would be targets of a concerted campaign of kidnapping and intimidation.

Under any other circumstances, the Islamicizing of the conflict might have been yet another disturbing development in an already wildly fractured situation. But in the hothouse of the Lebanese civil war, Hezbollah's fierce brand of anti-Americanism became not just a Shia or Iranian cause but a Palestinian and therefore pan-Arab cause as well. In the years since the embassy bombing, the cause has taken on many faces, including that of the vast al-Qaeda network, but the anger remains undiluted. Not only is anti-American thinking still prevalent today in the Middle East, but it has become the uniting force for radical Muslims the world over.

Former high-ranking members of the Reagan administration have confirmed that how to respond to the embassy bombing and the bombing of the marine barracks was a subject of debate at the time. There was a clear split within the White House between those who believed that force was the best response and those who argued that the use of military power would only add to the problem by antagonizing America's remaining friends in the Arab world. The lessons of Vietnam, along with the horrific loss of life in both attacks, no doubt helped cement the decision to follow a policy of disengagement. In the end, the choice was made to pull all American troops out of Lebanon.

It's no coincidence that I chose to make the 1983 bombing of the American embassy in Beirut central to the plot of *An Accidental American*. This is a novel about U.S. involvement in the politics of the Middle East, and the embassy bombing has shaped American policy in that region as few other events have. Disengagement is no longer the United States' response of choice when dealing with Islamic extremism. In light of the September 11 attacks, it comes as no surprise that American foreign policy leans heavily on the swift use of military might. But the effects of the decisions made in the wake of the Beirut bombings are also at the root of this powerful policy shift. Those in Washington who argue in favor of unilateral military action can point to the message that the earlier withdrawal sent: namely, that the United States could be intimidated by terrorists.

Writing about events in which real people lost their lives is always a delicate undertaking. Sixty-three people were killed in the embassy bombing, and it is not my intention to dishonor them. While I do aim for historical accuracy, my main focus as a writer is on my characters. Truthfulness for me means looking back on the events of history through the flawed lens of human perception. This means creating characters who are as real as possible, and whose motives are often less than pure and always complicated. I strongly believe that I can best respect the real inhabitants of history by struggling to portray my fictional inhabitants as honestly as possible.

Most of my fictionalization of the embassy bombing in *An Accidental American* adheres closely to the facts. The van used to transport the explosives to the embassy had, in fact, been stolen from the embassy pool the summer before the bombing. It is universally acknowledged that the Syrians, as well as the Iranians under the guise of Hezbollah, were behind the attacks. Among the people killed that day were the CIA's chief Middle East analyst, Robert C. Ames, and station chief Kenneth Haas. Both Ames and Haas were brilliant men and rising stars, and the consequences of their deaths are still being felt within the intelligence community. But the idea that a rogue CIA official was actually behind the bombing is entirely fabricated, as are all the characters involved.

In recent years, there seems to be a growing uncertainty concerning what, exactly, separates fiction from nonfiction. The meteoric rise of the memoir and other forms of "creative nonfiction" has further blurred an already fuzzy line between minor embellishment and outright fabrication—while the popularity of a certain kind of fiction, which claims to illuminate long-concealed truths, has led readers to confuse clever fabrication with fact. In the wake of this uncertainty has come outrage and even anger. I have to admit, I don't see what all the fuss is about. Stories are meant to transport—at its best, historical fiction can even offer us a wise perspective on our own condition—and if readers are denied the joy of suspending their disbelief, they might as well not read at all.

This doesn't mean, however, that we should substitute the watered-down truths of historical fiction for the real thing, or the musings of a fiction writer, whose ultimate loyalty lies with his or her story, for the more measured presentations of historians and journalists, whose allegiances are with the truth. We live in a world in which the costs of ignorance are simply too high.

ABOUT THE AUTHOR

■ ■ ■

ALEX CARR lives with her family
in Lexington, Virginia.